The
Martian
Patriarch

A science fiction novel

by Robert A. Vella

This is the story of Marc Bolton, a man who unknowingly becomes the critical focal point in the history of three very different worlds. From 2075 to 2095, his journey marks the past, present, and future evolution of Man. Caught in the middle of an interplanetary struggle, he is torn between the opposing forces that form the essence of his being. The difficult ordeal he must endure is filled with uncertainty and anguish. The profound fate that befalls him was born in the heart of a distant star. And, the lives of millions lay in the balance. Can one man bear such a burden and discover himself at the same time?

Table of Contents

Chapter 1
Specters in the Night

Marc Bolton watched the live news event unfold
on his telecom monitor. It was early summer, 2075.
The interplanetary transport ship *Maxwell Montes* was
preparing to leave Earth orbit for a scheduled
resupply mission to the Moon Base. He was amazed
by Mankind's technological achievements. It had
been 106 years since Man took his first tentative steps
on another world. Now he lived permanently on the
Moon, Mars, and in orbiting stations that circled high
above his birthplace. Space travel was no longer a
rare event. Ships of all sizes scurried between the
Earth and Moon on a daily basis. The large self-
sufficient colony on Mars was visited at least six times
a year. Manned exploration of the outer solar system
was progressing steadily, and there was even talk of
sending robotic explorers to other star systems.

The transport's powerful fusion-pulse engine
ignited, ejecting a stream of white-hot plasma at
fantastic speed. The huge vessel lurched forward and
quickly disappeared into the blackness of space. Yes,
it was quite remarkable what we had achieved,
Bolton mused; but, what of our future? What will
happen when there are no more worlds to conquer?
What will become of us when we've spoiled all that
we have? Bolton only needed to look at the Earth for
an answer. Malnutrition and disease, once confined
to impoverished regions, were now common around

the globe. Competition over dwindling resources was kept from escalating into destructive conflict only by the heavy hand of the *Terran Council*. Sadly, Bolton feared that Man's worst enemy was himself.

Upon cleaning up the aftermath of his evening meal, Bolton went to sleep. He dreamed of a utopian realm where people flew effortlessly within turquoise-blue satin clouds. It was an escape from the shame he harbored for the sick society to which he belonged.

As fiery meteors streaked through the midnight sky, Bolton was suddenly awakened by an unknown voice calling his name. Jumping from his bed to confront the intruder, he felt warm drips of blood coming from his nose. Switching on the room light, he saw his pillow covered in a deep red stain. Holding his nostrils closed, he thoroughly searched his apartment only to find no trace of any intrusion. Bolton was perplexed. The voice was so real, so close, not at all like what would be experienced in a dream.

Somewhat shaken, Bolton telecalled his friend Christine. Sleepily, she turned on her monitor.

"Marc, what's wrong? You look terrible."

"Something happened just now. I'm not sure what it...," he stuttered.

"Wait," she interrupted. "I'm coming right over."

Christine Bakerman was a field archaeologist for the University of Georgia. She and Bolton have had an ongoing intimate relationship for the last five years. Her job required her to travel much of the time, and this has kept the pair from forming a more permanent union. Aside from that, the two cared for each other a great deal, and had forged a solid friendship.

Bolton opened the front door, and the casually dressed Christine entered. Taking him by the arm, she asked, "What happened?" He replied with a step by step recount of his experience.

"It must have just been a dream, don't you think?" she suggested. "And, you certainly have had a history of nosebleeds, you know."

"Yes, I suppose it was a dream," he replied. "But, I tell you that voice sounded so real."

"Sounded?" Christine inquired.

"Well," Bolton continued, "I don't believe I actually heard anything. It was as if someone had placed the message into my mind."

"Marc, are you talking about *telepathy*?"

"I know," he admitted. "Seems a little crazy, doesn't it?"

Christine nodded in tacit agreement. She gently lowered him back onto the bed, and laid down beside him.

"Let's get some rest, shall we?"

The piercing rays of the early morning June sun burst through the windows and illuminated the interior like a battery of floodlights. In unison, the numerous houseplants arranged throughout the apartment jumped to attention as if they were soldiers acknowledging the entrance of their commanding officer.

Christine joined Bolton in the kitchen, who was making a pot of coffee.

"Marc, I was wondering... if you would like to come with me on my Bolivia trip in September. I know you're fascinated with the ruins down there, *Tiwanaku* and *Pumapunku*, and I sure could use your help. Besides, it would be nice to spend some time together – something we haven't had much of lately."

Bolton looked deeply into her eyes. "You know nothing would make me happier, but you are aware of my situation."

Christine sighed in exasperation. "Damn the Council! Haven't you given enough to them? They treat you like a scientist held hostage. When was your last vacation anyway? Two years ago, or was it three?"

"We've been over this before," he replied.

"Yes, we have indeed," she retorted sternly. "Yet, you continue to let Krichek's bureaucratic goon-squad walk all over you. Surely, you've proven your worth to them time and again. Doesn't that warrant at least a modicum of freedom?"

"Freedom is a commodity not readily offered by the Council. Chris, you know what's going on there. What's really bothering you?"

The statuesque woman was clearly losing composure as the tears welled up inside. "I'm worried, Marc. Not for us, but for you. I realized long ago that our life together would never be what both of us wanted, and I've accepted that. I guess it's a reflection of the troubled times we live in. What I'm gravely concerned about is you, my love. Deep down inside that dispassionate servile facade of yours, is an intensely ethical man who is at odds with his official duties. Sooner or later, that internal conflict will be resolved in a manner that will pose a great threat to the Council. It is that resulting danger, to which I fear."

The two fell into each other's arms, softly embraced in a silent and lengthy interlude. No one noticed the coffee alarm.

While driving to work, Bolton looked to the south of Sutter City and viewed the vast white-capped inland sea of California. Off in the distance, he saw the rusted tops of skyscrapers still standing in what used to be the city of Sacramento. He regarded them as sentinels, guarding the gates of a bygone era.

Marc Bolton was a technology analyst for the *Terran Council*. He was born on September 10, 2035 in San Francisco. His immediate family was killed in the *Great Flood* on June 24, 2052. Found wandering alone on a hilltop isolated by the floodwaters, he was rescued several days later by a fishing boat lucky enough to be at sea during the deluge. Bolton attended college, receiving an engineering degree from the University of Nebraska. Later, he earned a master's in computer science from the Western Institute of Technology (W.I.T.). Hired by NASA in 2060 just before the revolutionary upheaval, he was subsequently recruited in 2066 by the *Terran Council*.

After settling into his office, Bolton prepared to continue a research project to identify possible power supplies for a Moon-based 500 megawatt 1 micron free-electron laser. Though a devoted worker, Bolton was feeling hesitant to assist in the development of such a powerful weapon. He could only speculate how the Council intended to use a device perfectly capable of striking targets anywhere on the Earth's surface. One fact was certain. Although unknown to the public, the Moon was being converted into a large military base. For what reason, Bolton could not be sure. At the time, there were no known rivals capable of aggression towards the *Terran Council*.

The twelve-member *Terran Council* was the preeminent governmental body on Earth. The sequence of historical events leading up to its formation started with the *Great Flood*. Overpopulation began adversely affecting the global environment in the *Industrial Age*, escalated during the *Information Age*, and reached a critical tipping point in what later became known as the *Dystopian Age*. Eventually, technological innovations had begun to reduce the per capita emissions of greenhouse gases and other harmful pollutants, but this was offset by the continued growth in the world's population. Average surface temperatures rose steadily until the last of the Greenland glaciers quickly melted away, and the West Antarctic ice shelves collapsed in rapid succession. The latter event destabilized the massive West Antarctic continental ice sheet, allowing it to break up and flow into the oceans. All this happened concurrently, which triggered a sudden surge in sea levels that transpired over a brief period of a few months – astonishing even those who had issued the most dire climate warnings. Coastal and lowland communities were insufficiently prepared to evacuate the millions of inhabitants, and were inundated long before their hastily conceived plans could be implemented. What made matters worse, was the unexpected increase in the frequency and intensity of violent storms. As a result, the actual flooding was fiercely episodic rather than gradual. The environmental domino effects were ghastly. Global weather patterns changed abruptly, turning most of the surviving agricultural areas into useless wastelands. Regional wars broke out from numerous disputes over dwindling resources that collectively grew into worldwide revolution in 2061. The anarchy had to be stopped. The greatest military power, the United States of America, finally suppressed the rebellion under the ruthless leadership of Janus Krichek. In 2065, he founded the *Terran Council* which assimilated all national governments under its domain.

Bolton's work was interrupted by a telecall.

"Hello Marc," said the caller.

"Han Li, my good friend! How the hell are you?" answered Bolton.

"Fat and sassy," replied Han. "Listen, I know you're busy, but I'm in *The City* and was wondering if you could join me for dinner sometime soon… if that's ok."

"Are you kidding me?" Bolton chuckled. "How about tonight?"

"Perfect. There's an excellent restaurant here in the Transamerica pyramid called *The Archipelago*. Marc, did you know this building is scheduled for demotion next year?"

"No I didn't, Han. I'll be sorry to see that iconic structure come down. What a shame! But it's understandable, I suppose. What is truly surprising is that it lasted this long. I'll meet you there at nineteen-hundred hours, okay?"

"Great, see you then buddy," acknowledged Han.

Bolton turned off the monitor feeling happy to see his old friend again. He met Han in college where they became inseparable companions. At that time, a close friendship was especially important for Bolton. Having just lost his family, he was alone in a world full of tragedy and hostility. He recalled the gracious manner in which Han's family warmly welcomed him into their house during those breaks from school. Without such a friendship, Bolton wondered if he would have had the strength and determination to continue his education.

Han Li (pronounced "Hahn Lee") was a climatologist for the Inter-Mountain West branch of the Goldstone Atmospheric Monitoring Service (G.A.M.S.). This independent firm provided highly accurate weather forecasting and climate analysis primarily for governmental agencies and private corporations. He was one of the most respected scientists in his field, frequently in demand on the lecture-circuit. Han's greatest contribution was his development of the *Precipitation/Temperature Correlation Curve*. This hypothesis, stated that the total amount of global precipitation that falls to earth, begins to decrease when the average global surface temperature surpasses seventy-four degrees Fahrenheit. Below that figure, precipitation rates – for interglacial periods – are proportionally linked to evaporation rates. Above seventy-four degrees, evaporative effects become so strong that precipitation increasingly falls as *virga*, which never reaches the Earth's surface. The flattened, bell curve Han created to illustrate this relationship became popularly known as the *Li Dry-Line Graph*, and his published scientific paper became required reading in most academic circles.

The magnetic train terminus at Sutter City was a beehive of activity, connecting the *Terran Council* capital with the pacific northwest, inter-mountain west, desert southwest, and the coastal islands. Bolton's route to San Francisco would take about thirty minutes over the inland sea causeways.

Bolton's train quickly accelerated to over 200 mph. Upon reaching its cruising speed, the passing of regularly spaced electromagnetic transducers created a soft rhythmic vibration within the passenger compartments. Reclining back into his seat, Bolton drifted off into a somnolent state. The images of twenty-three years past were still vivid in his mind. He could see his powder-blue house at the end of an undulating suburban street lined with deep-green cypress trees, and his dark muscular father proudly embracing his lovely golden-haired mother on the second floor balcony. Down below on the lush lawn, his effervescent nine year old sister fiendishly tried to douse the happy couple with a water hose.

Suddenly, the speeding train screeched to a halt throwing Bolton over the seat in front of him. The interior lights flickered off and on as the deep groans of passengers meandered through the compartment. Bolton picked himself up checking to see if he was hurt in any way, and then assisted a lady lying next to him. The intercom crackled with an embarrassed voice.

"Ladies and gentlemen, the causeway in front of us appears to be damaged. In a few minutes, we will be reversing direction in order to use the causeway to the south of us. Please aid any passengers who might be injured. An attendant will be coming around soon to check on you. Please remain calm, and accept our sincere apologies for this mishap."

Luckily, no one was seriously hurt. Within a short time, the train began moving again. With the exception of a few sporadic complaints, the passengers returned to their quite demeanor.

Bolton noticed a man approaching him.

"Hello, Mister Bolton. That was exciting, wasn't it?"

The man looked familiar, though Bolton couldn't remember his name.

"Yes, but that kind of excitement I can live without."

Taking an adjacent seat, the large round man continued the discourse.

"You'll forgive the intrusion, Mister Bolton, my name is Douglas Fairchild. I am a political adviser to the Head Council on the floor above your office."

"Oh yes, you're the one who gave that speech last month regarding the threat of Asian separatism," Bolton recalled.

"That speech got me noticed by Councilman Hoster. He said I am now in line for the next Council seat that becomes vacant. That's great, isn't it?"

Bolton was unimpressed. "Yes, if that pleases you. I am a scientist. I have no political aspirations."

Fairchild was in a talkative frame of mind. He continued with a purposeful question.

"Mister Bolton, may I call you Marc?"

Bolton barely nodded in approval.

"Marc, what if I told you that the causeway damage that almost killed us was a deliberate act of sabotage by an extremist faction within the *Asian Federation*?"

Bolton was reaching his limit of tolerance.

"Mister Fairchild, if you do have specific intelligence information to support that charge, I must question your very presence aboard this train. If not, I must point out your foolhardiness of making such an accusation in public about a political institution so vital to the interests of the Council. Now, if you would excuse me, I'd rather finish this trip alone."

"As you wish," Fairchild replied grimly. "However, it is never foolhardy for the Council to try to discover the political inclinations of its employees. Is it now, Mister Bolton?"

With that stern rebuke, the once jovial Fairchild arose from his seat after giving Bolton a long, icy-cold stare. If he had expected a fearful reaction from Bolton, the large round man would have been supremely disappointed.

As the train slowed down upon its arrival in San Francisco, the unknown voice Bolton perceived the evening before, replayed itself yet again in his mind. Was it a dream? Was it a hallucination? Those questions repeated over and over in a conscious attempt to comprehend that which was incomprehensible. What began to scare Bolton, though, was that his intuition knew the voice was neither.

Getting around San Francisco, especially at night, was not quite as easy as when Bolton was a child. The city had become nothing more than a cluster of natural, and manmade, islands connected by a maze of viaducts and elevated expressways. The financial district, once dominated by the wide corridor of Market Street running through it, was now under twenty feet of salt water. Several of the original skyscrapers were saved by retrofitting their structures to a marine environment, which allowed continued use of the floors above the water line; but, their occupants were gradually relocating further inland.

It was only a matter of time before the once majestic city was abandoned to the fish.

Bolton hopped aboard an electric taxicab that delivered him to the Transamerica building's tenth floor at 19:52 hours. He took an elevator up to the sixteenth floor, and saw Han Li sitting patiently in the lobby.

"Han, I'm so sorry for the delay," Bolton apologized. "There was some sort of problem on the causeway."

"I know," Han replied. "I saw it on the news." He stood up and gave Bolton welcoming hug. "It's so good to see you again, Marc! Are you hungry? Let's go eat."

"What do they serve here?" asked Bolton.

Han laughed. "I'm not sure, but it better be good. Did you notice the prices?"

The Archipelago was adorned with historic memorabilia of San Francisco before the flood. Marble statues of the city's famous sports figures stood in glass cases arranged around the circular room's oak walls. In the center of the restaurant an intricate model of the city, as it was in the year 2000, was gloriously displayed with special lighting. There were a multitude of pictures capturing the architectural beauty of the *Palace of Fine Arts*, the *Civic Center*, the *Golden Gate Bridge*, the *Presidio*, and other notable places. The remarkable paintings were a remembrance of the city's influential people, including politicians, entrepreneurs, journalists, and philanthropists.

Bolton scanned the menu and saw an interesting variety of fresh fish and common salt grain entrées. One item caught his attention – risotto. This Italian-style rice dish was almost impossible to find anymore. The *Great Flood* effectively destroyed all the low-lying fresh water habitats that were once the world's great rice producing regions.

The waiter brought two classic gin martinis to the table, garnished with a lemon twist, a favorite cocktail of the two friends.

"Cheers, Han. Just like old times, eh?"

"And, cheers to you. But it's not really like old times, is it Marc?"

"No, I suppose not. After we each left Lincoln to pursue our careers, we haven't had much opportunity to see each other. This feels like a family reunion, of sorts, to me."

Han immediately perceived the underlying sadness in Bolton's remark, and decided some levity was in order.

"Marc, do you remember the time when we were stood-up on that double-date Margie Wilkins setup for us?"

"How could I forget? What a fiasco! What were their names, Tammy or was it Terri?"

"Tamara and Julia," Han replied.

"That's right," Bolton continued. "After I told Julia to meet us at the playhouse because we didn't have a vehicle, they decided to ditch us!"

"So then, big guy, we ended up side-by-side in the middle of the theater packed with romantic couples, watching that tear-jerker of a love story! I guess those people must have thought we were pretty gay, huh?"

"I'm sure they did after you put your arm around me, Han."

Han couldn't stop giggling. "Oh yeah… isn't that when you stood up and had a hissy fit?"

"Yep," Bolton said sheepishly. "And, that's when they kicked us out."

The meals arrived amidst the laughter. They were thoroughly enjoyed.

"Tell me about this seminar you're attending tomorrow," inquired Bolton.

"It's titled, *The Global Climatology Solutions Forum*," Han replied. "The *Terran Council* is sponsoring the event with the hope of finding agreeable solutions to the current climatic conditions that are restricting agricultural productivity. They have chosen scientists and industry representatives from all over the world. It is a noble agenda, but…"

"What is it, Han?"

"The issues are too complex, Marc. Furthermore, the Council is pushing the ridiculous idea that climate can be artificially modified regionally for specific purposes. Despite all the climate-related disasters that have occurred this century, they still refuse to accept that this is a global problem which can only be solved with macro solutions. Besides, can you imagine getting all those stubborn factions to agree on a unified course of action?"

"No, I cannot," admitted Bolton. "How close do you believe we are to your seventy-four degree dry-line threshold?"

"Temperature-wise, we're ten degrees Fahrenheit away. If and when we'll ever hit that mark is an open question. It took a century and a half to reach the current five degree increase. However, the rate of increase is continuing to rise exponentially, due to collateral factors, in spite of technological advancements that weaned us off the fossil fuel energy use that initially caused the problem."

"What's your best prognosis, Han?"

"Honestly, I just don't know. No one does. But if you asked for my personal opinion, I would say that the planet has been disturbed from its natural balance by the misuse of technology, and is probably dying. If the temperature rise is not abated, it will eventually get to the point where a Venus-like runaway greenhouse effect is generated. Thermal conditions would excite the atmosphere sufficiently to allow water molecules to chemically decompose, which would then be stripped away by the solar wind. If Earth loses its water, it loses its ability to support life."

"Earth is dying," Bolton mused aloud. "That thought is far from being an isolated one, these days."

"And, how about you?" proffered Han. "What sort of clandestine projects has the Council assigned you to, lately?"

Bolton just smiled coyly, knowing that Han understood he was forbidden to discuss his official duties.

"Let me guess. You are developing a new computer system to replace high-priced climatologists, like myself," Han speculated jokingly.

"You know that's impossible," Bolton chuckled. "If we ever built a computer that made as many wrong predictions as you do, it would never pass beta testing!"

Han happily retreated. "Okay, big guy, you got me! Dessert?"

During a conversational lull necessitated by the sheer sinful lusciousness of the sweet preparations before them, Bolton's mind wandered as if it were somehow detached from his physical senses. Without purposeful intent, he focused in on the thoughts emanating from his close companion.

Bolton suddenly snapped back into sensory awareness, and blurted out a confirmatory pronouncement in the form of a question, "*Tropospheric distillation?*"

The two men looked at each other in utter disbelief.

Chapter 2
Seeds of Change

William Brown, Director of the *Terran Council's Developmental Sciences and Technology Department*, performed his periodic review of the department's open projects work log. Methodically, he scrolled through the listing of analysts displayed on his monitor. A blinking entry, highlighted in bright yellow, caught his attention. The analyst's name was Marc Bolton. Looking closer, Brown noticed that Bolton's last activity date was three days old - April 3, 2076. The log entries for the intervening days listed Bolton's status as "unknown."

After activating the personnel locator program, Brown discovered that Bolton's office was empty, and that he had not checked into the building that day. The Director's temper had risen sharply. Bolton's current assignment was a project to enable the Moon Base to acquire raw materials by mining Earth-crossing asteroids. This project was given top priority by none other than Janus Krichek, the Head Council, because it was becoming increasingly costly to supply the growing Moon Base from Earth. Brown contemplated the ramifications to him if the project was not completed on time, and this thought caused him great consternation to say the least.

The burly Director spun around in his desk chair a little too quickly, and knocked his telecom device to the floor. Angrily, he picked it up and tried to reach

Bolton at his residence. But, there was no answer. Brown then contacted the department's internal security team. He issued an order instructing them to locate Marc Bolton as soon as possible, and have him brought to the Director's office immediately. The use of force was authorized.

Five grey-clad security officers walked up the steep shrub-lined pathway leading to Bolton's apartment complex. Finding the entrance gate locked, one of the men violently kicked it open. The wooden gate slammed against the side of the building with such impact, that several neighbors came out to see what had happened. They arrived at a door that matched the one shown on their locator device.

"Number one-zero-two, this is it," said the leader.

After knocking on the door several times, the leader nodded to one of the officers who crudely broke in using a crowbar and some brute force. Bolton was lying face down on the living room floor. The leader rushed over, and turned Bolton onto his back.

"He's unconscious," declared the leader. "Notify the Director we're taking him to the hospital."

The leader shook Bolton by the shoulders, while barking orders at him as if the unresponsive man was either drunk or under the influence of a controlled substance.

"Wake up! Come on now, wake up!"

His eye lids began to flutter and some imperceptible moaning was heard. When Bolton opened his eyes, the leader lifted him up to a seated position.

"What happened to you?" the leader demanded as he closely examined the barely cognizant forty year old technology analyst.

"I… I don't… know," mutter Bolton.

During the ride to the hospital, Bolton became more lucid. "Where are you taking me," he asked.

"The hospital," answered the leader. "Do you know you've been missing the last two days?"

Bolton responded with a negative gesture.

"The last thing I remember was reading a scientific journal in bed," stated Bolton.

"You weren't in your bed when we found you," the leader informed him.

"I cannot explain that, sir," Bolton respectfully replied.

At the hospital, Doctor Sally Jorgensen placed Bolton under a biometric scanner while nurses attached various electrodes and tubes to his body. In an orderly sequence, specialists began reading aloud the data being displayed about Bolton's medical condition.

"Electroencephalogram indicates subdued, but normal brain activity."

"No electrocardiographic irregularities. Blood pressure is one-thirty-one over sixty-seven. Three-minute heartbeat interval is holding at an average of seventy-nine."

"Patient is moderately dehydrated, and electrolyte levels are correspondingly low; although, still within the normal range."

A number of questions were fired at Bolton from every direction. In detail, he described everything he did and consumed in the two days prior to his blackout.

After reading a blood analysis report, Doctor Jorgensen verbally recorded the emergency room log entry.

"Subject identification number is S-U-T-M-1-5-6-0-9-7-1-0-3-6-C-M. Vitals are stable. No trauma discovered. No blood abnormalities. Foreign microbe levels are nominal. Evidence of minor brain function inhibition possibly due to *Electro-Synchronous Synapse Reflection*, although symptoms have ceased. Subject transferred to monitoring station at eleven-thirteen. Recommend release if no change occurs within two hours."

Shortly after 13:00 hours, Doctor Jorgensen visited Bolton in the recovery room. "How do you feel?" she asked while reviewing the latest figures on his medical status.

"I feel fine," replied Bolton. "What happened to me anyway?"

"Well, I can't say definitively," the dumpy, red-haired woman of fifty-two years responded. "There really isn't anything wrong with you. Regarding your blackout, my speculative diagnosis suggests you might have been exposed to an electromagnetic field that somehow synchronized with, and temporarily amplified your brain waves. The effect would be analogous to overloading an electrical circuit, which for people, would feel like an electric shock. Although extremely rare, we have seen this happen before - particularly to individuals who were in close proximity to military and communications facilities. However, no serious or long-term residual effects have ever been documented. I don't think you need to worry about this unless it reoccurs."

Bolton nodded in recognition, but knew that his apartment was nowhere near any such facility.

The doctor continued. "I'm releasing you from the hospital, but ordering you to go home and rest this afternoon. The officers who delivered you instructed me to notify your employer, which I'll do shortly. Good day to you, Mister Bolton."

Bolton thanked the doctor, and then requested taxi service at the front desk.

An unusual downpour drenched Bolton as he approached the broken front door of his apartment. Upon entering, he noticed that some household items were out of place. He surmised that the officers must have conducted a routine search of his home when they found him. As he glanced down at the living room floor, Bolton saw a dark stain on the carpet. He touched it, and rubbed his fingers back and forth. There was no doubt the stain was partially coagulated blood.

Four weeks later, Bolton left work early to pick up Christine at the airport. She was returning from a field trip in Saskatchewan, and he hadn't seen her since early March. It was unusually hot, even for this time of the year, as temperatures had approached one hundred and ten degrees for three consecutive days. As he drove along the turnpike, Bolton noticed a large patch of bright orange poppies nestled at the bottom of a hillside. Oak trees dotted the golden landscape, and millions of love-struck male crickets filled the air with musical harmony. He wondered what California must have looked like before Europeans settled here, when the land was wild and free.

At the arrival gate, Bolton saw Christine walking down the sloping ramp. They gently embraced and whispered some sweet-nothings to each other that only couples understand. He picked up her luggage, and they strolled arm-in-arm through the concourse towards the exit.

"What grand discoveries did you find up north," he asked curiously.

"Nothing truly grand, but we did uncover some human artifacts that appear to be incongruous with our understanding of that time period," answered Christine.

"What time period is that?" prompted Bolton.

"Our preliminary estimate is between twenty-five and thirty thousand years ago during the Paleolithic, or *Old Stone Age.*"

Stepping onto the people-mover, Bolton probed further. "Let's see, that must be the glacially-dominant Pleistocene epoch."

"Yes, you stud of a man, the Pleistocene. Now, are you going to take me home and ravage me all night, or should we continue this interrogation properly in a laboratory?"

Bolton pursed his lips and made a gesture as if he were closing the zipper of a hand bag.

That evening, they shared a bottle of champagne and a simple meal expertly prepared by Bolton. Their passionate desire for each other forged into a white-hot interlude that lasted until the early morning hours. Exhausted, the couple finally drifted off into a heavenly sleep intertwined like a litter of kittens.

Much too soon, the alarm sounded rudely reminding Bolton that he was obliged to show up for work. He groggily made his way towards the bathroom. Pausing at the door, he looked back and saw Christine still sound-asleep with her long strawberry-blond hair knotted into an amusing mass. He started to giggle, but it was abruptly cut short by the pounding in his head.

"Coffee," he mumbled.

That day at work was an uneventful one for Bolton. Aside from a slight alcohol-induced hangover, and not getting enough sleep, he was his usual self - analyzing and extrapolating volumes of scientific data at an extraordinary rate. His intelligence, and ability to concentrate on a single task, was considered remarkable by his peers. These traits made Bolton an extremely valuable asset for the *Terran Council.*

When he returned home early in the evening, Christine greeted Bolton warmly with a glass of chilled white wine.

"Oh, thank you," he said. "I guess the champagne has worn off by now."

They both sat down on the midnight-blue sofa facing a picture-window that overlooked the courtyard and garden. Christine started running her fingers through Bolton's hair without saying a word.

"Chris," he began, "I'd like to hear more about your field trip. What was so unusual about the artifacts you discovered up in Saskatchewan?"

"Well, 'artifacts' might not be the correct word to describe some of the items we recovered from excavation pit number two. They appeared to be extremely precise hand tools that Doctor Bovelli believes were manufactured from high-grade titanium-alloy steel. We haven't got the metallurgy results back yet, but in any case, the tools couldn't have been produced by the human civilizations known to have existed during that period. In fact, this find predates the earliest known evidence of human habitation in the Americas by several thousand years!"

"Wow!" reacted Bolton. "What did the tools look like to you?"

"Surgical instruments," Christine replied. "But, not like any I've seen before. They did not appear to be designed for the human hand."

"What?" he interjected.

"As you know, the two movements of the thumb relative to the other four digits, called *opposition* and *apposition*, allow the human hand great dexterity in manipulating physical objects. Tools such as scissors, a type of lever, are designed to utilize the convergent motion of the thumb, index and/or middle fingers. One of the artifacts in the collection was labeled as 'scissors' because it has the same familiar double-pivoted shearing blades. However, it was designed to operate in a completely different manner. This artifact has three separate micro-pneumatically operated finger grips, with the outer two radially offset by thirty degrees and inclined inwardly."

"You just lost me, Chris."

"Imagine this," she suggested. "Take a tennis ball and try to hold it with just your index, middle, and fourth fingers. You'd have to spread those fingers out very wide to do it, wouldn't you?"

Bolton nodded in the affirmative.

"Now, imagine using that grip to squeeze the tennis ball. That is how this artifact is designed to work; although, its dimensions are such that a human would have trouble operating it – our fingers are just not long enough."

"That's amazing," exclaimed Bolton. "How did your team explain these findings?"

"We didn't, Marc. The obvious conclusion could not be published. It would have caused a firestorm of controversy, and brought the wrath of officialdom down upon us like a ton of bricks. So, we just released a summary report that only included geologic date estimates of the excavated strata, and an inventory listing of the artifacts retrieved without revealing any detailed information."

"That was a pragmatic and perfectly understandable decision," Bolton observed. "However, I'm on pins-and-needles in anticipation of hearing what you personally think about this incredible discovery."

Christine smiled, and softly massaged his bare forearm.

"Assuming our dates are correct, and assuming the artifacts are not anomalous – meaning, they were originally laid down in those layers at the time of deposition. And, assuming our functional analysis of the artifacts is accurate, the only deduction that can be made is that the 'hand tools' could not have been produced from the technological knowledge available to Homo sapiens anywhere on Earth during that timeframe."

"Chris, you can speak more plainly than that."

"Alright, humans didn't make those tools. At least, stone-age humans didn't. Now, are you asking me to speculate about who actually did make them?"

"Sure, why not? This conversation is fascinating!"

"You're making fun of me, aren't you Marc?"

"No, no! Absolutely not! You know better than that."

"Yeah, I know better than that," she said sarcastically while giving Bolton a look of playful suspicion.

"I suppose that the tools could have been made by an advanced humanoid species unknown to modern science that either went extinct or has kept itself hidden from us. That possibility isn't too farfetched, I imagine. Wilder still, is the idea that highly evolved human travelers from the future went back in time and inadvertently forgot some of their tools. Or…"

"It was extraterrestrials," interrupted Bolton to complete her sentence.

"Yes. Have you ever wondered about the history of human technological advancement? It is not a gradual increase of incremental steps widely dispersed over a long evolutionary period. Instead, it is marked by seemingly random leaps of great innovation interposed between lengthy intervals of technological stagnation."

"Granted, although, that random pattern can be easily explained by non-extraterrestrial factors such as the stimulating effects of erratic climate changes and war."

Christine arose from the sofa and took a few small steps in noticeable contemplation of Bolton's comment.

"That," she stated, "was also my opinion… up until recently. But after I saw it with my own eyes, considerable doubt has since been raised in my mind."

"It?" asked Bolton, as he too got up from the sofa.

"Marc, I hope you'll appreciate the confidential nature of what I'm about to tell you. I'm afraid of what might happen if this were to leak out."

Bolton reassuringly caressed her.

"We found a body. Err, not a complete body… a skeleton, really, wearing some type of environmental suit. Whatever the material was, it had hardly deteriorated at all. The colors were still vibrant. Inside the helmet, there were tiny electrical components – like microprocessors. The hands looked bird-like, each having three extended claw-tipped digits. The head was humanoid in shape, but the brain cavity was much larger. We found it curled in a fetal position, although I estimated its erect height at no more than four feet."

Bolton sat back down on the sofa, and stared through the picture-window in stunned silence.

A month later, Bolton completed the asteroid mining plan for the Moon Base. He had identified hundreds of accessible Earth-crossers of various types, and defined specific methods in which to mine them. The asteroids were categorized by size, shape, composition, plus rotational and orbital characteristics. This provided a cost-basis analysis for the first phase of the project to identify suitable targets. Asteroids having great mass, asymmetrical shapes, high angular momentum, or extreme velocity differences with the Earth-Moon system, would require more time and energy to move them into lunar orbit. The second phase prescribed the use of inexpensive unmanned rockets to rendezvous with selected asteroids, and release preprogrammed vector-thrust pulse engine modules close by. Each module would use on-board sensors to determine the asteroid's center of gravity, and then attach itself to that point on the surface. Bolton plan recommended that, with minor modifications, the current *Planetary Surface Cargo Shuttle* (P.S.C.S.) hardware could be employed for this purpose as a cost savings measure. The third phase would be initiated by the transmission of *go signals* from control stations located on the Moon, or elsewhere, instructing each module to begin its automated engine firing sequence to change that asteroid's velocity into eventual orbit around the Moon. The fourth and final phase mandated the concurrent construction of orbital mining platforms. These facilities, the most costly components of Bolton's plan, would process the asteroids while in lunar orbit. Raw materials such as iron, nickel, various organic compounds, and even water, would be extracted and stored until transferred to the surface by cargo shuttle.

After reviewing the asteroid mining proposal documents for the umpteenth time, Director William Brown telecalled Bolton in his office.

"Bolton, the plan looks fine. I just received confirmation from the Head Council's Chief of Staff. You are to meet privately with the Honorable Janus Krichek this afternoon at fifteen-hundred hours in the south building, tenth floor, room five-five-zero-zero. Any questions?"

"Privately, sir?"

"I said, privately! Don't you hear too good?"

"Yes sir! Fifteen-hundred hours. Thank you, sir."

Bolton was intrigued by the prospect of meeting the de facto absolute ruler of the world, but he was also cautiously apprehensive. If he were to make a bad impression, or say something inappropriate, the consequences could be most unpleasant.

Bolton recalled viewing a biography of the great leader when he was in college. The pirated copy was given to him by his late uncle Richard, who had mysteriously disappeared after being caught distributing subversive propaganda against the government. After his uncle was arrested, Bolton destroyed the copy to avoid the possibility of prosecution. Now, he tried to remember the particulars of what he had watched on several occasions.

Janus Franz Krichek was born on July 30, 2009 in Graz, Austria. His family immigrated to the United States of America in 2019. They settled in central Texas where his father worked as a prison guard. Young Janus had a deeply troubled adolescence. He frequently got into physical confrontations with school administrators and local law enforcement. As a young adult, he became a staunch Christian fundamentalist, and developed extreme conservative and nationalistic political convictions that occasionally strayed into fascist doctrine. Lacking a remarkable intellect, Krichek nevertheless used his incredible determination to land a job with the *Central Intelligence Agency* (C.I.A.), which was up-to-its-neck in counterterrorism operations at the time. After several years of subservient toil in the agency, an opportunity to satisfy his insatiable desire for power finally appeared when the established governmental order began to break down in the aftermath of the *Great Flood*. Chaos was spreading everywhere, and political vacuums were sprouting around the world like wild mushrooms in a misty forest. Charging headlong into this void went Janus Krichek. In 2055, he was appointed Director of the C.I.A. without even being confirmed by the Senate. When the crisis grew into global revolution in 2061, heads of state and other important political figures either went into self-imposed exile or were hunted down and murdered. Humanity desperately needed a strong leader with the courage to restore order. Krichek managed to seize control of the powerful U.S. military, and immediately organized a successful coup d'état that culminated in the assassination of President Mariana Rowena Argüello-Sanchez. Within four years, he had solidified his authority by having millions of dissidents put to death; and in 2065, he shrewdly proffered official administrative positions, on the newly formed *Terran Council*, to several key regional dictators that had similarly rose to power around the globe. Regardless of his cruel methods, Janus Krichek would go down in history as one of the most powerful and important rulers of all time.

Bolton passed through two security checkpoints as he approached room 5500. The first was a humiliatingly invasive procedure where he was intensively probed and scanned after being forced to strip naked. The second was a thorough verification of his identity that included a blood-sampled DNA test, and a battery of psychological questions designed to establish his current mental state. After being cleared, one of the escorting security guards unlocked a massive steel door leading to the Head Council's office. There was an eerie hissing sound made when the door slowly cracked opened, as the air pressure equalized between the two rooms.

"Marc Bolton," announced the guard.

Janus Krichek swiveled around in his impressive desk chair, and stared intently into his visitor's eyes. Bolton noticed the tough, brawny features of the great ruler. His thick black hair was silver-streaked and combed straight back atop a hard, chiseled face. The eyes were slate-grey, and the brows were wildly bushy. The uncomfortable silence continued. Bolton struggled to maintain his composure, but was becoming noticeably ill at ease.

The Head Council finally spoke, "Sit down son. Relax."

Bolton immediately did so.

"Your asteroid mining plan for the Moon Base has got my staff buzzing," Krichek remarked. "It's a very creative solution, I must say."

"Thank you kindly, Your Excellency."

"The expression of gratitude is not required of you, Bolton. I expect this kind of work from you, and was simply acknowledging a job well done."

"I understand, sir."

"Good. I have a new assignment for you that is vital to the security interests of the *Terran Council*. Among hundreds of prospective candidates, you were selected because of your unique combination of scientific knowledge, its practical application, and an unwavering devotion to this administration."

Bolton had no reaction.

Krichek turned to his monitor, and activated a command icon with his large chafed index finger. "I've been studying your career. Let's see... oh yes, you developed the artificial intelligence software that we use to predict potential hot-spots of political instability throughout the world - quite ingenious. That program has been a real help to us. Tell me, how did you create it?"

"Sir, *knowledge-based* systems using *inference-engines* have been in existence for nearly a century. I just wrote a stand-alone version with a polling interface linking various remote data bases in order to..."

"Fine, that' fine," interrupted Krichek. Now, where was I? Yes, here it is. You designed the mark-five parallel power grid currently under construction for the Moon Base. Excellent work, my boy! And, ten years of service to boot!"

Krichek paused for a moment while scratching the back of his prodigious head. "You must be wondering what your new assignment is."

"Yes, sir," Bolton acknowledged unemotionally.

"I want you to go to the Martian colony and keep us informed of their scientific and technological activities. You see, they have been less than cooperative in this regard. For reasons of interplanetary political stability, Mars must not be allowed to further develop itself independently. There have been far too many wars. We do not need another one. Do you get my drift?"

"Absolutely, sir."

"There are times when I feel the Martian *Board of Regents* forgets they are a subordinate arm of the *Terran Council*. This is a seriously unfortunate situation," the Head Council warned.

Instinctively, Bolton knew he couldn't turn down this spy mission as he was now privy to an official state secret. There simply was no practical alternative other than agreeing to perform the assignment.

Another conversational lull widened as Krichek searched for any hint of hesitation in Bolton's facial expressions, but the man sitting before the Head Council was as unreadable as a solid rock wall. Conversely, Bolton began to concentrate on the great leader's thoughts like he unintentionally did with Han Li the previous year. Bolton's mind was suddenly awash in images, ideas, and emotions that didn't belong to him. He narrowed his focus so that he could extract something pertinent from the maze of mostly troubled thoughts, and to his amazement, he realized he had done exactly that. As the mental congestion faded away, Bolton now understood that Krichek planned to overthrow the Martian *Board of Regents* – violently, if necessary. The cadre of spies he was sending to Mars was, in reality, an intricate *fifth-column* infiltration operation.

"Son, are you still with me?" demanded Kricheck.

"Yes sir. I'm sorry, sir."

"It is imperative that humanity, wherever it resides, works together under one leadership," lectured the Head Council. "Can I count on you to execute this assignment to the best of your ability?"

"Sir, I will put forth every effort within my capacity."

"Good. My staff has setup a schedule for your briefings over the next few weeks. You will be contacted at the appropriate times. In the interim, you are not to discuss this matter with anyone outside my personal staff, nor are you allowed to travel beyond the confines of Sutter City. This assignment has the highest security classification, and its confidentiality will not be compromised under any circumstances. Is that clear?"

"Perfectly, sir."

"Excellent. If you do a good job on Mars, there could be a high-ranking position on the Council waiting for you when you return. Now, you may return to your normal duties."

Bolton briefly stood at attention before turning to leave.

On the way back to his office, Bolton tried to mentally prepare himself for the coming adventure. He knew that the path of every life was marked by a split in the road. The direction chosen would determine the difference between two opposing realities. For him, it would occur on the eve of his forty-first birthday. His options were unambiguous: conformity and personal gain, versus morality and certain danger. The former was the pragmatic choice to make, but for him, meant a lifetime of guilt. The latter required the courage and conviction to place principle over consequence. It was not a facile decision, but Bolton felt that no human soul would be complete without enduring such an ordeal. Like a Native American's ritual rite of passage, he would confront himself without trepidation.

What perplexed Bolton much more was his recent and occasional ability to read the thoughts of others. Initially, he told himself it was just a trick of the mind, but later came to realize that the experiences were indeed quite real. Although he couldn't adequately explain it, he was certain that this ability was growing inside him like an infant using trial and error to learn how to talk. As time went on, Bolton became less concerned about why it was happening, and more acceptant of the fact that telepathy was just an intrinsic part of his natural being.

Later that evening, Bolton met Christine at her home. He was ostensibly watching one of his favorite classic films, *From Here to Eternity*, but was too preoccupied to enjoy it. He found it difficult to put the right words together and tell her what needed to be said. Across the family room, Christine was studiously reviewing some archaeological papers. Bolton worried that he'd never see that gentle face and soft contours again after he left for Mars. He wished he could capture this moment and store it away for safe keeping. Fighting back the emotion, he nervously approached his lover.

"Chris, there's something I must say to you."

She gave him an affectionate, though apprehensive look.

"There has been a change in my job responsibilities for the *Terran Council*. They're sending me away, and I'm afraid we won't be able to see each other for a while."

"Where are you going, Marc, and how long will you be gone?"

"I cannot reveal my destination, and have no idea how long I'll be there. I don't even know when I'm leaving," Bolton sadly admitted as a teardrop ran down his cheek.

Christine arose and tenderly touched his face. "Darling, how much time do we have left?"

"A few weeks, maybe a couple of months at the most, but there won't be much warning when I get the orders."

"You know I'm leaving for the Yucatan next week, don't you?" Christine submitted rhetorically.

"Of course," he replied.

"Isn't there anything you can do?"

Bolton just shook his head while rubbing the water from his eyes.

"Oh Marc, I'm so afraid!"

High above the pale-yellow house, a large thundercloud blew in from the southwest obscuring all traces of the once-brilliant sun. A pall of gloom cast over the residents of Sutter City, but for two of them, the darkness seemed especially cruel.

Chapter 3
Just another Star in the Sky

It was Christmas day, 2076. Marc Bolton sat alone studying in his quarters buried a mile and a half beneath the *Ruby Dome* summit in the old Nevada desert. For eight weeks, he had been locked up at this secret military base in preparation for his mission to Mars. Being agnostic, this Christian holiday did not hold any religious meaning for Bolton; but, it had always been a traditional special occasion for him to be with family and friends. He fondly remembered those pleasant holidays spent with Christine's parents, and with Han's bubbly family whom he felt very much a part of. Isolated here in this sterile and regimented martial community, depression was as much of a daily companion as the stone-faced soldier who was Bolton's personal guard.

Volumes of printed reports were neatly arranged on top of a large desk in the room. Bolton was required to memorize all pertinent information regarding the Martian Colony, and the false identity he would be assuming, because he would not be able to take any of those records with him. Wading through this mass of paper was slow and tedious work, but was necessary as his computer access had been denied for security reasons.

Bolton read a dossier of the nine-member Martian *Board of Regents*. Carolyn Jones, Chairperson of the Board, was born in Algeria in 2011. She was of mixed racial and religious heritage. Her family fled to North America in 2020 to escape ethnic persecution. Bolton saw a highlighted comment noting her exceptional intelligence. Jones was the Canadian ambassador to France from 2041 to 2049. She resigned that post in order to lead a consortium-backed effort to colonize Mars. In 2050, she founded the *Board of Regents* to administrate the fledgling colony. Jones was overwhelmingly elected as the Board's first Chairperson, an office she has held ever since. Bolton made special note of the last entry, describing her attitude as hostile towards the *Terran Council*.

The next name on the dossier was that of Ivan Tcholich. Bolton already knew some of this man's past. He was widely revered as a genius in the field of nuclear physics by the age of twenty. Along with the now-deceased Arnold Janowitz, Tcholich was credited with the historic breakthrough in nuclear fusion power generation. These two men patented the *Janich Pulse Reactor* in 2043, which was still the primary means of interplanetary travel. Intrigued, Bolton continued to read further. Tcholich was born in Russia in the year 2020. Known as *Ivan the Terrific* in the scientific community, he was recruited by the Martian Colony in 2051. Shortly thereafter, he was appointed to the *Board of Regents* as Member of State – a position second only to the Chairperson. He also currently held the prominent Minister of Science seat. Once again, Bolton viewed the last remark as biased political commentary. The *Terran Council* regarded

Tcholich as a dissident, and intended to prosecute him as such if he ever returned to Earth.

Curiously, the dossier contained very little information about the other seven members of the *Board of Regents*. Bolton read the names listed in descending order of seniority: Robert Toscani, Magdalena Alvarez, Candice Butler, Vejay Dadaki, Marilyn Lee Kim, James Henderson, and John Severs. Each member had a closing annotation, which labeled their political inclinations as somehow philosophically antithetical to that of the *Terran Council*, except for one – the *Board of Regents* newest member John Severs.

In his analysis of the Martian colonization, Bolton recognized one apparent fact that stood above all others. Nearly all of the high-ranking people responsible for the migration to Mars, including financiers, organizational leaders, and key scientific personnel, were considered visionary intellectuals who had been chastised for predicting a worldwide environmental catastrophe earlier in the century. Beginning in 2049, it took them only three years to establish permanent human habitation on Mars. Without question, this was an impressive achievement by any standard, and it sent shock waves through the ranks of earthbound critics. By early 2052, they had recruited six thousand highly skilled technicians to join the colony. In June of that year, the advent of the *Great Flood* initiated a series of ecological disasters that had been accurately foretold by the Martian founders. Bolton found he admired their wisdom, rational objectivity, and proactive strategy in securing their collective future.

Bolton put down the dossier after realizing that it was time for his afternoon meeting. As he walked down the well-lit hallway, he was met by Jonathan Killanobrey – the *Terran Council's* Intelligence Chief.

"Ah, Mista Bolton," Killanobrey said in broken English. "I believe today is da day when you assume you mission identity. No more Marc Bolton. From now on, you be a new man. Are you ready?"

"Yes sir."

"Good. This is da one, room one-nine-seven."

Upon entering, Bolton saw eight uniformed intelligence agents seated around a massive circular stainless-steel table. Killanobrey motioned for Bolton to take a seat opposite the men. The room was uncomfortably cold, dreary and austere.

The bald man seated in the center of the agents, stood up to address Bolton. His uniform was adorned with numerous medals and patches that Bolton couldn't identify, as they didn't appear to be consistent with regular military honors and attire.

"Mister Bolton, as of today, you are now Franklin Sharp. All identity data bases have been modified. Facial and speech recognition systems, retinal and fingerprint scanning repositories, everything that could reveal your true self has been accounted for except individuals who know you personally. We have verified that no one you're likely to encounter on Mars has any knowledge of Marc Bolton."

"Furthermore, you are hereby ordered to avoid all contact with anyone who could identify you, and instructed to deny all knowledge of the person known as Marc Bolton. If you violate either the terms or intent of these directives, you shall be considered as committing treasonous acts against the *Terran Council*. The penalties for charges of this kind rise to the level of capital punishment. Additionally, your family, friends, and acquaintances would be regarded as accomplices after the fact, subjecting them to a lengthy imprisonment and confiscation of their financial and material assets. Do you understand?"

"Yes sir, I do understand," Bolton replied.

"Then, let us proceed with the interview," the bald man motioned with a wave of this hand.

A ruddy-faced man on Bolton's extreme right began the questioning, "What is your purpose for traveling to Mars?"

"I am on temporary loan to the Colony to assist them in the procurement of raw materials."

"Who is your consignor?"

"Rafe Jorgensen, Chairman of the *Terran Council's Interplanetary Liaison Commission*."

"What is the length of your assignment?" another agent asked.

"One year," Bolton answered.

"Is that an Earth year or a Martian year?"

"An Earth year, Martian timekeeping is never used for interplanetary contracts."

"What qualifications do you possess that warrants this high profile and highly desirable assignment?"

demanded yet another agent who had an ugly scar traversing his cheek.

"I have a Master's degree in Industrial Engineering from Whitehall University."

"Bullshit!" yelled the bald man. "You're nothing but a corporate stooge on a mission to steal Martian technology!"

Bolton tried to remain calm, suspecting that the intensity of the mock interrogation would escalate. Soon, the questions were being fired at him so rapidly that it was difficult to discern which agent had uttered them.

"Bolton, that girlfriend of yours Christine, is a hot piece of ass!"

"My name is Sharp, Franklin Sharp, and I don't know anyone named Christine."

"When you're gone, we're going to pay her a little visit!"

"How do you feel about the Head Council?"

"I have the utmost respect and admiration for His Excellency," stated Bolton.

"So, you've met him? What is he like?"

"No, I've never met Janus Krichek."

"But, you just said…"

"I said I respect and admire him, as any loyal citizen would."

"Liar, liar, you're a goddamned liar!"

"Do you miss your deceased parents?"

"Yes, I miss them. But, they are still quite alive living in London."

The agent with the facial scar got up and grabbed Bolton by the ear. "You're a fucking freak" he yelled, "a cowardly degenerate freak! What do you even keep that girlfriend for?"

"I don't have a girlfriend. I'm a happily married man with two children," Bolton avowed defiantly.

The grueling trial dragged on for two more hours. When it was over, Bolton was taken to the medical facility and treated for several bruises and abrasions. Jonathan Killanobrey, however, was thoroughly satisfied with his performance. The forgery of Franklin Sharp appeared to be effectively complete.

On December 26th, Bolton looked out the window of the military aircraft as it descended into the Phoenix spaceport. He had never experienced space travel before, and this was the first time he had seen such a facility. He was amazed by its size and complexity. Sixteen silver-winged aerospace planes were neatly arranged around a geometric grid outlining underground terminals, transport tubes, and maintenance stations. On the opposite side of the long runway, Bolton could see the commercial airport bustling with people and vehicles moving to and fro. Off in the distance, massive communications towers protruded up into the western horizon. Resting on his lap was a brochure boastfully proclaiming that forty percent of the world's space traffic flowed through the Phoenix spaceport.

After passing through security, Bolton relaxed in a lounge adjacent to his departure gate. The two-and-a-half hour layover shouldn't be too uncomfortable here, he thought. The colorful food and beverage bar was equipped with personal audio and video entertainment consoles, as well as monitors airing a variety of popular television shows. Telecoms were distributed evenly about, and there were sleeping rooms close by in a secluded area.

As he sipped on a blended orange-melon drink, Bolton felt a supple hand touch his shoulder. Pivoting around, he was greeted by the familiar smiling face of Han Li.

"Sit down and shut up!" Bolton ordered under his breath.

Han was startled, but complied with his friend's command.

"Say something casual like you don't know me," whispered Bolton.

"Excuse me, do you mind if I join you?" a bewildered Han asked.

"Not at all, be my guest. My name is Franklin Sharp, and you?"

"Han Li," he replied while weakly shaking Bolton's hand. "I presume you are also booked on this Mars flight?"

Now it was Bolton's turn at confusion. "Yes... I am. The colony is in short supply of raw materials. I will be assisting them in their procurement efforts. And, what is bringing you to the Red Planet, Mister Li?"

"The colony wants to explore the prospects for terra-forming Mars. Being a climatologist, I have some expertise in atmospheric modification."

"I see," Bolton added before leaning closer and continuing in a subdued voice. "Han, we are in great danger. If the local surveillance crew gets any indication that we know each other, they'll report it to headquarters and learn your identity. Then, we're dead. So, play along with this charade until I notify you otherwise."

Han acknowledged with a reassuring facial expression.

"Please tell me more about terra-forming Mars," Bolton said normally as he reclined back into his chair.

"Alright, may I call you Franklin?"

"Sure."

"The colony wants to fundamentally alter the climate by increasing the atmospheric pressure sufficiently enough to allow bodies of liquid water to form on the surface. This would also increase ambient temperatures, and possibly create the conditions necessary for rudimentary plant life to exist out in the open."

"How could that be done? I mean, wouldn't terra-forming require many thousands of years to accomplish?"

"Not necessarily. We have already seen the rapid effects of inadvertently enriching the Earth's atmosphere with greenhouse gases from the burning of fossil fuels. Although doing the same thing on

Mars is neither feasible nor desirable, there are other alternatives. Mars has three known reservoirs of carbon, in addition to its CO2-rich atmosphere, that reside within its lithosphere. The Martian regolith, or soil - if you will, is comprised of various silicate compounds containing carbon at a rate of roughly four parts per million. More sporadic in distribution, although still significant, are sedimentary deposits – where water once flowed in the ancient past – having carbonate-infused layers with much higher concentrations approaching three hundred parts per million. But the most viable source of carbon dioxide exists within the so-called cryosphere as clathrate compounds in the Martian permafrost which extends to a depth of over one mile in places."

Bolton revered Han's scientific passion. It was a major foundation of their friendship. The two could easily converse for hours discussing intellectual topics, even in a surreal setting like this one.

"Interesting, and what mechanisms would be employed to liberate the carbon?"

"Heat," replied Han. "While the Martian carbon cycle is vastly different than the Earth's, due to its lack of a biosphere and active hydrosphere, CO2 is still cyclically exchanged between the atmosphere and surface. This phenomenon, resulting from diurnal and seasonal temperature oscillations, has been directly observed on Mars since the early days of robotic exploration. Artificially applying heat to the previously described matrixes will upset the natural equilibrium and increase the atmospheric concentration of carbon dioxide. As the pressure of the atmosphere becomes greater, temperatures will rise correspondingly releasing even more CO_2 in what is called a *positive feedback* effect."

"Considering the breakthrough in nuclear fusion, the power required for this objective is readily available," Bolton added.

"Yes Franklin, and I think solar might work just as well. But, the generation of power isn't the problem. The critical issue is how to apply the energy to heat the matrixes. I have two theoretical proposals I'll be submitting to the colony. The first entails the use of orbiting satellites to reflect solar radiation onto the surface, and the second calls for fusion-powered deep mine heat exchangers to activate and vent the permafrost."

"That's amazing, Mister Li."

An attractive young attendant interrupted the conversation and faced Bolton. "Pardon me, sirs. Mister Sharp, there is an urgent telecall for you at the departure gate reception desk," the voluptuous brunette pronounced as she pointed in the appropriate direction.

"Thank you," Bolton responded as he walked away from the lounge rather warily.

The attendant began to follow him, but was sidetracked by a smitten Han Li.

"Are all the ladies who work here as strikingly gorgeous as you?"

She smiled coyly, before replying. "They are much prettier than I. If you wait long enough I'm sure you'll have a chance to meet some of them."

Han was beaming like a birthday boy who had just received a cherished gift. "I would prefer getting to know you better. Perhaps we could share a cocktail or two when your shift is over."

"I don't believe you have the time," she suggested sarcastically while leaning over him in teasingly close proximity and diverting his attention to an obviously noticeable wall clock. "Very soon you will be bolting up into the wild blue yonder. And from my vantage point, you'll just be another little star in the sky."

Han laughed to himself in amusement, and lustfully admired the attendant's curvaceous form as she proudly strutted away.

The reception desk clerk directed Bolton towards a secluded telecom booth adjacent to the departure gate. He pressed the call-waiting transfer link and soon recognized the face of Madeline Bailey, the Intelligence Chief's operations manager.

"Franklin Sharp here," Bolton said nervously as he wondered if his chance meeting with Han Li was detected by the *Terran Council*.

"Listen," the annoyed middle-aged woman commanded. "I'm going to make an exception to security protocols just this once. Your friend Christine Bakerman has been asking a lot of questions regarding your whereabouts. She's emotionally upset, and we fear her persistent inquisitions might become public. We need to calm her down, so I'll be connecting you to her shortly. But, I remind you not to divulge any information about your mission. You are to reassure her so that she doesn't become a problem for us, and nothing more. Is that understood?"

"Yes madam."

"Alright, I'm connecting you now. Your conversation will be monitored, and I suggest you keep it brief."

After a momentary delay, Christine's image was displayed.

"Oh Marc, thank goodness! I've been worried sick about you. They won't tell me anything. Where are you? What's going on? When can I see you?"

"Chris, all I can say is that I'm safe and well. You know there has always been a great amount of trust and respect between us. I'm asking you now to have faith that I'll be able to take care of myself, as I have faith that you will do the same for yourself. This situation will work itself out eventually. When it does, I'm hopeful that everything will return to normal."

"What are you trying to tell me, Marc?"

"Remember the last night of our Lake Tahoe vacation?"

Christine did remember. In fact, it would have been impossible for her to forget. That trip was culminated with an intimate dinner when they pledged to each other to carry on individually should the insanity of the world come between them.

"Yes… I remember," she murmured as her eyes began to tear up. "But, why didn't you tell me you were taken to the hospital last spring because you blacked-out again? Didn't you feel I had the right to know? I only found this out recently when I stumbled upon the medical report in your apartment."

"I should have told you," admitted Bolton. "I was in denial, and very embarrassed about it. And, I didn't want to worry you too much. But, I was wrong. Please forgive me, Chris."

A warning buzzer sounded indicating the imminent termination of the telecall.

"Marc, come back for me!" she bawled.

"I love you, Christine," he declared just as the monitor went blank.

There are times in every person's life when a cascade of seemingly random events merge into a powerful force driving one beyond their ability to control their own destiny. Like an ocean vessel encountering a gigantic rogue wave, the only available course of action is to remain level-headed and ride it out. For Marc Bolton, the inertia pushing him towards an uncertain future on the Red Planet was now severely challenging his composure with somber remorse.

As he took a seat next to Bolton inside the surprisingly spacious aerospace plane, Han perceived emotional distress in his longtime friend. His first instinct was to inquire into that which was troubling

Bolton, but he quickly dismissed the idea knowing intimately that he shouldn't press into the matter. Instead, he gave him a familiar smile, a gentle pat on the back, and topics of discussion sure to distract away his melancholy. If there was only a single essential quality of true friendship, it must be that silence and understanding are not mutually exclusive.

"Franklin, I couldn't help but notice your bruises. Are you a fighter, or just ran into some bad luck lately?"

Bolton's expression revealed a token annoyance with the question. But before he could respond, their seats began to vibrate as a high-pitched whine signaled the ignition of the aerospace plane's two scramjet engines. As the frequency of the small vibrations increased, Han issued forth some contrived nervousness.

"This craft seems a bit shaky. How old is it?"

"It's been in operation for forty-two years, with an excellent safety record," Bolton stated plainly.

"Forty-two years! That's ancient! They might as well have strapped us to the top of a rocket and blasted us off into oblivion like they did in the twentieth century! I'd feel better in a shuttle. Why couldn't they use those?"

"Mister Li…"

"Call me, Han."

Bolton's exasperation was elevating. "The P.S.C.S. shuttles were designed for planetary bodies without dense atmospheres. They are not aerodynamically sound, making them difficult and expensive to use here. However archaic, the aerospace plane was specifically designed for Earth orbital transfer, and it has performed quite well in that role. You shouldn't be worried, the fleet is appropriately maintained."

"Glad to hear that, Franklin," Han remarked in smug satisfaction.

Bolton looked at his friend with inquisitive scrutiny. When he realized what Han was up to, he smiled warmly and shook his head in amazement. "You're a real prick sometimes, Han," he said rather sheepishly.

As the 130 foot long aerospace plane accelerated down the runway, the scream of the scramjets rose to a nearly ear-splitting crescendo. It lifted off the ground at a 45 degree angle, and Bolton could see the spaceport rapidly fading away as he looked out his window. In the wink of an eye, the craft passed through a puffy white cumulous cloud as wispy contrails whipped around the forward canards. Almost twenty miles up, the sky turned a deep midnight blue and Bolton could no longer hear the rush of air past the fuselage. At that moment, the liquid fuel rockets fired pressing the passengers hard back into their seats. After several seconds, the rockets ceased marking the acquisition of Earth orbit.

The sensation of weightlessness and the utter blackness of space gave Bolton a feeling of youthful exuberance. His childhood dream of experiencing spaceflight had finally come true.

Han Li, however, did not appear to be as enthusiastic. His head was pointed down as if he was lost in deliberation, and he was wringing his hands like a defendant on a witness stand. When their eyes met, Bolton unexpectedly recognized the emission of his friend's thoughts just as he had on the other occasions. Only this time, it wasn't as much of a surprise to him.

"What memorandum?" asked Bolton.

Han was incredulous. "How did you know what I was thinking?"

"To be honest, I'm not sure."

"Mar… Franklin, you did this once before. Remember San Francisco?" demanded Han in a low voice.

"Yes, I remember. And, it has happened with other people as well."

"Are you telling me you can read minds?"

"No not really. But, every once in a while the thoughts of others I'm in close contact with seem to pop into my head. I don't know what to make of it, although it's been occurring more frequently the past few months."

"So, it happens randomly – meaning you are not in control?"

"Yes, in the beginning. However, I'm learning that by placing my consciousness in a particular state I can increase the likelihood of reception."

"I'm stunned," Han revealed. "How long have you been having these experiences?"

"Over a year now, I think."

"I've suspected for some time that telepathy might be a latent human trait."

Han's conjecture was overshadowed by the pilot's voice broadcasting over the intercom. "Ladies and gentlemen, we'll be docking with the interplanetary transport ship *Argyre* in approximately twelve minutes. We hope you have enjoyed the flight so far, and suggest you take this opportunity to savor the spectacular panoramas as we slowly rotate into synchronous orbital position. As a safety reminder, please remain belted into your seats and refrain from allowing unsecured personal items to float about the cabin. Thank you."

Bolton's attention returned to the document Han had been thinking about. "Han, please tell me more about the memorandum you found in the Transamerica building, if you don't mind."

Although he felt somewhat violated, Han proceeded to explain. "I was studying in an unused conference room when the workmen who were removing a partition discovered a small broken wall safe. Everyone was curious, so we opened it and found an unsealed envelope inside. The workmen said they had no instructions regarding any findings of property, as that floor had been officially cleared out. So, I took it upon myself to see what the envelope contained. I unfolded a single page letter dated November, 3, 2066. It was a memorandum from the Head Council to the Adjutant General – Western North America. Severs, I think his name was. Yes, John Severs."

Bolton recalled from his research that the addressee of the memo had the same name as the newest member of the Martian *Board of Regents*.

"Essentially," Han continued, "it was a request for a specific classified report on the Martian Colony."

"Do you remember the identification code of the report?" queried Bolton.

"No. There was a lengthy alphanumeric reference number listed, but I couldn't even begin to recite it. After one of the workmen saw who had sent the memo, he grabbed it from my hands and burned it to ashes with a cigarette lighter. He was very upset, warning the rest of us to keep our mouths shut – if we knew what was good for us – and ordering one of the other workmen to immediately dispose of the safe. It was quite a scene!"

As he thought to himself for a moment, Bolton realized that Janus Krichek's curiosity of the Martian colonists dated back to at least the time of the *Terran Council's* formation – eleven years prior. Why he was so concerned back then about a small group of utopian-seeking pioneers, wasn't at all apparent.

During the docking maneuver, Bolton and Han got an excellent view of the *Argyre*. It was an incredible sight. The interplanetary transport ship was 750 feet long with four massive 500 foot diameter habitation rings spinning leisurely around her axis. At the front end, a planetary surface cargo shuttle was mated to the command module. Its opposite end housed the engineering control station, nuclear power plant, and a powerful fusion pulse engine. There were communications and scanning antennas located fore and aft, as well as defensive laser turrets. The ship's standard capacity was 2050 persons, of which 77 were crew and 120 were military personnel.

"Wow!" exclaimed Han as the bright rays of the sun illuminated the mammoth light-grey vessel. "I forgot. How long does it take to travel to Mars again?"

"I believe our transit time is seventeen days," replied Bolton. "We'll eventually reach speeds approaching a quarter of a million miles per hour."

"Fascinating, that large round structure with the exhaust nozzle must be the fusion drive. It is based on the *Janich Pulse Reactor* technology, right?"

"Yes, that's correct Han. The module you see immediately in front of it is a conventional nuclear fission power plant, with ten deuterium storage tanks attached around its exterior. It also houses two turbine generators. One is reserved for the ship's electrical supply, while the other produces the fusion engine's magnetic containment field."

"Franklin, although I understand the basic fundamentals of nuclear physics, it escapes me how the engine can generate sufficient thrust to propel such a large vessel without rupturing the containment field."

"Ah, you're alluding to the historic breakthrough that Janowitz and Tcholich made decades ago. Tcholich got the idea from Germany's V-1 pulse-jet buzz bomb developed during World War Two. He proposed using a variable-geometry, pulsating magnetic envelope to initiate the fusion reaction and vector the resulting high-energy helium plasma as thrust. In the first phase of the cycle, the containment field constricts deuterium fuel down into a dense highly-pressurized state. In the second phase, the fusion reaction is triggered by the firing of powerful laser beams simultaneously converging on the fuel. In the third and last phase, the containment field relaxes into a geometric shape allowing the energy to be focused through an exhaust port thereby creating propulsive thrust."

"I see," said Han. "So, the explosive force of the reaction never has a chance to build up against the containment field because it is allowed to vent in a controlled direction."

"Yes," Bolton added. "This is, if the system functions properly. It is a tediously delicate process having great inherent instabilities, and extremely low tolerances, which can only be run by a highly sophisticated and sensitive computer. Random imbalances can, and have on rare occasions, caused the system to fail catastrophically."

"I've never heard of any catastrophic failures," Han admitted with a noticeable expression of concern.

"Well, news of those events has been sequestered for obvious reasons. But, fear not Han. The kinks in the system have been worked out years ago, and there are now safety systems in place having a perfect operational record."

"That's reassuring. But, you mentioned that the engine thrust 'pulsates.' From the promotional videos I've seen, the exhaust stream looks continuous."

"The time interval between each cycle is just a few milliseconds. The human eye is incapable of discerning it," Bolton responded.

As the aerospace plane maneuvered into position, Bolton and Han were able to view the *Argyre* from an end-on angle. With the habitation rings spinning around them, it appeared as if they were heading straight into a giant vortex. Soon thereafter, the docking locks contacted with a dull thud.

The pilot once again addressed the passengers over the intercom. "For your safety, please keep your seatbelts fastened until you receive instructions to transfer to the *Argyre*. We hope you enjoyed the ride, and wish you a pleasant and memorable voyage to Mars."

Chapter 4
To the Pillars of Ares

Getting aboard the *Argyre* was an embarrassing experience for Bolton. Because of the weightless environment, people and cargo must be moved into the ship by a conveyor mechanism. Bolton didn't secure his harness properly, and he slipped out of it half way into the airlock. Instinctively, he tried to regain his grip on the harness by pushing off the conveyor platform with his legs. But in zero gravity, that is never a wise thing to do. His reaction sent him tumbling end over end, and he was soon ricocheting off the walls like a pinball in an old-fashioned arcade game. It took the cargo crew several minutes to retrieve him. The delay solicited an angry tongue-lashing from the stowage officer who was already behind schedule. Fortuitously, Bolton was not injured in the mishap.

The loading and unloading of an interplanetary transport ship was a time consuming endeavor. Safety regulations mandated that the interior and exterior doors of the air lock could not be open simultaneously. Normally, about ten people could be moved at a time. The transfer of the aerospace plane's 81 passengers, along with their baggage and commercial cargo, required nearly two hours to complete.

As he traversed through the *Argyre's* cavernous storage hold, Bolton noticed how efficiently cargo was organized and manipulated within the ship. The crew used modular lattice-works to secure variously sized containers and bulk items. The lattices were attached to steel ribs protruding from the inner surface of the cylindrical hull, which could be assembled into almost any conceivable configuration. The movement of cargo within the hold was accomplished by robotic arms, conveyors, and manually operated pulleys and opposable tethers.

After a brief 150 foot elevator ride to the main deck of habitat ring two, Bolton and Han reacquired their lost equilibrium as they began to feel the effects of simulated gravity. Han had coped with the physics of zero gravity far better than Bolton, who should have remembered Sir Isaac Newton's *Third Law of Motion* – that for every action, there is an equal and opposite reaction.

As the two men walked along the corridor leading to their individual quarters, Han's curiosity regarding his friend's recent bizarre behavior could not be subdued.

"You know," he paused. "When you have some free time, I think we should experiment a little with your telepathy. Perhaps, we can get an idea how effective it is in different situations, and how well you can control it."

"Look Han," Bolton retorted. "I wasn't sent to Mars to be some sort of guinea pig for your private research. Now if you'll excuse me, I want to unpack." He entered his room and abruptly closed the door leaving Han outside in bemusement.

Bolton threw his bags on the bed with unrestrained force. He turned around deliberately, and examined himself closely in the dresser mirror. He was ashamed by his angry reaction towards Han. He knew it was unwarranted, but was unable to comprehend what had provoked it. Something inside him didn't feel right, as if a fundamental change was taking place within his being. No, not a change, he corrected himself, more like a metamorphosis with its own sense of identity and purpose. From his college days, Bolton recalled a species of wasp that incubates inside the living body of a caterpillar. The host goes about its normal activities until the day comes when the parasite rips it apart to be born into the world.

"Ridiculous," Bolton said aloud in a vain attempt to restore some sanity to his perceived paranoid delusion. But suddenly, another errant thought popped into his mind. He remembered the 'dream' he had nearly two years past, when the voice inside his head called out to him by name. "Marc," it said, with an inflection intended to get his attention. Yes, that's it, he realized. Just like how his father used to talk when he wanted Bolton to do something. "Marc," he recollected his father once saying, "get in here now and wash your hands. It's dinner time."

It dawned upon Bolton that all his telepathic experiences occurred after the 'dream' incident. "Was there a cause-and-effect relationship?" he postulated to himself. "But how could that be? What could be responsible for his perception of receiving an external mental communication, and also given him the apparent ability to read the minds of others? Why did he experience severe nose bleeds during both the 'dream' and second 'blackout' episodes? Had a physical transformation taken place?" Bolton struggled to uncover a reasonable answer, but could not. The problem just didn't make any sense to him, because it existed outside his practical nature and subjective view of reality.

Nonetheless, Marc Bolton was not an individual who would submit to the indifference of ignorance. He was instinctively compelled to resolve problems and understand the universe around him to its fullest extent. If an orthodox approach couldn't adequately explain his dilemma, then he would expand the boundaries of cognition to the point where objectivity supplanted the trappings of personal experience.

Christine had proposed that the conventional interpretation of human evolution might be fundamentally incomplete, and that it could be missing a crucial contributory factor of extraterrestrial origin. If an alien species had indeed performed human engineering in the past, it was logical to assume that activity could still be happening. Bolton let his mind clear and stared vacantly at his image being reflected back by the mirror. Seconds seemed to pass like minutes as if time itself was being stretched out. He sensed the soft white light inside the room appear to slow down and contort into multi-colored eddies. The contours of his face became obscured with distortion, and he felt a sensation that his consciousness was growing beyond the physical constraints of his body. In the mirror, a different face appeared replacing the one Bolton was accustomed to. It was expressionless, frail, and yet somehow familiar. It was also not at all human. Then in a brief instant, Bolton's mind snapped back to his corporeal reality; however, the transition was too abrupt. A sharp pain pierced through his temples, his brown eyes fluttered, and he collapsed to the floor unconscious.

Han Li heard the initial P.L.A. alarm informing all passengers to proceed immediately to their assigned L.S.R., or Launch Safety Room. The *Passenger Launch Assembly*, or 'play' as referred to by the crew, was initiated twenty minutes before main engine ignition would send an interplanetary transport off on its journey. The L.S.R. was a pressurized compartment that could be jettisoned away from the ship in the event of a serious launch malfunction. Each interplanetary transport carried fifty L.S.R.'s that could individually support up to forty people for as long as a week. They were commanded by a crewman trained to maneuver it in space using attitude control jets. Although no such disaster involving passenger flights had yet occurred, the P.L.A. was a precautionary safety protocol incorporated into standard operating procedures.

When the L.S.R. filled up with passengers, Han Li saw that Bolton was not among them. He checked the passenger list and verified that Franklin Sharp was assigned to that room. After notifying the crewman, Han was allowed five minutes to try and find him.

Meanwhile, Bolton had regained consciousness and arose from the floor. He had no recollection of what happened, aside from remembering the sharp pain in his head that knocked him out, and which was now completely gone. Surprisingly, he felt pretty good. There was no residual grogginess or disorientation, but he mistakenly believed that several hours had elapsed.

The door buzzer sounded. Bolton pressed the command switch, and the door rolled up smoothly into its ceiling compartment.

"Didn't you hear the P-L-A alarm?" Han asked inquisitively.

"No, I think I passed out."

"Are you okay, big guy?"

"Yes, I feel alright now."

"Well, come on then. We need to go to the L.S.R. pronto!" Han instructed while ushering Bolton out of the room with a firm hand on his friend's shoulder. "They're about ready to light this damn candle!"

Bolton complied, but without any outward display of urgency. Moreover, he seemed to be oddly detached from the excitement that normally goes along with an interplanetary transport launch, and his movements looked mechanical – almost robotic in its lack of fluidity. Han's concern was progressing into genuine worry.

"Franklin, I think you should pay a visit to the doctor tomorrow. Sometimes people don't react well to space travel. You better get yourself checked out."

Bolton was unresponsive.

The L.S.R. crewman, Tech Sergeant Madeline O'Mara, began issuing the standard prelaunch passenger instructions. "May I have your attention, everyone! " The crowd noise immediately subsided. "Thank you. Flip your right arm rest cover over, and you'll see a green acceleration pill in the compartment. Please swallow it now. You have all been advised of the bodily effects associated with an interplanetary transport launch. I will reiterate. The main engine will fire for two hours. During that time you will experience constant three-g acceleration. You will feel sluggish, heavy, and your blood flow will slow down. It might become difficult to think and speak clearly, and you may suffer blurred vision. You must resist the urge to sleep, as that increases the odds of slipping into a coma. If those seated next to you appear to be sleeping, you must wake them up immediately. As you know, I will not be able to assist anyone during the acceleration. If your neighbor needs attention, do whatever you can to help, but do not attempt to leave your seat for any reason. When the engine cuts off, you will feel zero gravity even though we will be traveling close to a quarter million miles per hour. Keep your seat restraints on. You will be given further instructions at that time."

As Sgt. O'Mara secured herself to her duty station, the final launch alarm bellowed throughout the ship.

All the passenger seats automatically reclined into a horizontal configuration. Shortly thereafter, the *Argyre's* habitation rings stopped spinning and were locked into place, putting everyone on board in a state of weightlessness.

"I'll take your advice and see the doctor tomorrow," Bolton told Han. "Also, it's very reassuring to know that you'll be here with me, Han. If I didn't know better, I'd swear you arranged it just to look after me."

"It's my pleasure, big guy… it's my pleasure."

The *Argyre's* massive fusion engine ignited sending a deep shudder reverberating through the great ship. The weight of hundreds of pounds seemed to press down upon its prone occupants as the muffled roar grew in intensity. Astern of the ship, the brilliant blue-white Earth gradually receded into the cold blackness of space. Bolton remembered a quote from the famous author of *Beckoning Worlds*, Sir George Easterly: "Though I know not what I'll find… though I know not why I go… Off! Off! Off! Off to the Pillars of Ares!"

Acceleration sickness affected some people greater than others. The symptoms were usually mild bouts of lethargy, vertigo, sensory dysfunction, and nausea. More severe and persistent effects such as delirium and psychosis occurred very infrequently; however, paralysis and even death resulting from brain hemorrhaging remained statistical possibilities that had to be considered for all personnel. To reduce the instance of serious health problems aboard interplanetary transports, all passengers and crew were required to pass a vigorous medical screening in order to weed out susceptible individuals.

As Bolton began to regain normal awareness from his trance-like state, he noticed the effects of weightlessness on his body telling him that the main engine had cutoff. He heard groaning noises in the room, and smelled the foul odor of regurgitation wafting through the air. Then, there was a loud clunking noise followed by the sensation of gravity. Several small items, which had not been properly secured, instantly fell to the floor and made a clattering sound.

Sgt. O'Mara stood up from her seat and scanned the L.S.R. "Mister Huggington!" she shouted. "You were instructed not to eat anything four hours prior to your arrival on the *Argyre*. Look at the mess you made!"

Several passengers in the vicinity of Alexander Huggington were visibly upset, as they were now wearing some of the odorous products of his untimely sickness.

"Calm down everyone and remain seated," ordered O'Mara. "Let's give ourselves a few minutes to get re-acclimated. Take deep regular breaths. That's it. Now, stretch out your arms and legs. Wiggle your feet and clinch your fists a few times. Very good, continue those exercises a little longer and I'll raise your seats back up. When I allow you to stand up, make sure you are feeling okay before leaving the room. Also, I'm advising you to abstain from any strenuous activity for at least eight hours. It's probably a good idea for you to eat pretty soon, but you should restrict it to a light meal and drink plenty of fluids."

The activity in the L.S.R. gradually increased, and Bolton likened it to a beehive arousing from an overnight slumber as the morning sunlight warmed up its confines.

"Alright everyone, you may leave now," instructed Sgt. O'Mara. "Except you Mister Huggington, get over here and help me cleanup this disgusting mess!"

Bolton and Han left the L.S.R. together having few residual effects from the two hour long acceleration.

"How do you feel, Han?"

"Tired, very tired," he replied. "I think I'll grab a snack and go to bed. How about you?"

"Not too bad at all," replied Bolton. "I think I'll stroll around for a while and check out the facilities."

"Right, see you later then," Han said while stepping into his quarters.

Each of the *Argyre's* habitation rings contained three separate levels. The main deck occupied the middle level. It housed the passenger quarters, commissary, medical station, laundry and other personal services, and several lounge areas. Above it was the inner deck which included a computerized library, meeting rooms, crew quarters, a communications station, and various administrative offices. The outer deck was the lowest level containing the machinery spaces, storage areas, and some recreational facilities.

During his tour, Bolton admired the quality of the ship's accommodations. The library was first-rate having expansive data bases, efficient file servers, and virtually all available presentation mediums. The technology of the data links with remote sites like the Earth were impressive, considering the distances involved, but were tightly controlled by internal security protocols. In many ways, the working environment aboard the *Argyre* rivaled anything found on the Earth, including the *Terran Council's* state-of-the-art offices in Sutter City. However, it was obvious that the ship was no twentieth century-style luxury liner. Its entertainment options were few, its creature comforts rather Spartan, and its culinary style was similar to the banal simplicity favored by military boot-camps.

The artificial gravity resulting from the centrifugal forces generated by the rotating habitation rings varied noticeably as Bolton traversed through the different levels. With the rings spinning at a constant 3.42575 revolutions per minute, the main deck – at a radius of 250 feet from the ship's axis – essentially had the same gravity as would be experienced on the Earth's surface. The inner deck, with a radius ten feet shorter, had four percent less simulated gravity; and, the outer deck had four percent more at 1.04001g. A person weighing 150 pounds on the main deck would be six pounds lighter on the upper level and six pounds heavier on the lower level. Bolton joked to himself that if he gained a few pounds on the trip he could always spend more time on the inner deck to mitigate the guilt.

To his surprise, the recreational facilities on the outer deck were modestly impressive. There was exercise equipment, squash courts, a hologram game arcade, billiard tables, card tables, a small theater, and a spectacular listening room with a transparent floor. The latter captivated Bolton. He relaxed in a soft recliner listening to his favorite classical jazz, and gazed in awe as brightly colored stars and planets moved across the floor under his feet. "What a concept! The ultimate in stress relief," he thought. The hours passed by easily. Bolton could think of no better place to be.

The next day, Bolton visited Major Ellis Raystreet who was the highest ranking medical officer aboard the *Argyre*. After listening to Bolton's description of his most recent blackout episode, and reviewing the medical records of one Franklin Sharp, the doctor began a routine and progressive series of tests designed to identify any physiological abnormalities that might have caused the problem. When completed, all the test results were negative – meaning that his patient was in excellent physical and mental condition. Unconvinced, Raystreet decided to perform two additional tests: An electroencephalogram to monitor brain wave irregularities, and a DNA diagnostic analysis to expose foreign radical mutations.

It took Doctor Raystreet another two hours to acquire a meaningful E.E.G. tracking and the DNA results back from the *Genetic Code Profiler*, or G.C.P. During that time Bolton became rather short-tempered, particularly with one of Raystreet's assistants whose sadistic enjoyment in her patients' discomfort was disquietingly evident. After the doctor had thoroughly reviewed the data, he called an impatient Bolton back into his private office to give him his findings.

"Sorry about the delay, Mister Sharp, it was unavoidable. Why don't you have a seat?"

"Thank you," said Bolton.

"As I said before, all of the tests indicate that you are in good physical health. We couldn't find any pathological evidence whatsoever. You have no bacterial or viral infections, no indication of toxic exposure, and no signs of disease or significant trauma. The CAT scan of your brain revealed no thrombosis, arterial embolism, or hematoma which could cause a stroke. Having had the chance to observe you for several hours, it is also my opinion that you are not suffering from any mental dysfunction or psychological condition."

"If there's nothing wrong with me, then what's causing the blackouts? Could it be what they diagnosed in Sutter City last spring?"

To refresh his memory, Raystreet displayed Franklin Sharp's medical history on his monitor. "Let's see," he paused while browsing the records. "This is it. April third, twenty-seventy-six, subject unconscious approximately sixty hours due to probable *Electro-Synchronous Synapse Reflection*. Patient released following establishment of criteria specified per association guidelines - signed by Doctor Jorgensen, Sutter City Medical Center."

Raystreet's hesitation revealed his skepticism. "No, I cannot agree with that diagnosis. I'm quite familiar with ESSR having worked on planetary transports the past several years. Although rare, it is more prevalent in space environments due to the higher levels and wider spectrum of radiation. However, I can say with reasonable certainty that your current condition is not consistent with ESSR."

"What is it then, Doctor?"

"Officially, I cannot make a diagnosis. I just don't know what caused your last blackout, and therefore will not speculate on the prior occurrences. My noncommittal position notwithstanding, I'd like you to see an interesting discovery I stumbled upon. Please come over here, Mister Sharp, so that you can view the monitor better."

Bolton walked around the doctor's desk and stood over the man's shoulder.

"You see the three lines on the EEG graph?" Raystreet asked rhetorically.

"Of course," replied Bolton.

"They each represent what we in the medical profession call a *Standard Pattern Map*, which is a synthesis of your conscious brain activity in a controlled setting that uniquely identifies individuals much like fingerprints and retinal scans. It is not definitive, as of yet, due to the brain wave changes a person experiences with age or when they are affected by uncontrolled stimuli. However, it is a valuable research tool in clinical settings."

"So what do they mean, Doctor?"

"The blue line is a file record from twenty-sixty-six. The solid green line was taken in Sutter City by Doctor Jorgensen. The solid yellow line is today's reading. Now, considering how old you are and the time span of the recordings, the evolution of the patterns should match the blinking green and yellow lines I'll put on the graph now…"

"But they don't match," observed Bolton.

"Correct," noted Raystreet. "Though, they *should* match. Here's something else I'd like to bring to your attention. This display shows your DNA profile from the same twenty-sixty-six file record. Watch what happens when I overlay it with your DNA sample taken earlier today."

"What?" Bolton exclaimed.

"Yes Mister Sharp, those prominent DNA sequence anomalies are truly shocking, aren't they?"

"How can that be? I assure you, Doctor, that I am the same person I've always been."

"Well, I believe you. The differences between the two records are not sufficient enough to suggest that you are anyone other than Franklin Sharp."

"Then, what the hell is happening to me?"

"Assuming your medical records are accurate, and that my equipment is working properly, I must conclude you represent an unprecedented example of selective genetic transformation. Your gamma wave readings above one-hundred hertz have never been seen before on an EEG. Your mutated DNA sequences are... well... unknown to human genetics. My best guess is that your brain is in the process of developing a new cognitive function all on its own! It is a theoretical impossibility. I'd like to have your permission to study this further."

"Sorry Doctor, but I'm afraid my cooperation with such a research project resides outside the boundaries of my current assignment. May I ask what report you will be submitting to the *Terran Council*?"

"Only my official comments, Mister Sharp. It would be unwise of me to include any of the speculative content we discussed."

"Agreed, then I will thank you for the professional attention you gave to this matter, and wish you a very pleasant day."

"My pleasure," the doctor replied. "And, I recommend you come back and see me if the need arises."

"I will, thank you Sir," Bolton said matter-of-factly before leaving the office.

That evening, Bolton had dinner with Han in the commissary. The preparation of food aboard the *Argyre* was typical of interplanetary transports, having been done with little creativity. The fare was served in the traditional military way with cafeteria-style hot plates in a queued assembly line. Though properly cooked, the flavors were generally bland

and the textures unrefined. Nothing on the menu was exciting, but the variety was sufficient to keep everyone reasonably satisfied.

"Did you see the doctor today?" Han asked as the two sat down on a flimsy molded plastic dining table.

"Yes, he performed an exhaustive battery of tests and couldn't find anything wrong with me."

"That's odd. People usually don't lapse into unconsciousness without some sort of cause."

"I know, I know, but the fact remains there is no medical problem."

Han was incredulous. He stopped eating momentarily and appeared offended by Bolton's remark. "Franklin, I consider it in bad taste for friends to withhold information from each other."

Bolton put down his fork which had just skewered a piece of potato pancake better suited for another less palatable venue. "Alright Han, I'll come clean. But what I'm about to tell you is rather far-fetched. I don't even know if I believe myself."

"Big guy, you are not a person inclined to fantasy. I know self-analysis on your part is never pursued without objective reason and brutal honesty. Please continue."

"The doctor discovered that my brain is undergoing an unknown form of genetic and functional mutation. He called it 'medically impossible' if I recall correctly. Somehow, deep down inside I've been aware of the changes even though my conscious mind seemed oblivious to them. That doesn't make much sense, does it?"

"I'd say yes," Han rejoined. "Consciousness is nothing more than the collective intercommunication between brain functions. When we sleep, that communication generally shuts down resulting in our perception of unconsciousness; but, the individual brain functions are still active. For example, the *Primary Auditory Cortex* doesn't turn off during sleep. It continues to process sounds, as well as the regions of the brain that react to sound, such as the *sub-cortical* area, *auditory brainstem*, and *mid brain*. Signals are continuously sent and received. If the *cortical* area recognizes a threatening noise, intercommunication restarts and the individual will, quote, wake up."

"So, are you're saying that the mutating area of my brain hasn't yet started to fully communicate with the other brain functions?"

"Precisely, and I'm contemplating the probability that the mutation is directly related to your telepathic experiences."

Bolton gazed around the commissary and saw a woman who appeared to be playfully scolding her male companion much like Christine used to do with him. He felt the onrush of sadness, but fought off the emotion with his legendary fortitude. Marc Bolton did not fear his pain, though he did work very hard to compartmentalize it. To him, a discomposed mind was an anathema.

"Han, if what you're saying is true, then whatever telepathic potential I may have should become more integrated into my cognitive being as time goes on."

"Absolutely," replied Han. "Like a child learning how to ride a bicycle, it will eventually become a natural activity requiring little effort or thought."

"What do you make of my blackouts, which have also been accompanied by other odd symptoms like persistent nosebleeds?

"I'm treading on unfamiliar ground here, but those may be physiological or psychological reactions to the process of metamorphosis occurring in your brain. They might be analogous to the *growing pains* experienced by children that feel like lower-leg shin-splints common in adult runners. Medical science cannot definitively explain the phenomenon, yet it exists nevertheless."

"Han, how is it that you are consistently able to provide meaningful insight into my life that I would otherwise struggle to acquire?"

"Perhaps, it is I who can read *your* mind," Han quipped with an infectious laugh.

"Okay, Mister Li. Let's get down to the heart of the matter. We've covered *what* is happening and *how* it's happening, but not *why* it is happening."

"That is a difficult question, isn't it? I suspect that you already know the answer; however, let me try to coax it out of you. To my knowledge, there are only three causes of genetic mutation. The first results from random mistakes made during the copying of DNA in preparation for cell division. In evolution, the individual mutations are minor, but can lead to substantial changes in time if they are favored by natural selection. The second cause is DNA damage triggered by external factors such as particle or electromagnetic radiation. These mutations are typically destructive, being responsible for severe diseases like cancer. The third cause of genetic mutation is the intentional manipulation of DNA by an outside intelligence. As far as we know, only humans are capable of this."

"How would you classify animal husbandry and selective breeding?"

"I would include those in the first cause of genetic mutation, while conceding the debate over whether intelligent choice should be considered as natural selection. But getting back to the question of *why*, let me say this. It is highly unlikely that the rapid changes you are experiencing could have been caused by natural selection, selective breeding, or radiation damage. That leaves DNA manipulation as the most plausible cause. Furthermore, if we make that assumption, then the next question is *who*."

Bolton picked at his food which was now cold and even less appetizing than it was before. He did not respond to Han's implication.

"I appreciate your reluctance to explore that possibility," continued Han. "However, who modified your DNA is an intriguing question, is it not? I do not believe the *Terran Council*, or any other organization, is capable of intentionally producing telepathic humans through genetic engineering."

"I don't either, Han."

"Well then, Franklin Sharp, let me leave you with one final thought for this evening. When you come to understand the underlying reasons for your passage to Mars, you will learn the identity of who sent you."

Han's prophetic comment made a distinct impression on Bolton. There was much more behind the strange turn of events that put him aboard this ship than just the omnipotent derangement of Janus Krichek and random chance. Instinctively, Bolton knew the answer could only be found from within his own self. To do so, he would need a key to unlock that which was growing inside him. Since knowledge was the universal key to understanding, he headed straight for the library.

The contemporary definition of parapsychology stated that it was the archaic study of paranormal, supernatural, and psychic phenomena, not explainable by conventional science. There were three distinct historical eras punctuating this discipline. The first was born in the late nineteenth century and concluded a hundred years later. The second era began in the nineteen-eighties and continued into the decade preceding the *Great Flood*. The modern era of parapsychology marked its abrupt demise as an accepted field of study when the autonomous purview of science was replaced by governmental control.

Called parapsychology's *Golden Age*, the first era had its inception with the foundation of the *Society for Psychical Research* in London, circa 1882. It was distinguished by an adherence to the principles and empirical processes of discovery established by the *scientific method,* and there was a determined effort to dissociate true psychic phenomena from spiritualism and superstition. The major areas of study included clairvoyance, precognition, telepathy, and psycho-kinesis. Bolton was especially interested in the following publications: *Thought Transference* (1946) by Whately Carington, *The Reach of the Mind* (1947) by J. B. Rhine, and *Extrasensory Perception* (1961) by Fabian Gudas. Although the research results were inconclusive in proving the existence of psychic ability, Bolton found this material relevant to his own experience and gave him a much broader field of reference.

The second era saw parapsychology slip out of mainstream science and into realm of diverse factional interests who were not necessarily interested in learning its truths. In his 2024 best seller, *The Rise of Counter-Information,* H. E. Steinholtz documented the corrupting influence of corporate power on the established institutions of society through the skillful use of propaganda and misinformation. Particularly hard hit were democratic governments, education systems, and the scientific community, which were unfairly vilified as ineffective and untrustworthy behemoths that threatened economic prosperity and personal freedom. The public was coerced into believing that all organized endeavors should directly support capitalistic enterprises, else be considered as malignantly seditious. After a brief cultural backlash against this corporatist ideology beginning in the late 2030s, it rebounded a decade later and subsequently provided the political power base for the ascendancy of Janus Krichek. As a consequence, parapsychology had lost its legitimacy and decayed into the domain of charlatans, soothsayers, and mysticism. Bolton decided to ignore the work done during this era.

Even though the modern era was devoid of any serious studies on parapsychology, Bolton did stumble upon one book recently written by Magdalena Alvarez – a current member of the Martian *Board of Regents*. Titled, *Nascent Connections to the Cosmos*, it proposed the hypothesis that the human brain contained embryonic structures having the potential to tap into a ubiquitous cosmic level of consciousness that exists extra-dimensionally – that is, outside the constructs of Einstein's space-time continuum. Bolton thought the novel was unabashedly speculative, but also intellectually provocative. And, he became aware that it had one other notable aspect – having been banned from further publication by the *Terran Council*.

Bolton had spent the better part of four days studying the history and research techniques of parapsychology, paying special attention to the subject of telepathy. He learned that although psychic aptitude is generally not evident in the human population at large, a small percentage of individuals do possess a latent capacity for developing it. To varying degrees, such skills emerged through the performance of a mental exercise regimen designed to stimulate specific abilities, although it was extremely rare for any person to cultivate multiple psychic talents concurrently. Apparently, an aptitude for precognition, for example, had no relation to one's aptitude for telepathy – just as the ability to see does not increase the ability to hear. However, there was indication that the reverse was true. People who lacked any of the five traditional human senses (sight, hearing, taste, smell, and touch) had a higher incidence of psychic ability. Bolton surmised that the brain instinctively reacts to sensory deprivation by utilizing its remaining active and/or dormant senses to a greater extent.

At the conclusion of his research into parapsychology, during which time he had little contact with any of the passengers and crew of the *Argyre*, Bolton rested peacefully in his quarters in a state of near-sleep. A silent voice spoke to him once more, "phase one is complete," it said. This time, there was no surprise, no pain, no loss of consciousness, and no bleeding from his nose.

Chapter 5
Yesterday's Child

In college, Bolton and Han regularly played *racquetball* together. It fostered a healthy competition between the two friends and was a great way for them to get vigorous exercise. The game also had the benefit of being played indoors, allowing it to be enjoyed year-round and protected from the extreme weather now common in the Great Plains. Aboard the *Argyre, squash* was a more popular sport since it had the space-saving advantage of a smaller court; but, the ship's recreational area did have one compartment large enough to be configured for racquetball. The crew had no problem putting one together after Bolton requested it.

Playing racquetball - or any other activity involving a moving ball or similar object - within the spinning habitation rings of an interplanetary transport, was a bizarre experience for those unaccustomed to space travel. First of all, the court's floor was concave in shape like the inside surface of a bowl, and its walls inclined inward towards a convexly shaped ceiling. Secondly, the court was oriented perpendicular to the direction of angular momentum, so a dropped or struck ball would appear to curve in mid air from the perspective of the player. This effect is called the *coriolis force*. On the *Argyre,* its counter-clockwise rotating habitation rings combined with its forward-facing racquetball court meant that players would always perceive balls in play curving to their left. Thirdly, running and jumping without losing one's balance was problematic for the very same reason, and Bolton described it as trying to jog on a treadmill that was fastened to a merry-go-round.

After some sloppy practice and a few bruises suffered from falls, Bolton and Han managed to complete a best-of-three games match with Han prevailing 15-8, 13-15, and 15-10. It was like everything else aboard the *Argyre*, even the simplest tasks had to be relearned through trial and error. And the experience of watching a racquetball roll uphill after being placed on the center of the court, finally made Bolton realize why every item on the ship – no matter how small or insignificant – always had to be properly secured.

"It seems as though I left my game back on Earth," Bolton mentioned as the two sweaty men gingerly walked off the court.

"I'm glad for that," admitted Han. "If you had made me work any harder, I'd need a stretcher right now!"

"Yeah, that was a little rough," Bolton chuckled. "But, you are definitely adjusting to space travel much better than I."

"Yesterday's child," Han mused.

"Come again?"

"Yesterday's child," Han reiterated, "Giuseppe Petroni's futuristic story of coping in a radically new world."

"I'm afraid you've stumped me on that one."

"The story told of a man, Brandon Wilder, who was raised in a traditional culture built upon strict religious doctrine. When a historic discovery shattered the very foundation of their spiritual beliefs, the people cast out the old order and remade the world in a drastically new way – one based solely on the concept of empiricism. Try as he did, the change proved too great for Wilder. Stripped of his former high standing, he wallowed in self-pity before succumbing to his inner demons. Upon his death bed a solitary observer asked, "Are there no tears to be shed for yesterday's child?"

Bolton shook his head in mock displeasure. Then, the two ersatz combatants shared a laugh as they entered the dressing room.

"Han, I've been thinking about your suggestion."

"My suggestion," Han pondered as he unlaced his shoes. "Oh, you mean about experimenting with telepathy?"

"Yes," Bolton acknowledged. "I would like to try it if you are still willing."

"Sure, I'm still willing. I've got Colony business to attend to this afternoon, but how about after dinner?"

"That's good. Shall I come to your quarters around, say, nineteen-thirty hours?"

"Perfect. You will be gentle with me, won't you big guy?" Han mimicked lightheartedly.

"I'm serious, Han. I wouldn't have asked you if I didn't feel this was important," Bolton retorted while stepping into a constricted shower stall.

"Alright, alright, I get it. But just try to keep your perspective on this, okay? I mean, neither of us really knows what we're dealing with here."

"You're right as usual, Han. I guess that's why I'm a little apprehensive.

Shortly thereafter, Bolton went to the commissary for lunch. The midday service had recently begun and there were few customers in the dining room. He was fond of the chef's interpretation of *congee*, or *juk* in Cantonese, which was a thick rice porridge topped with fried bread and fresh herbs. Because of the shortage of rice, however, this version used tapioca instead. Bolton thought it was an acceptable substitute, and appreciated the simplicity, warmth, and digestibility of the dish. He ordered a bowl and sat down by himself at one of the empty tables.

Before long, a woman about his same age approached Bolton.

"Mind if I join you?" she asked politely.

"Not at all, please sit down."

"What's that you're eating... some kind of mush?"

Bolton tittered. "It's the *congee*."

"It looks very plain and unappetizing to me."

"I suppose it is plain, but I doctored it up with soy sauce and hot chili oil."

"My name is Teresa... Teresa Jones. And you?"

"Franklin Sharp. Jones, eh... you wouldn't by chance be related to Chairperson Jones, would you?"

"She's my aunty. I've been trying to join her staff on Mars for several years, and my request was just approved last month."

"You must have a valuable skill, Teresa. Martian visas are hard to come by these days."

"I'm a horticulturalist specialized in non-terrestrial environments. And, what is sending you all the way out to Mars, Franklin?"

"The *Terran Council* is temporarily assigning me there to assist in the procurement of raw materials. It's a space engineering project."

"Impressive," the attractive woman avowed in recognition. "Then, you'll be working directly with the *Board of Regents*."

"I assume so," Bolton professed.

"Hmm... perhaps we could socialize a little when we're not working. I mean... well, I don't know anyone on Mars except for my aunt and a couple of her associates."

"That would be fine, Teresa. I'll be a stranger on Mars as well."

"Great! I'll look you up on the visitor's register. It's nice to know I'll have someone to unwind with on occasion. The Colony has a real stodgy reputation."

"Yes it does," Bolton added with a nervous laugh.

"You know, it just kind of hit me."

"What's that, Teresa?"

"You're an extremely handsome man, Franklin. I've heard that Martian men are scrawny. You look quite... muscular."

"Well thank you, but I..."

"Sorry," Teresa interrupted him. "I didn't intend to be so forward, but you're not wearing a ring so I thought you were single."

"I have a lady friend back in Sutter City."

"Is she pretty?"

"I think so, and smart too."

"You must miss her a great deal."

Bolton paused for a moment and stared across the room. "Yes, I do miss her so."

Now it was Teresa's turn to feel uncomfortable. "Umm... well ah, what's her name?"

"Chris... I mean Christine."

"That's lovely. Franklin, sometimes when the world separates us from our loved ones, it's important to keep on living life to its fullest. Christine would want you to come back to her happy and strong, not downhearted and weak."

"Those are words of wisdom. Thank you."

"Then I hope you realize that sharing a bit of yourself on a planet tens of millions of miles away won't affect your special relationship with Christine in the slightest. Maybe, it might even help it grow."

"Agreed," Bolton said with a smile.

"So I will leave you now, Franklin Sharp. You know how to get in touch with me. Hope to see you soon on the Red Planet. Ciao, honey!"

Bolton was at a loss for words, but managed to murmur a faint, "Wow!"

At 19:25 hours, Bolton arrived at Han Li's quarters. He was unsure about how this telepathy experiment would transpire, but was convinced there was no better partner to conduct it with other than Han. What troubled Bolton most was not whether it would work, but at what he might find. The human mind is a complex and unpredictable biological mechanism that is not always in harmony with the conscious intentions of the person to which it serves. Extraneous thoughts occur at random, and are sometimes primitive and appalling to our individual and collective sense of decency. The mere existence of a fleeting and impulsive thought such as murder has little correlation to actual behavior. People continually evaluate the merits of their thoughts by considering them in the context of the real world. This is referred to as personal choice. Healthy individuals have the ability to generally make wise decisions, and persons deemed mentally ill typically do not. Since Bolton knew Han so well, he postulated that his interpretation of his friend's thoughts would have a greater chance to succeed in determining cognitive relevance; however, he understood the need to temper his own reactive emotions so that he wouldn't jump to erroneous conclusions.

"Hello Han. Are you sure you're still up for this?"

"No, but I'm game nonetheless. We can use that table over there. I've been telling myself that I must be very brave to allow someone to read my thoughts. But, you know, I don't feel so brave."

"It's alright. I'm not feeling confident either. Shall we continue?"

The two men sat down facing each other on opposite sides of the small empty table.

"Han, in order to prevent me from accidentally corrupting the results of this test by subconsciously manipulating the conversation, you should control the procedure. And, I would suggest avoiding familiar thoughts we have in common."

"Alright, do you have any guidelines you want me to follow?"

"No, you know what to do. If this works, maybe we can vary it a little by changing the distance between us, interposing physical and mental barriers, and closing our eyes or facing in different directions."

"Sounds good, and since we're only testing your ability to *read* thoughts, I shouldn't make any conscious effort to *send* them to you."

"Exactly, please begin."

A few seconds elapsed as Han thought repeatedly about how much he disliked the astringent taste of raw unripe persimmon.

"Did you get anything?"

"Nothing," Bolton admitted. "Try something else."

Han then constructed a mental image of a pleasant schoolyard experience he had as a child.

"What about now?"

"Zilch," Bolton said with mild exasperation.

"Perhaps you are trying too hard. Do you remember your state of mind during the telepathic episodes?"

"Yes, I recall my mind began to wander as if my consciousness had disassociated from my body. Then it seemed to focus directly on the person, and that's when I was able to read their thoughts."

"Try that then. I'll give you a few moments to prepare yourself."

Bolton found it remarkably effortless to slip into the detached mental condition. Within seconds, the psyche of Han Li had completely filled his consciousness. There was no mistaking what he had received.

"Why Han, I'm surprised at you having such amorous desires for that pretty young attendant back at the Phoenix spaceport. You're nearly old enough to be her father."

"Amazing, that's absolutely amazing!" Han exclaimed. "Let's try it again."

This time, Han thought about the name and office number of a colleague at his employer's headquarters in Colorado knowing that Bolton should have no prior knowledge of that information.

"You were thinking of Michael Dartannon in office number seven-fourteen."

"His last name is actually d'Artagnan, but that's close enough for me. Can you not see words?"

"Only if the subject specifically visualizes them, I think. I perceive the same images, sounds, ideas, and emotions as you do. You thought of the person who is your coworker, not of the spelling of his name. I just tried to interpret what I thought his name should sound like."

"Interesting," Han observed. "I'm going to try something different this time. Are you ready?"

Bolton nodded as he prepared himself. Han decided to formulate an abstract thought in a foreign language. There was a noticeable delay in Bolton's response.

"You thought of a cat wearing red shoes. Then, you translated it into French which I believe is pronounced, 'Le chat portait des chaussures rouges.'"

"Correct, but I didn't know you spoke French."

"I don't, Han."

"What? I speak French fluently, and I thought of that sentence *in* French."

"That might possibly be just a myth, Han. I recognized two separate thoughts. The first was the cat and the second was the translation."

"Did you perceive a second translated thought in English for the previous examples?"

"No, I didn't. However, I believe I understand what's going on here and we can test it. I want you to think of something else while mouthing it in English without actually speaking. I'll keep my eyes closed so I won't see your lips move."

Han complied by silently mouthing 'The-silver-cloud-drifted-away.'

Bolton opened his eyes. "The silver cloud drifted away. Yes, just as I suspected, there were two separate thoughts this time. Apparently, people conceive original thoughts and then construct the language to express it in an additional mental step. But, a person is more accustomed to their first language and that's why it requires less time compared to a less familiar second language."

"I understand now and it should have been more obvious to me beforehand," Han conveyed. "Before young children learn how to communicate with language, they are still actively thinking; and, the same is also true for animals which are incapable of human speech. Theoretically then, your ability to read minds shouldn't be limited to humans."

"An astute analysis, Han, I'll have to remember that."

The experiment in telepathy continued on into the wee hours of the morning, and much ground was covered. They learned that Bolton's ability to read minds was not affected by the direction the subjects were facing or whether they had their eyes closed. However, distance and/or intervening obstructions did appear to be a limiting factor; and when Han deliberately put up a mental block, Bolton had difficulty penetrating it.

The *Argyre's* passengers had an easier time coping with the deceleration into Martian orbit than they had with the launch seventeen days earlier. The same could not be said for the ship's crew however, especially for Captain Choi Deiterbrock. Trajectory calculations did not include an adjustment for the effects of a solar flare the ship encountered on

January 10th. Navigator Francis LaChapret had preprogrammed the maneuver on the 6th, but was not informed of the solar event due to a communications foul-up. When the *Argyre* completed its engine burn, it was on a head-on collision course with the Red Planet. Alarms sounded and panic reigned in the command module. Quick action by the pilot officer, Lieutenant Cheryl Kowicki, averted disaster but sent the ship beyond the orbital acquisition point. It took the command crew another two days to correct the mistake. The delay had to be officially entered into the ship's log – much to the dismay of its career-minded captain.

Bolton used the extra time to become familiar with the Colony's structural arrangement. The main administrative complex was located in a low basin of the *Chryse Planitia*, an area of flat volcanic plains 24 degrees north latitude and 45 degrees west longitude. Named Lowellton in honor of astronomer Percival Lowell, the city housed more than 300,000 residents. 80 percent of its structures were built underground to insulate the population from the harsh conditions on the surface.

Roughly 400 miles to the west, just north of the *Kasei Vallis* canyon, was the Sharonov Shuttle Terminal. This was the Colony's primary spaceport. It was connected to Lowellton by a subterranean magnetic train line, and the Regency Air Transport Service – a small fleet of liquid-fuel rocket planes reserved for official use.

East of Lowellton were located the Colony's industrial centers, McLaughlin, Rutherford, Maggini, and Pasteur. McLaughlin was the largest with over 40,000 workers. The newest was Pasteur, some 2500 miles from Lowellton. An additional spaceport was situated in the *Curie* crater, which marked the center of a vast transportation network linking the entire region. The magnetic trains used here ran on the surface and were designed for heavy bulk transport.

Positioned 800 miles south of Lowellton was the DaVinci power station. Lying almost directly on the equator, it supplied 75 percent of the Colony's electrical power. The terrain was crisscrossed with canyons carved out by the liquid water that flowed there long ago in the Martian past.

The Colony was also building a new settlement, named Galilaei, some 400 miles east of DaVinci. Their plan was to develop it as a centralized food production facility using the latest agricultural technologies. Bolton surmised that Chairperson Jones' niece Teresa was scheduled to be assigned to that project.

Everyday life in the Martian Colony was devoid of the physical freedoms taken for granted on the blue planet Earth. One could not walk on the surface of Mars, for example, without a protective environment suit. Even in mid-summer, the temperature is bitterly cold. The thin oxygen-poor atmosphere meant certain death if breathed. All precaution had to be taken to avoid contact with the direct rays of the sun, as just a few moments of exposure could result in serious eye or skin damage from the high levels of ultraviolet radiation. Colonists needed to spend much of their time exercising or wearing cumbersome weighted garments to prevent their muscles and bones from atrophying in the weak Martian gravity – only 38 percent as strong as Earth's.

Another aspect of Martian society new to Bolton was the Colony's measurement of time. A day on Mars was 40 minutes longer than on Earth. Because of the similarity, a Martian day was also divided into 24 equal periods called *Mars-hours* which were each slightly longer than the Earthly equivalent. Correspondingly, there were *Mars-minutes* and *Mars-seconds* defined in the same ratio. Colonists in the industrial centers had begun using the colloquial slang *mour, min,* and *mec* in place of the prefixed words, and this improvised nomenclature quickly spread throughout the Colony as a de facto standard. However, some colonists used the word *day* to describe a Martian day, and referred to a 24 hour period on Earth as an *Earth-day*. Likewise, *month* and *year* were employed in a similar fashion. The usage could be confusing to an outsider.

The official *Martian Calendar* was created to promote the unique cultural identity of the Colony, and to provide a comparable timekeeping system as the widely used *Gregorian Calendar* on Earth – which had important social significance. It was similar in many respects to the original 20th century *Darian Calendar*, but quite a departure from the heliocentric systems favored by science such as the *universal time* analogue called *Coordinated Mars Time* or MTC.

The Martian year was approximately 667.8 Martian days in length, which was equivalent to 687 Earth days. It was divided into 23 months of 29 Martian days each. Four out of every five Martian years, the last month in the Martian year contained an extra leap day to synchronize the calendar with the actual orbital revolution of the planet. Martian months were named after the first 23 letters of the Greek alphabet, which are: *Alpha, Beta, Gamma, Delta, Epsilon, Zeta, Eta, Theta, Iota, Kappa, Lambda, Mu, Nu, Xi, Omicron, Pi, Rho, Sigma, Tau, Upsilon, Phi, Chi,* and *Psi.* The capitalized transliteration of each was commonly used as an abbreviation: *A, B, G, D, E, Z, E̱, TH, I, K, L, M, N, X, O, P, R, S, T, Y, PH, CH, PS.*

The seven-day week was incorporated into the *Martian Calendar* for nostalgic reasons, although it didn't have the same cultural meaning on the Red Planet. The same names were carried over: *Sunday, Monday, Tuesday, Wednesday, Thursday, Friday,* and *Saturday.* There were 95.4 weeks in a Martian year.

There were further delays in transferring the *Argyre's* passengers and cargo to Mars due to mechanical problems encountered aboard the ship and a resultant logistical disagreement between Captain Deiterbrock and the spaceport's managing director. It wasn't until January 24th that Bolton was scheduled to take the planetary surface cargo shuttle's fifth trip down to the surface. As he gathered his belongings, Bolton's excitement for going to Mars was subdued by the uncertainty he harbored for his covert mission. There was no question his sympathies resided with the courageous founders of the Colony, who he had grown to respect and admire over the past few months. However, his practical nature warned him to be cautious. The reality was that he would be presenting himself under false colors to a potentially hostile reception. Furthermore, his action or inactions could pose great risk to others. If he were to obediently fulfill the objectives of his mission, it meant the certain end of the *Board of Regents* and the new human culture evolving on Mars. If he were to betray Janus Krichek, everyone he loved on Earth – including Christine and Han's family – would be in grave peril.

There were other emotions at work here as well. Bolton was as devoted to his duties as a person can be short of becoming a mindless slave to his master. Whether it was the obligation of professionalism, an innate sense of personal responsibility, or an obsession for achievement, Bolton was compelled to perform his assignments to the best of his abilities. Five years prior, he was part of a team that successfully infiltrated a private venture in Beijing, China that was developing a powerful particle-beam weapon which could have destabilized the world's military balance. The *Terran Council* used the information obtained to quickly seize control of the project. Bolton considered his role in the technological coup as an affront to his moral character, especially when he learned how many people were killed; however, he did his job all the same.

As is often the case - the line between loyalty and ethics can be quite thin when practical realities are taken into account. Fortunately for Marc Bolton, he held no delusions. He knew all too well that the *Terran Council* was an oppressive dictatorial force, and that its notorious leader was capable of despicable acts of cruelty. He also knew that the human society on Earth was in a degenerative state, and its prospects for survival would be marginal without such overt control. Conversely, Bolton was aware the situation on Mars was completely different. The Colony was prosperous, growing, and seen from an Earthly perspective as being an avenue of escape from terrestrial misfortune. This perception generated tremendous jealousy in Janus Krichek and his court of close confidants. They would not rest until the inconvenient juxtaposition of Mars was removed, and Bolton understood that meant its virtual destruction. Therefore, Bolton had decided to keep his mind open and clear for the time being. He would allow his actions to be determined by the circumstances as they unfolded. His uncertainty would have to be overcome by sheer will and determination, and when the time was right, Bolton knew he would have to make a critical choice.

As he strapped himself into the seat next to Han in the shuttle, Bolton noticed his friend's hair was floating wildly upward in the weightless conditions.

"Looks like you've been spending too much time in the reactor room lately," he commented with deliberate self-amusement.

"Ha, ha, ha, and if you're working on a second career in comedy, I'd say you better hang on to your day job there big guy," Han retorted sarcastically.

The heavy outer door of the planetary surface cargo shuttle locked shut with a dull thud, and Han's mood suddenly turned more somber.

"Listen, I realize there must be a good reason why you haven't told me why you've come to Mars, and I won't start asking questions even now. But, I'm getting this uneasy feeling that we won't be seeing each other anytime soon, and that prospect bothers me."

"Han..."

There was a loud bang as the shuttle detached from the *Argyre*.

"No, don't say anything," Han interrupted. "You've never been very good at goodbyes. Just remember you can reach me at the Ministry of Science, section number four-four-zero, level six. Got it?"

Maneuvering thrusters fired that pitched and rolled the shuttle into descent position. Outside the viewport, the image of the great interplanetary transport ship gradually exited the frame and was replaced by the spectacular ruddy features of the fourth planet from the sun.

Bolton smiled warmly as he shook his friend's hand. "This isn't goodbye, Han. Although, I wouldn't mind it too much if you wished me luck. I think I'm going to need it."

"Alright, best of luck to you. But in my opinion, whatever happens down there won't be the result of luck. It is your intelligence and intuition that will be the determining factors."

The shuttle's main engine fired redirecting the bulky, ungainly vehicle towards the surface of Mars. Bolton could see the frosted tops of the Tharsis ridge below him, and the brilliant-white north polar ice cap on the edge of the horizon. As the descent continued, the lengthy Vallis Marineris came into view stretching out like a gigantic crack splitting open the planet. Soon, a red glow obscured the breathtaking scenery as the shuttled encountered the ethereal upper reaches of the Martian atmosphere. When the intensity of the vibrations substantially increased, Bolton found it difficult to keep his teeth from clattering.

Bolton looked down below the shuttle as far as his vantage point allowed, and observed ominously dark rusty clouds roiling over the surface. Immediately, the pilot addressed the passengers through the intercom.

"May I have your attention, please. There is a dust storm developing over our landing site. It appears to have spun up from the cold air mass moving southwest from the Acidalia Planitia. It's going to get a little bumpy, but be assured there is no danger. The highest wind gusts of fifty miles per hour are well within our safety range."

'Bumpy' was a bit of an understatement as far as Bolton was concerned. The shuttle was rocked repeatedly, and seemed to be on the verge of flipping over at one stage. When they finally landed and the engine shut off, all that could be seen outside was an angry mass of swirling dust roaring like an un-caged animal. Bolton heard the sound of countless tiny sand grains battering against the hull of the vessel.

"Welcome to Mars," said the pilot with a noticeable intonation of relief.

"Some welcome!" Han blurted out. "I'd rather have been greeted with a punch in the face!"

The efficiency of the Sharonov shuttle terminal crew impressed Bolton immensely. They had secured the shuttle to the docking gate and connected the pressurized unloading ramps within five Mars-minutes of landing. It required only another seventeen Mars-minutes to disembark the 190 passengers and all the cargo. There wasn't much conversation amongst the crew. Everyone seemed to fully understand their assigned tasks, and went about performing them with dynamic professionalism.

Because of the frequency of space-sickness associated with prolonged exposure to artificial gravity interspersed with periods of weightlessness, all arriving travelers were initially sent to an adjacent medical facility called the Acclimation Room. They would be kept there for at least four Mars-hours to allow their bodies to adapt to Martian gravity, and to receive any necessary medical treatment. It was a rather unpleasant experience for Bolton. Along with many of the other passengers, he developed severe nausea and vertigo, and had to be given fluids intravenously to prevent dehydration. The air in the room took on a malodorous quality, and there were few smiling faces anywhere to be seen.

Bolton learned from the administration desk that Han had been released from the Acclimation Room shortly after arrival as his friend had suffered few ill effects from the transition to Martian gravity. He negotiated his way towards the central lounge where he was scheduled to meet with a representative from the *Board of Regents*. Walking proved to be a challenge for Bolton. His equilibrium had not yet fully recovered, and he was exerting more force with his leg muscles than was required. Consequently, he lost his balance and tumbled to the floor a couple of times, and his gait resembled more of an awkward skipping hop than a smooth stride. A helpful bystander pointed out an overhead sign that instructed people to walk slowly and use the hand rails for support.

The central lounge was a large circular room with several self-serving refreshment stations arranged around its perimeter. Bolton took a seat and waited patiently for the *Board of Regents* representative. This spot was ideal for people-watching, as it was located in the hub of the spaceport. It wasn't long before Bolton was able to distinguish the physical difference between colonists and visitors. Natives appeared to be taller than average, slight of build, and had very pale skin. Their eyes looked unusual to Bolton as well, being quite large by comparison and having a bluish tint in the sclera. How interesting, he thought, that this much biological change could occur in just two generations of humans. Bolton also wondered if there were any other variations not so visually apparent.

One of these young Martian natives approached Bolton and asked, "Franklin Sharp?"

"Yes."

"Greetings, my name is Jasum Bardomule. I am with the Ministry of Science, and will be escorting you to Lowellton. Can I get you a gravity suit to help you walk?"

"Oh, no thank you. I think I'm getting the hang of it."

"Alright then, shall we?" Bardomule suggested as he motioned towards a corridor exit.

The two men left the lounge and took an escalator down several levels into the spaceport complex.

"I understand you will be assisting in the new mining project," stated Bardomule.

"Yes, I have some ideas I'd like to propose to the Ministry. Isn't nitrogen one of the elements in the shortest supply?"

"Correct, there aren't many natural sources on this planet. The atmosphere contains roughly three percent nitrogen; however, that option has been ruled out because it conflicts with our long-term goal of increasing atmospheric pressure. Without nitrogen, we cannot grow plants. Without plants, we cannot live. It is a critical issue, don't you agree?"

"Absolutely," Bolton acknowledged while making particular note of the young Martian's cool, unemotional demeanor.

At the bottom of the escalator they entered a transit station. Bardomule ushered Bolton into a silver and green magnetic train much smaller than those used on Earth.

"We'll depart in five mins," he said while looking at the digital display in front of their seats. "And, we're due to arrive in Lowellton at nineteen-fifteen mours. That's a mour and twenty mins travel time."

Realizing that Bardomule was using Martian time, Bolton did a quick calculation in his head. "Let's see, that's over three hundred miles per Earth-hour."

"Yes, the lower gravity and air pressure enables our trains to travel faster than is practical on the Earth, and we use less energy too."

When the train began moving, Bolton had to acknowledge the ride was much smoother and quieter than other equivalent mass transit systems he was familiar with. Like everything else he had experienced so far on Mars, it was markedly efficient.

"Mister Sharp, I was told you were stationed on the Moon Base. What was it like living there?"

Using the knowledge gained during his preparation for this mission, Bolton responded with a contrived story. "The lifestyle there is typical of a military community. All activities are highly regimented, and there are restrictions of every sort. The landscape is excruciatingly monotonous, nothing but grey dust covered hills under a coal-black sky. One even gets tired looking at the Earth and stars after a while. I was very glad to leave."

The train emerged from its underground tunnel to travel on the surface for a while. It was Bolton's first up-close glimpse of the rugged Martian terrain.

"You must feel the same about this barren, unforgiving environment, Mister Bardomule."

"I can't say that I do, sir. This is my home. It is all that I know. To me, the landscape here is varied and wondrous. Just look over there at that protruding crescent-shaped ridge. We call it Sagan's Smile. When the angle of the sun is just right in the month of Epsilon, its late-afternoon rays eclipse the top of the rim and illuminates the ridge's steep interior flanks. It looks as if the sun is grinning at you. It's a marvelously spectacular effect. You should see it for yourself."

"Perhaps one day I will," Bolton supposed.

"As a planetary mining engineer, what kinds of projects were you assigned to on the Moon?"

"I was primarily involved with the procurement of raw construction materials. The silicate-rich lunar soil is excellent for making a type of cement called lunite. It is strong, durable, and has good insulating qualities. However, since it is susceptible to hydrolysis – or chemical weathering – when in contact with ionized water, it was used mostly for building exterior structures. Deeper below the surface, the Moon contains a variety of valuable minerals mined primarily for transport to the Earth. My greatest contribution was the development of a robotic mole that employed a chemical process to extract specific mineral ores, for which I received an honorary military commendation."

"Yes, that patent was included in your dossier – a remarkable piece of engineering, I must say. We are sincerely grateful that the Council agreed to send you here to assist us."

"The Council agreed? Are you implying that the *Board of Regents* solicited my services from the *Terran Council?*"

"Certainly Mister Sharp, the official request was issued by none other than the Chairperson herself."

"Carolyn Jones specifically asked to have me sent here?"

"Of course, I assumed you knew that. Are you surprised?"

"No, I didn't know that. And yes, it is quite a surprise. The Council is not an organization known for explaining their reasoning to anyone, let alone to their employees."

Surprise was an inadequate way to properly describe what Bolton was feeling at that moment. Profound incredulity would have fit better. It was logically implausible for Carolyn Jones, or anyone else for that matter, to have known who Franklin Sharp was prior to the fabrication of that persona. He simply did not exist until after Bolton was assigned to this mission. The only possible wildcard was John Severs, who could have suggested that name to the *Board of Regents* beforehand; however, that would have necessitated either of two preconditions: 1) Severs knew ahead of time that the Board was going to send a formal request and communicated this information to the *Terran Council,* which then quickly constructed the fictional history of Franklin Sharp and instructed Severs to lobby the Board for him. Bolton would be cast into the role afterwards only because he fit the profile of Franklin Sharp. 2) The entity of Franklin Sharp had already been created specifically for Bolton, and the Council was awaiting an opportunity to plant him on Mars. This required Severs to have had a mandate to act more autonomously than is usual for agents of the *Terran Council.*

Bolton considered these possibilities and then discounted both of them. The first explanation involved too much random chance and good fortune to be believable. The second explanation was even more absurd. The operational characteristics of the *Terran Council* mirrored the personality of its leader. Janus Krichek was a reactionary micromanager, not a delegator and certainly not a sophisticated planner. His distrust of everyone around him made it unlikely that he would have given John Severs the authority and information necessary to carry out such an intricate plan. So, Bolton was at a loss. If neither of these scenarios was true, then what could account for the *Board of Regents'* aforementioned knowledge of Franklin Sharp? Bolton recalled something Han had said to him aboard the *Argyre*, 'When you come to understand the underlying reasons for your passage to Mars, you will learn the identity of who sent you.'

The remainder of the train trip to Lowellton was uneventful. Bardomule provided Bolton with general information about the workings of the city, specific directions, and an itinerary for the next day's activities. It was dark when they arrived, so Bolton wasn't able to enjoy the scenery. He was thoroughly exhausted when he finally checked into his room, and sleep overcame him shortly thereafter.

The next morning, Bolton woke up to the gentle sounds of Martian music playing from the telecom. The song was a melodious soulful instrumental reminiscent of the lighthearted rhythm and blues tunes from the mid 1960s which Bolton was quite fond of. He enjoyed a light breakfast of dandelion coffee and an unidentifiable protein bar supplied to his room, and got cleaned up for his 9:00 meeting. Water was an extremely scarce commodity on Mars, and there was no conventional plumbing in the Earthly sense. His room had a single water dispenser and a vacuum-operated toilet similar to those used on space vessels. All indoor facilities recaptured moisture directly from the air through a combined heating/cooling/dehumidification system. Afterwards, an underground automated people mover delivered Bolton to the governmental complex located several hundred yards away in the center of the city.

The meeting attendees were Ministry of Science administrators and technicians headed by Ivan Tcholich, and two other *Board of Regents* members – Marilyn Lee Kim and John Severs. Name plates had been placed around the large circular table for identification and assigned seating. Bolton wondered if anyone was aware that Severs was a former Adjutant General for the *Terran Council*.

After everyone took their seat, Tcholich stood up to formally initiate the meeting. The fifty-six year old legend appeared rather nondescript to Bolton. His facial features were surprisingly plain, lacking the unique character of notable geniuses such as Einstein, Hawking, and Janowitz.

"Thank you all for coming to this important gathering," the co-founder of the *Janich Pulse Reactor* began. "Firstly, I would like to welcome Mister Franklin Sharp to our Martian home. His work over the past decade has revolutionized the science of planetary mining. I am very thankful for his presence here today."

There was a chorus of dignified applause throughout the room, but Bolton noticed that the stern-faced John Severs sat quietly with his arms crossed.

"Without further ado, I'll turn over this meeting to our scientific operations director Madam Bess Harcourt."

Bolton recalled that Harcourt had been a highly respected physicist on the Earth, but became disillusioned with the scientific community in the years following the *Great Flood*. She was recruited by the Colony in 2060.

"Thank you, Minister Tcholich. Let me begin by summarizing our dilemma. Our colony has a severe shortage of two basic elements, nitrogen which we need for growing food and hydrogen which is our primary source of energy. Currently, we are recovering these resources from our recycled waste; but that method will soon be unable to sustain our growing world. Latest estimates indicate the problem will become critical within eight sols, or Mars-years. After that, the self-determination of this colony is now considered to be problematic. Before we move on to cover detailed analyses and specific proposals, does anyone have any general questions at this point?"

"Yes, I would like to make a comment," Severs proclaimed as he stood up facing Ivan Tcholich in an obvious affront to Harcourt's authority. "Minister Tcholich, the *Terran Council* can adequately provide the various nitrogen compounds we require as well as elemental hydrogen. Since we have developed new agricultural techniques that are sorely needed on Earth, I hereby repeat my recommendation that an equitable trade be arranged to our mutual benefit."

Ivan Tcholich did not respond.

"Honorable Member Severs!" Harcourt barked. "This is an official meeting of the *Board of Regents*, and is subject to formally established procedural rules.

You will direct your comments to the Chair. Is that understood?"

"Yes Madam," Severs acknowledged politely.

"Now regarding your statement, the issue of trade with the *Terran Council* has already been excluded by legislative act B-R-S-0-0-2-6-0-5-6 dash A. If you recall, it was voted on by all Board Members including yourself. That option is officially off the table for this project. Are there any other questions? Good, we will break until ten-hundred mours."

Leaving the room, Bolton recognized that the identification number of the legislation director Harcourt had spoke of contained a Julian date denoting its creation – the fifty-sixth day of year twenty-six on the Martian calendar. He also realized that he would need a Martian timepiece to give him the proper timekeeping perspective, and to be punctual.

He found an administrative supply shop within the complex that had watches and clocks of various types. Although he knew that the Board was paying for all his expenditures, it was surprising for him to learn that there was no free market system on Mars. People did not earn income, profits, or accumulate personal wealth. They each had individual and occupational accounts that registered expenses only. The relative value of goods and services was set by the Ministry of Trade which adhered to the *Mars First*, or *Tharsian Principle*, placing the general welfare of the Colony as the government's highest priority. People could work in any productive capacity they wished, pending Ministry of Labor approval, or were assigned duties based on their unique abilities. Luxury did not exist on Mars. Everyone lived essentially the same, and the narcissism of greed was an anathema to their society. Bolton remembered a famous quote from Chairperson Jones issued in response to sharp criticisms that the newly formed *Board of Regents* was nothing more than a return to communism: 'What we are building here has no Earthly equivalent, nor should it. Mars will serve its own interests, in its own way, and welcomes those having the foresight enough to join with her.'

The meeting resumed with a two mour period where the attendees reviewed a detailed scientific study of the Martian atmosphere and lithosphere, and then broke for lunch. Upon returning, Harcourt brought the meeting back to order.

"Please be seated everyone. Thank you. We will now open up the discussion for the presentation and dissection of specific proposals. Who would like to begin?" After a lengthy pause, Bolton raised his hand.

"Yes Mister Sharp."

"I have two ideas I'd like to present."

"Let's take them one at a time," instructed Harcourt.

"Analysis of the Tharsis volcanic region indicates the presence of nitrites, sulfides, acids, and possibly organic compounds. The underground chemistry there looks promising as a source for both elemental requirements."

"We concur, Mister Sharp," Harcourt's senior geologist, Alexander Wellington, responded. "But the question of extraction remains."

"Yes, I was getting to that. We are all aware that active volcanism causes dissolved gases, such as hydrogen sulfide, to come out of solution at the surface releasing them into the atmosphere. In the late nineteenth century the *Frasch Process* was developed, which emulated this natural volcanism, to mine sulfur using superheated water and compressed air. Currently in Europe, they are employing similar methods to mine other minerals. With some adaptation, I believe that basic process can be utilized here on Mars."

"I'm familiar with that mining technique," Wellington acknowledged. "It does work; however, our limited water resources combined with our thin atmosphere and the additional chemistry required, makes it a more complicated proposition."

"I'll profess to that observation, Mister Wellington. Although, I'm sure you'd agree that any solution to this problem will be both difficult and expensive."

"What is your second proposal, Mister Sharp?" asked Harcourt.

"Asteroid mining, Madam," Bolton answered.

John Severs jumped to his feet and loudly exclaimed, "Preposterous! Madam Harcourt, why are we wasting our time with these outlandish notions when the appropriate solution is so obvious?"

"May I respond, Madam Harcourt?" the previously reticent Ivan Tcholich requested.

"Certainly Minister Tcholich, please do so."

"Tell us, Member Severs, why do you consider asteroid mining preposterous?"

Beads of sweat began forming on John Severs' brow as he contemplated his reply. "Well, it is common knowledge that asteroids are mostly rock and metal. Chasing after these wayward remnants of the solar system in search of light elements like hydrogen and nitrogen is absurd, in my opinion."

Tcholich displayed a quizzical expression. "I find your astrophysical knowledge distressingly lacking, Member Severs. In fact, stony and metallic bodies comprise only about a quarter of the main asteroid belt. The remaining asteroids are carbonaceous chondrites, of which at least two sub-groups are rich in water and organic matter. Now if the Chair concurs, I would like Mister Sharp to proceed with his proposal."

"Please continue Mister Sharp," Harcourt motioned as the irritated John Severs was forced to bite his tongue.

"As Minister Tcholich accurately described, there is a large number of asteroids having the chemical composition necessary for this project. They are particularly abundant in amino acids and ammonia, the latter of course is comprised entirely of nitrogen and hydrogen. They are also easy to reach due to their close proximity to Mars, and I need not restate the significance of another source of water for the Colony."

"Mister Sharp, how could we travel to these scattered asteroids, mine them, and transport the desired materials back to Mars in a cost effective manner?" asked *Board of Regents* member Marilyn Lee Kim.

"That would not be necessary," claimed Bolton. "We wouldn't go to them. We would bring them to us instead."

There were puzzled expressions all around the meeting room.

"Let me explain. We would use the propulsive and navigational components of current P.S.C.S. technology - I mean our cargo shuttles - to assemble automated robots. The robots would rendezvous with the asteroids, attach themselves, and then move them into a high Mars orbit. There they would remain until the asteroids could be processed by a self-propelled orbital mining station, which admittedly, would have to be built from scratch. The remaining cargo shuttles are perfectly suited to transporting the mined products down to the surface. This leaves the issue of disposing the unused asteroid matrix outstanding, but I don't consider this to be an insurmountable problem."

Surveying the reaction from the meeting attendees, Bolton was pleased to see almost unanimous approval. The lone exception was a stupefied John Severs.

"Thank you very much, Mister Sharp," Harcourt congratulated him. "That is a most promising proposal. I believe we have enough for my staff to contemplate for now. You will all be notified of future meetings as they are scheduled, and may officially submit – in writing - any questions, comments, or ideas, beforehand. I'd like to express the Board's sincere gratitude to everyone for the excellent work performed here today. Mister Sharp, someone from the Ministry will contact you tomorrow. Until then, please make yourself comfortable in our humble Martian home. This meeting is hereby adjourned."

Chapter 6
The Rapture of Mars

In the weeks that followed, Marc Bolton was heavily involved in the asteroid mining project. The *Board of Regents* had approved it after several days of intense debate, appointing Franklin Sharp to the lead technical position directly under Bess Harcourt. The vociferous - although numerically stunted - opposition was predictably led by John Severs, who used virtually every dirty trick in the book to discredit the merits of the plan and its author. This further reinforced Bolton's supposition that his assignment to Mars, ostensibly as a covert agent for the Head Council, was at least partly initiated by some other and as of yet unknown motive.

Severs' criticisms were not baseless, however. There were two important safety issues to be resolved. Placing asteroids, even small ones, into Martian orbit was an inherently dangerous undertaking. A mistake, malfunction, or act of sabotage, could send one of these mountainous space rocks crashing into Mars with dire consequences for the Colony. Secondly, a desirable method of disposing the left over debris had to be developed. Leaving this refuse in place was not a viable option since it would be extremely hazardous to space travel, and would eventually de-orbit posing a great threat to people and structures on the ground.

The first concern was addressed by Harcourt's staff with the addition of redundant navigation and propulsion systems. If something were to go wrong with the primary functions, they would be used to make necessary course corrections or to execute abortive maneuvers. This solution did increase the cost estimates, but not enough to outweigh the overall benefits of the proposal.

Bolton provided an innovative solution to the second problem. He designed lightweight orbital container modules that would store the mining debris. When they filled to capacity, the containers would be sent on a collision course with the planet Jupiter by utilizing low cost ion engines which were already being produced for robotic science exploration missions. The Ministry of Science was ecstatic about this cheap and effective way to utilize Jupiter as a giant vacuum cleaner. It would also not go unnoticed by the *Board of Regents*, whose opinion of the man they knew as Franklin Sharp had risen markedly since his arrival.

During this time, Bolton had become aware that John Severs' superfluous involvement in the project, now named *Archimedes* in honor of the famous Greek inventor, was increasingly evident. It was clear that he was trying to gather as much information as was possible from his advantageous – albeit indirect – position on the Board. Even more distressing to Bolton, was Severs' persistent requests to meet with him privately. To this point, he had managed to avoid such an engagement by being unresponsive and occupying the preponderance of his time with *Archimedes*; but, Bolton understood that he couldn't keep up these evasive tactics forever. Whether Severs had been informed of the true identity of Franklin Sharp, Bolton did not know; therefore, he planned to use this fact to frustrate any attempt by Severs to bring Bolton into his confidence. The former Adjutant General would be kept at bay, for as long as possible.

On a windless afternoon when the skies over Lowellton were particularly clear and free from dust, Bolton left work early to visit one of the city's observation decks. These were elevated platforms that afforded unobstructed views of the capital and surrounding landscape. Bolton was very fond of them, and he spent a considerable amount of his free time there in tranquil contemplation. As he gazed over the majestic Martian panorama, a familiar voice broke the silence.

"Beautiful, isn't it?" the distinguished woman said.

"Oh Madam Harcourt, I didn't hear you come up here. Yes, it is very beautiful. I love this location."

"Call me Bess. I loathe unnecessary formality. Tell me Franklin, what do you think of our Martian architecture?"

"There's a special uniqueness in its simplicity," Bolton articulated as he surveyed the city's skyline, "nothing but domes, pyramids, and dragon's teeth above the surface, vaults, catacombs, and great halls below. It is an architectural symbiosis between the medieval past and the technological future."

"A keen observation, I'm sure. And, what would you say about our people and culture?"

"I am still trying to get a handle on that, Bess. Outwardly, colonists – especially the younger ones – give the appearance of being emotionally cool and dutifully workmanlike; however upon closer inspection, that description becomes woefully inadequate."

"How so?" she pursued.

"Well, let me explain it this way. On Earth, modern culture reflects an externalization of customary belief systems which are inherently subjective. Contemporary art, for example, is more indicative of *how* we perceive existence rather than an appreciation of *what* the essence of existence actually is. Likewise, popular music expresses our inner passions, colloquial language expresses our competitive nature, and current lifestyle trends express our proclivity towards self-indulgence. It is all so demonstratively egocentric. Conversely, Martian culture seems to exhibit more altruism, intellectualism, and objectivity. For lack of a better analogy, I'd say it resembles a kind of cross between ancient Buddhism and the eighteenth century Age of Enlightenment."

"An interesting and thoughtful examination, Franklin, and I've never heard anyone put it quite that way before – remarkably perceptive. Now, which culture do you prefer, Earth's or Mars'?"

Bolton's confusion caused him to pause for a moment. "Prefer?" he mused. "I haven't considered the cultural differences between the two worlds as a *choice*, Bess. I was simply making a distinction. Besides, Mars is still very new to me."

"I see. So, your analysis was strictly objective. Didn't you just describe that as a Martian trait?"

"Yes, I suppose I did."

"You are not at all what we expected from the *Terran Council*, Franklin. Aside from your obvious technical expertise, you have displayed a focused, energetic, and unbiased approach to your work. Those are extremely valuable qualities which this colony needs more of if it is to survive as an independent society. There may soon come a day when such a choice will be presented to you. Perhaps, it is an idea you might want to contemplate in the meantime."

"Perhaps it is, Bess. There are some aspects of the Colony's administration that I'd like to learn more about. The people of Earth see Mars as an enigma, because they cannot reconcile their leaders' inflammatory rhetoric regarding the *Board of Regents* with the conspicuous desire of so many who want to come here. For instance, information describing your governmental structure is often distorted by official propaganda. Janus Krichek, himself, once referred to Carolyn Jones as a 'totalitarian in a spacesuit.'"

"Ha, ha, ha, I remember! That sound bite was a big topic of discussion throughout the Colony, and was re-aired numerous times on the *Mars Today* and

Sol News shows. Krichek the consummate totalitarian, accusing a political rival of being the same... what a laugh! But in response to your query, shall I give you a brief synopsis of our form of government?"

"Please."

"As you know, the *Board of Regents* is our highest governmental body. The role of the Chairperson is that of a referee to ensure the inner workings of the Board, and is not a chief executive in the classic sense. The Board itself is tasked with the responsibility of approving legislative acts by a simple majority vote of its members. Legislation is written by the departmental ministries for science, industry, labor, trade, health, education, and justice, who also perform the everyday duties of administering the Colony's activities within their purview. Each of the nine Board Members, and the seven department Ministers, are directly elected by the citizenry every two Mars years."

"That makes the Martian system a form of democracy," added Bolton.

"Indeed, it is representative, constitutional, liberal, and non-partisan. Although, our specific unitary state system has no Earthly precedent as far as I know. There is no regional representation or authority. Judges, legislators, and administrators are not elected to office - anyone can apply for those positions."

"I was unaware that the Colony has a constitutional foundation; and, are you saying there are no political parties?"

"The actual document is on public display in the Hall of Records. You should go there sometime and read it. And yes, we have no recognized political parties even though they are not explicitly prohibited. It's just that they serve no useful purpose in our system. Anyone can run for elected office if they qualify for the ballot by getting a minimum number of signature endorsements, and all qualified candidates receive the same amount of air time to get their message out."

"Can candidates win an election by a plurality of the vote? Also, doesn't Minister Tcholich currently hold two elected offices?"

"If no candidate receives a majority of the vote, a runoff election is held for the two candidates with the highest vote counts. All *Board of Regents* members are also allowed to run for one Ministry office, but the votes are cast separately. To date, Tcholich is the only Board Member to have successfully done so."

"Tell me Bess, why did the Colony exclude the profit motive from its economic system?"

"That was the most contentious debate that occurred during the establishment of the Colony, Franklin. Corporate interests had a fit when they realized they could play no part in writing our Constitution. But the conditions of their contracts were carefully worded by our founders to preclude any legal claims to Martian property, persons, or organizational entities. The corporations involved in the transport to, and initial construction on Mars, assumed they would be able to leverage their capital to influence the Colony's foundation for their long-term benefit and control. However, they were wrong."

"So, the Constitution merely became an instrument to free the Colony from corporate domination? Wasn't that a rather heavy-handed solution?"

"No, there's much more to it than that. You must read the text to fully understand the founders' philosophy and what they were trying to accomplish. In their view, capitalism had morphed far beyond what Adam Smith had envisioned in the eighteenth century. With the advent of industrialization, it became the ruling aristocracy's primary weapon to secure their power and subjugate the lower classes. As long as there were new lands and peoples to conquer, the insatiability of capitalism could be sustained. But beginning in the early twenty-first century, there was nothing much left to exploit. Capitalism collapsed upon itself, and the world degenerated into anarchy. It was that mistake which our colony's founders vowed never to repeat on Mars."

"Fascinating, but what encourages your people to lead productive lives without the incentive of self-interest?"

"I would argue, Franklin, the people of Mars are acutely aware that their own self-interests are best served by the vitality of this colony. And, it is common knowledge that our fragile existence in this far-flung desolate wilderness ultimately depends on the productive contributions of all our citizens. Although, I must admit we are singularly fortunate in that no one ever dares come to Mars with the intent of being lazy; and that industrious attitude is evidently being passed on to our children."

"I can attest to that attitude, Bess. It is different here, and I would go so far as to say Mars is an extraordinary place in many ways. I'm finding myself eager to learn more about it."

"There is no doubt you will, Franklin, just as Mars is eager to learn more about you. Now, if you'll forgive me, I must get back to the Ministry. I've really enjoyed this discussion, and hope you didn't mind me tracking you down like this."

"Not at all, Bess, it was my pleasure."

"Good evening."

Shortly thereafter, Bolton returned to his room and saw there was a personal transmission waiting on his telecom. He routed the text of the communication to his monitor. It read:

TO: FRANKLIN SHARP.
ADDRESS: LOWELLTON LEVEL 8, MINISTRY OF SCIENCE, SECTION #150.
FROM: JANET CRABTREE, OFFICE OF INDUSTRIAL AFFAIRS, TERRAN COUNCIL.
DATE: MARCH 20, 2077.
---------------------- BEGIN MESSAGE ----------------------

YOU ARE INSTRUCTED TO SUBMIT A DETAILED
ACCOUNT OF WORK ACTIVITIES PERFORMED
TO DATE FOR THE BOARD OF REGENTS, TO THIS
OFFICE NO LATER THAN 0800 HOURS PST
MARCH 22, 2077.
----------------------- END MESSAGE -----------------------

This appeared to be a routine accounting-related order for workers contracted out to the Martian Colony. However, Bolton knew from his briefings that the first installment of information he should have covertly obtained about the *Board of Regents* was now due. Janus Krichek's intelligence team had taught Bolton a cryptographic technique called *Cyprus*, which allowed secret messages to be encoded within the body of superficial communication. It was a time-consuming process, and Bolton stayed up most of the night preparing his response.

The message he transmitted back to Earth did not contain anything damaging to the *Board of Regents*, although it surely could have. Bolton had learned that the exchange of technology between Mars and Earth, which was the fundamental basis for the trade relationship between the two worlds, was deliberately and secretively being phased out. The only logical conclusion implied a plan by the Board to eventually sever all political and economic ties with the *Terran Council* – a realization of Krichek's worst suspicions. If discovered, it would have been considered mutinous and likely would have incited an aggressive military reaction from the Head Council.

As he lay down on his bed, Bolton worried about how his message would be interpreted. He had worded it in such a way as to give the impression that his surveillance simply did not uncover any subversive activities. But considering the Council's palpable mistrust of the Board, Bolton deduced that they would conclude he had either not made sufficient effort to gather the information or had deliberately withheld it. He also speculated that, at this early point of his mission, the Council would presume the former unless another one of their agents had conveyed doubts about Bolton's loyalty. That is why it was imperative for him to not arouse any suspicion in John Severs.

Two days later, Bolton was having lunch with orbital transportation technician Felicia Eduardo. They were discussing safety protocols for the movement of liquid nitrogen and hydrogen from orbit to the Martian surface. Bolton had been working more closely with Eduardo than any other person associated with project *Archimedes*, and quickly had formed the opinion that she was exceptionally knowledgeable and possessed extraordinarily good judgment.

"Are we in agreement, Franklin, that the transfer of pressurized containers from the mining platform to the shuttles is the most critical aspect of this procedure?" Eduardo asked.

"Yes I concur," replied Bolton. "Although, the reactive stabilizers should be able to properly maintain the platform's orbital configuration even in a worst-case scenario. At least, that's what the numbers indicate."

"Agreed, but I'm more concerned about the shuttles. They don't have such a system. Should a container malfunction occur after they have been secured, the unpredictable propellant force could cause a shuttle to tumble out of control. Depending on the circumstances, its crew might have little time to react."

"Are you implying a possible collision with the mining platform?" Bolton inquired.

"Exactly, you are more familiar with P.S.C.S. design technology than I am. Is there anything that can be done?"

"I suppose the platform stabilization software could be modified for shuttle use; however, I am unsure how effective the P.S.C.S. attitude thrusters would perform in that capacity. They weren't designed to contend with velocity changes of that magnitude."

"I'll bring up this issue with director Harcourt," Eduardo stated. "Maybe she can procure additional resources to analyze it."

"Good, if you are finished with your cauliflower gratin, perhaps we should get back to the office now."

The two coworkers began to leave the cafeteria table when Bolton accidently bumped into a young lady walking behind him.

"Please excuse me," he apologized. "I have a clumsy habit of not looking where I'm going."

The unusually distinctive woman with bright green eyes and jet-black hair stared attentively at Bolton. Fixed upon her astonishingly captive gaze, his mind was suddenly awash in her pervasive thoughts. And, for the first time in Bolton's telepathic experience, he realized that the reverse had also occurred. The woman was reading his thoughts as well. Stunned by the unexpected encounter, she broke off mental contact and hastily scurried away without saying a word. Bolton was so thoroughly transfixed by the incident he almost appeared to be paralyzed.

Felicia Eduardo gripped Bolton by the shoulders and emphatically asked, "Franklin, are you alright?"

"Uh, yes... yes, I'm alright. Who is that woman?"

"I don't know her name, but she is often referred to around here as The Empath. What happened? You suddenly went completely blank."

"I don't know. I guess I was caught off guard for a moment. Why do you call her The Empath?"

"I've been told she has the ability to intimately connect with people's thoughts, almost like a psychic or something. I also have the impression that some folks are a little wary of her, and because of that, she tends to keep to herself most of the time."

"Where can I find her, Felicia?"

"She runs a hydroponic garden near the communication station on level one. Are you thinking about paying her a visit, Franklin?"

"Thanks for the lunch," Bolton said evasively. "We should meet again later this afternoon. We have other issues to discuss."

"Sure, I'll see you later then."

At the end of the day, Bolton retired to his room. Awaiting him was another personal message on his telecom. He issued the command to display it.

TO: FRANKLIN SHARP.
ADDRESS: LOWELLTON LEVEL 8, MINISTRY OF SCIENCE, SECTION #150.
FROM: JANET CRABTREE, OFFICE OF INDUSTRIAL AFFAIRS, TERRAN COUNCIL.
DATE: MARCH 22, 2077.
---------------------- BEGIN MESSAGE ----------------------
RECEIVED YOUR WORK LOG COVERING THE PERIOD THROUGH MARCH 20, 2077. YOUR NEXT REPORT IS DUE ON MAY 1, 2077, AND WILL INCLUDE ALL ACTIVITY FROM MARCH 21, 2077 THROUGH THE END OF APRIL. YOU ARE REMINDED THAT IT MUST BE COMPREHENSIVELY ITEMIZED. DETERMINATION OF RELEVANT DETAILS IS OUR RESPONSIBILITY, NOT YOURS.
---------------------- END MESSAGE ----------------------

The intended meaning of the message was a relief to Bolton. The Council's frustrated reaction was a good indication they had not suspected he was deliberately withholding information. Bolton had received a similarly worded communication when he was on assignment in Beijing. He knew the inner circle of henchmen surrounding Janus Krichek were intensely loyal, but intellectually mediocre – such as Janet Crabtree. She was simply not sophisticated enough to mask ardent distrust behind a veneer of exasperation - unless, of course, Crabtree had help composing the message from more capable individuals like those in the intelligence unit. Regardless, Bolton was convinced he had bought himself a little more time to operate independently.

With that worry put to rest for the time being, Bolton contemplated the significance of the lunch incident. Unlike his previous telepathic episodes, this one transpired mutually and on a much higher level of consciousness. Rather than a unilateral reading of another's mind, it was a genuine sharing of cognitive thought. Even though Bolton had eventually come to terms with his paranormal mental ability, he still felt some insecurity about it. It made him tangibly different from his point of view, separate and unequal from the rest of humanity. And, he absolutely did not like feeling that way. To be deemed a pariah - even if only by one's own self - was a lonely and lamentable place to be. Bolton had sensed a singular kinship with the woman known as The Empath. He was compelled to see her again, and he would try to do so without delay.

Finding the hydroponic garden Felicia Eduardo spoke of was no easy task. The city of Lowellton was not constructed in a rectangular grid having multiple decks stacked uniformly atop of one another. Instead, it was a maze of individual structures built into the Martian crust wherever geologically feasible, and connected by a network of tunnels and shafts. The term *level* referred to subsurface areas, and the term *floor* referred to buildings constructed above ground. Each had a number designation identifying its relative position from the Martian surface. Floor numbers ascended with increasing elevation, and level numbers ascended with increasing depth. *Departments* described separate entities in the city, such as the Ministry of Science; and, *sections* identified specific locations within each department.

After a couple of futile attempts, Bolton finally found the Ministry of Science communication station on level one. Just past it he saw a sign above a long up-sloping corridor inscribed with an advertisement for fresh vegetables and a call number for placing orders. There was an airlock at the end of the corridor with a telecom device mounted to the wall. Through the window, Bolton could see the woman tending to rows of juvenile green plants. He retreated out of her view and activated the audio call switch.

"Yes," answered the woman.

"Hello, my name is Franklin Sharp. I accidently bumped into you earlier today in the cafeteria."

"I remember, but your name isn't really Franklin Sharp, is it?"

Bolton felt a lump forming in his throat. "No, it isn't. I would like to explain. May I please enter?"

"Alright, but you must promise not to invasively probe my thoughts."

"Okay, how do I do that?"

"You do that by making a conscious effort to respect my privacy. If you cannot control yourself mentally, then I suggest avoiding direct eye contact until you figure it out. I'm opening the door now."

The heavy airlock door opened slowly after two loud clicks. Bolton carefully walked inside. The air smelled like earth, an odor he hadn't experienced in nearly three Earth months. The hydroponic garden had a transparent inclined ceiling, and through it a gentle-pink Martian sky blanketed a fiery-red setting sun. Strolling amidst the lush-green flora, Bolton could think of no more picturesque place to be.

"You must be a novice telepath, Mister Bolton. You are awkward in the use of your skills."

"What else do you know about me?"

"You are an undercover operative for the Terran Council on a mission to..." she hesitated momentarily and closed her eyes in concentration. "My, my, Mister Bolton, do I sense treason against the Council?"

Bolton hung his head low and turned away in shame.

"Do not be ashamed, my friend. You are welcome here. Come, let's sit down over there."

The two relaxed on a reclined bench that provided a spectacular view of the evening's sunset.

"Can you tell me exactly what happened to us earlier today?"

"You don't even know what you are, do you? Well, let me explain. There is an extremely rare human condition, of unknown origin, that allows certain individuals to develop extraordinary senses. Empathy usually manifests itself first. Such people can actually feel the emotions of others. Have you ever had a cold chill rush through your body when near an enraged person? Or, felt a tingling sensation in your spine when you see someone suffering from an injury or illness?"

"Yes, quite often," Bolton remarked.

"That is neural empathy, the sympathetic connection of your nervous system to another individual. It should not be confused with your own personal emotional responses. Empathy is a reflection of, not a reaction to, the emotions of others; and involves the same chemical and hormonal changes. I have been empathic as long as I can remember, but did not have my first telepathic experience until late in my adolescence."

"Then, what happened today was telepathy?"

"Yes," the young raven-haired woman replied, "the interpersonal exchange of cognitive thought through brain waves. Although I don't know this for certain, I believe telepathy is nothing more than an evolutionary development born from empathy. I have met many more empaths than telepaths in my life, and I've never known a telepath who wasn't also an empath. It appears that most empaths never progress into telepathy."

"But, why was our encounter so... shocking, if that's the right word?"

"That was mostly my fault, Marc. I don't run into many telepaths, even on Mars. I was daydreaming and carelessly stretching out with my feelings at the time. I should know better than to be that indiscrete."

I don't even know your name," Bolton intimated.

"Yes, you do. Maybe it's time for your first lesson. I want you to empty your mind of all thoughts except the desire to hear my name. If you feel adverse emotions, like the anxiety you are experiencing now, back off and start over. That's it, now turn and face me."

Bolton was suddenly enthralled by her serene beauty, and felt strong emotions come over him. He looked away out of embarrassment.

"Your name is Sir-tes," he pronounced somewhat sheepishly.

"Yes, but you already knew that. Now, tell me what we actually communicated."

"I sensed deep affection, though I know not from whom it originated."

"In this particular case, Marc, does that really matter?"

Sirtes took Bolton by the hand and they walked over to the side of the garden that faced west. The sun was now below the horizon, and a bright point of light shined slightly above the violet-shaded rim of Tharsis.

"That is Earth," she pointed out. "It is being warmed by the sun's rays. If Earth was not there, that spot in space would be ice-cold. Do you get my meaning?"

"Yes, I do. Sirtes, would you help me with my problem?"

"It isn't your problem, Marc. You must understand that. It is an elemental part of who and what you are. But yes, I would like to help you develop your telepathic skills. Do you like the view from my garden?"

"It's breathtaking, absolutely breathtaking."

For the remainder of Earth year 2077, Bolton devoted all his energies towards the development of the *Archimedes* project and the proper use of his telepathic skills under Sirtes' direction. He progressively became more comfortable living on Mars, to the point where his terrestrial cultural identity was rapidly fading from his psyche. Whatever it was that truly separated the Colony from its ancestral roots on the third planet, was now flourishing within the being of Marc Bolton. Furthermore, he had found love again for the second time in his life; but, what he was presently sharing with Sirtes was not the Earthy love he still passionately harbored for Christine. This new love was more spiritual than romantic, more impassive than expressive, and less emotionally fragile than he had ever known.

Concurrently however, there was a personal crisis brewing. Janus Krichek and his *Terran Council* had reached the limit of their patience with Bolton's poor performance in his assigned mission. For months Bolton had staved off detection by playing dumb, evading the unrelenting probes of John Severs, and even transmitting false information to mislead the Council. However, these tactics had worn out their usefulness. It wouldn't be long before they recalled him back to Earth and charged him with treason. His only hope would be to reveal his true identity to the *Board of Regents* and seek asylum, but that would be a big gamble because he wasn't sure how they might react. Timing was everything. If Bolton came out of secrecy before the Board was prepared to openly confront the Council, he would be symbolically sacrificed in order to preserve the eventual succession of the Colony. And obviously, coming out too late wasn't an option. In any case, Bolton now knew that his life, and possibly his friends' lives, would be in jeopardy. Events had overtaken whatever choices he may have once had.

This dangerous situation was further complicated by Bolton's promise to Sirtes that he wouldn't exercise his telepathic abilities until he was fully trained in its appropriate use. Her reasons for this restriction sought only to protect Bolton from himself. Sirtes understood well the human ego's appetite for power and control. Unrestrained, it was a self-corrupting force in an absolute sense. Even an unpretentious and selfless person like Bolton was not immune from the penchant to abuse power. Sirtes' mother was such an individual, who went insane when her insecurities pushed her to an obsessive desire to know what everyone around her was thinking at all times. The fear had fed upon itself until there was nothing left but an incoherent schizophrenic who had lost all connection to reality. Therefore, Sirtes was determined to prevent that fate from befalling her one and only telepathic protégé. Obligingly, Bolton chose not to read the minds of key *Board of Regents* members when doing so could have given him a clear path to action. Difficult as it was, he would later learn the wisdom of his decision.

Chapter 7
Transitions of Intellect

In his Ministry of Science office, Marc Bolton looked at the electronic calendar built into his desk. It was the sixteenth day of month Phi in the Martian year fourteen. Outside the controlled environment of Lowellton, it was the middle of autumn. Temperatures were plummeting as the angle of the sun dipped lower towards the southern horizon. The seasonal carbon dioxide frost was already condensing on the north polar ice cap. On Earth, it was early January 2078. California's Sierra Nevada mountain range was topped with a soft blanket of snow, and its shallow inland sea was being whipped into a frothy morass by strong northwesterly winds. Bolton thought it was marvelous that two unique worlds separated by millions of miles of space could be linked together in time simply by the action of a transient human thought.

Putting his dream-like dalliance aside, Bolton resumed working on the final stages of project *Archimedes*. He was developing a plan for a live test of the new P.S.C.S. emergency attitude correction system. There had been many problems encountered in converting the mining station's reactive stabilization software for shuttle use, but Bolton and the rest of the team satisfied themselves that those issues had been satisfactorily resolved. The live test would utilize a pressurized air tank attached to a shuttle's docking ring to simulate a liquid nitrogen container rupture. The remaining components of the plan would ensure there were procedures in place to protect the shuttle and its volunteer crew in the event of a malfunction.

Sporting a sarcastic grin, John Severs entered Bolton's office.

"Good morning, Mister Sharp!"

"Good morning to you, Member Severs."

"How's the project coming along?"

"Very well, Sir. Hopefully, we'll be launching our first robots towards the asteroid belt in a few weeks."

"That's good," Severs remarked rather insincerely as he pulled out a sealed envelope from his breast pocket. "On behalf of the entire *Board of Regents*, I thank you for the excellent work you have performed for the Colony. We are forever indebted to you. I just received this order for you from the *Terran Council*. Please read it now."

Bolton opened the envelope and read the letter to himself. It was an order for him to board the interplanetary transport ship *Hesperia*, due to arrive at Mars in three days, which would subsequently transport him back to Earth. The official stamp and signature were those of the Head Council, the Honorable Janus Krichek.

"Do you have any questions?" Severs asked facetiously.

Bolton was neither surprised nor upset by this order, as he knew it would have happened eventually. Unfortunately, he did not reveal himself to the *Board of Regents* in time. Now, he would have to pay for his treasonous acts.

It was also presently apparent to Bolton that the unscrupulous John Severs standing in front of him was every bit involved with the *Terran Council* as he had postulated. That meant this order likely posed an immediate threat to the autonomy of the Colony as well. If Krichek was willing to pull Bolton off *Archimedes* at this crucial stage, he probably wanted to kill the project altogether; and, he couldn't accomplish that without overthrowing the *Board or Regents* or at least bringing it under his direct control. Either way, it could spell the end of the remarkable fledgling Martian culture that Bolton had come to hold in such high esteem.

With so much potentially at stake, there was one card left for Bolton to play. He could use the telepathic skills he had mastered over the past few months under Sirtes' tutelage, to learn as much of Krichek's intentions as he could through the person of John Severs, and then warn the *Board of Regents* of exactly what was being planned against them. Bolton realized he would be breaking his vow to Sirtes, but the desperateness of the situation demanded it. Whether he was motivated by self-preservation or compassion could be argued another day, Bolton would do now what he was compelled to do.

"No Sir, I have no questions," he answered calmly. "It will be nice to see California again. Why don't you sit down, this might be our last opportunity to have a social conversation."

Severs was deeply puzzled at Bolton's emotionless reaction, which he had expected to be one of visible panic. And, although the former Adjutant General's cynical nature usually made him wary of his adversaries' open invitations, Severs' curiosity got the better of him this time. He politely sat down as instructed.

"Alright, I have a few mins before my next meeting. What would you like to discuss, Mister Sharp?"

"Please, call me Franklin. Since I'll be leaving soon, there's no more need to be so formal."

"Whatever you say, Franklin," Severs said with a mischievous grin.

"I've learned so much during my stay here on Mars. The expansion of the Colony is astounding, don't you think? It should set the cornerstone for the Council's future plans to develop the outer solar system."

"It should, as long as the Board fulfills its obligations to the Council."

"Excellent point Member Severs, and from what I've been able to see, you have done the most – by far – to ensure that it does. It must be a very difficult task trying to maintain the political alignment between Earth and Mars."

"Yes, it has been a struggle – almost like walking a tightrope. The Colony feels the need to go in its own direction, and the Head Council understands that, but it cannot be allowed to stray too far. Mars is too big an asset to lose control of."

"I see that now... quite perfectly," Bolton affirmed in a subdued tone.

Severs gave Bolton another quizzical facial expression and then stood up from his seat. "I must be going now. Good luck to you, Franklin. It's not likely we will be seeing each other again."

Bolton remained in his chair and did not reply. He had learned everything he needed to know. By getting Severs to talk about the relationship between the *Board of Regents* and the *Terran Council*, in addition to his role in it, Bolton easily read telepathically what Severs knew about Janus Krichek's plans for the Martian Colony. It was a stunning revelation. Aboard the *Hesperia*, there was a large Council delegation ordered to disband the Board and replace it with an interim administration under the dictatorial leadership of John Severs. His first act would be to remove all departmental ministers from office, and terminate any of their key subordinates who refused to pledge allegiance to the new regime. The delegation also included a substantial security force and a team of assassins to ensure the coup d'état succeeded.

That afternoon, Bess Harcourt called an impromptu meeting of the *Archimedes* project coordination panel. All of Bolton's responsibilities would have to be delegated to other technicians as soon as possible if the project was to remain on schedule. As the group assembled, it was obvious that everyone understood the seriousness of the situational change. To lose the project's creator, and its most integral technological contributor, at this late date put the ultimate success of the project in question.

As Bolton was presenting his itemized status report to the group, a sullen Ivan Tcholich entered the meeting room.

"Excuse me, everyone. I've just heard the news. Madam Harcourt, I was under the assumption that Mister Sharp was authorized to remain here until this project was completed."

"That is correct, Minister Tcholich," Harcourt replied. "However, the *Terran Council* has abrogated the agreement."

Tcholich studied the man he knew as Franklin Sharp for a few moments. "We need you, Mister Sharp. Is there nothing you can do?"

"No sir, I have my orders."

Turning towards the Minister, Director Harcourt proposed, "Perhaps if the Board requested a temporary stay until this matter could be discussed further…"

The Minister of Science just waved his hand in repudiation. "I'm afraid that's impossible, Madam."

Bolton surmised this might be his only chance to reveal his true identity and expose the impending menace to the Colony currently lurking aboard the *Hesperia*. He was confident he could trust Ivan Tcholich, Bess Harcourt, Felicia Eduardo, and a few of the other project technicians, but certainly not everyone in the meeting. If there was a covert operative of John Severs in the room, which Bolton considered a likely possibility, coming out openly here would be a terrible blunder. Severs would be quickly alerted, and he would take whatever actions necessary to preserve the delegation's mission and his own skin – no matter how extreme. No, the risk was too great. Bolton would have to find another way.

Several weeks earlier, Sirtes had taught Bolton how to telepathically place ideas in another person's mind. Though the technique was not complicated, it was much more problematic than simply reading the thoughts of others who unknowingly broadcast their brain waves into the interspatial medium. *Suggestive implantation*, as she called it, required intense and prolonged concentration to overpower the subject's own cognitive processes, and there was absolutely no guarantee it would work. People with highly active or disciplined minds would be difficult to get through to, and the probability of failure increased with physical distance. Although Ivan Tcholich was roughly ten feet away from him, Bolton decided to give it a try as he was undoubtedly running out of options.

After initiating eye contact with the Minister, Bolton began to rhythmically project the thought he was trying to instill. It took the form of a mantra: 'Must meet privately with Franklin Sharp very soon... He has vital information. Must meet privately with Franklin Sharp very soon... He has vital information...' Over and over he repeated the telepathic suggestion until Tcholich broke off eye contact and left the room without saying a word. Bolton intuitively felt he was able to get his message across, but there was no way for him to know for sure. Doubt crept into his mind, and he wondered if another opportunity would ever present itself considering the infrequency of Tcholich's public appearances. His second guessing would have to wait, however, as the meeting resumed and it demanded all of Bolton's attention.

Thirty mins later, Director Harcourt received a confidential telecall. She conducted the conversation in a sealed office adjacent to the meeting room. Upon returning, she addressed the group somewhat tersely.

"The remainder of this meeting is hereby postponed until oh-nine-hundred tomorrow. You are all dismissed." She walked over to Bolton who was gathering up his numerous hardcopy documents. "You will come with me, Mister Sharp."

The last attendees to leave the room, Harcourt quietly escorted Bolton down to level twenty which housed the Ministry of Science sections restricted by security clearance. They entered a large office where Bolton saw Ivan Tcholich standing next to a tall, slender, and elderly Black woman.

"Thanks Bess, I'll call you when we're finished," Tcholich told Harcourt who then departed. "Mister Sharp, let me introduce you to our Chairperson, the Honorable Carolyn Jones."

Bolton was awestruck. He had long wanted to meet the famous founder of the Martian Colony. "Madam, this is a great privilege for me."

"Please be seated Mister Sharp," she instructed.

"We did not know you were telepathic, Franklin. As I have informed the Chairperson, I'm convinced you tried to induce me into calling this meeting. Didn't you?"

"I sincerely apologize for that impropriety, Minister Tcholich. But, I had no other choice. It was imperative to speak with you in secret."

"For what reason," Tcholich inquired.

"To safeguard the autonomy of the Colony," Bolton revealed.

The Chairperson's eyebrows lifted in a surprised response. "Please explain," she ordered.

"My real name is Marc Bolton. I am an analyst for the *Terran Council*, and was sent to Mars under a false identity to monitor and report back subversive developments in the fields within my area of expertise – primarily science and technology. Specifically, I was ordered to examine how thoroughly the *Board of Regents* was cooperating with the mandate of twenty-sixty-five which proclaimed the Council's intellectual domain throughout the solar system."

"So, you're a spy," Jones noted. "That's not surprising. The Council has many agents like you that have infiltrated our colony."

"With all due respect, honorable Chairperson, I am no spy. Since my arrival on Mars, I have honestly dedicated all my efforts to the success of *Archimedes* and have deliberately withheld the information I was obliged to submit to the Council. Because of this, I will surely face charges of treason pending my return to Earth."

"Why would you take such a risk?" asked Jones. Are you actively working against the Council for some other political interest?"

"No, I don't have any other political associations. As to why I took the risk, that is a very good question; and, I'm not sure I understand the reasons myself. All I can really say is that I was *compelled* to do what I did."

Ivan Tcholich looked at the Chairperson with an air of sympathy. "Carolyn, one thing is certain. Mister Sharp... I mean Bolton... would not have worked so hard to develop *Archimedes* if he was acting on behalf of the Council. They are adamantly opposed to the project, and my Ministry experts have hailed it as a positively brilliant solution to our resource problem. Bess Harcourt - who is not one known to issue undeserved praise - has frequently extolled his value to the Colony, and has even suggested recruiting him for permanent residency. If there is deception here, it is at a level of sophistication I never would have thought possible."

Carolyn Jones was perceptibly confounded by the apparent paradox of Marc Bolton. "Alright," she agreed, "I'll assume you are telling the truth for the time being. Why did you say you wanted to safeguard the autonomy of the Colony?"

"There is a delegation of administrators, security personnel, and assassins, currently aboard the *Hesperia* who are to support John Severs in deposing the *Board of Regents* and seizing control of the Martian Colony."

The gravity of this revelation struck the two high-ranking Martian officials very hard.

"How do you know this?" Jones demanded.

"I deliberately probed the thoughts of John Severs when he delivered the Council's order regarding the change in my assignment status."

"Mister Bolton, just because you are able to read the minds of others doesn't mean what you perceive from their thoughts is valid or even useful. People think about all sorts of things, and much of it has no direct relationship to reality."

"That is true; however, there is little doubt in my mind that what I told you is indeed actual fact. Telepathy is like any other ability, experience enhances proficiency. After a while, one learns how to differentiate between primal emotion, behavioral intent, recalled memory, focused concentration, reactive responses, playful fantasy, and all other forms of cognition. If you're asking me could I be wrong, then my answer would be yes. If you're asking me if I am wrong, then my answer would be no."

"Carolyn, you know how I feel about Severs," Tcholich iterated. "What Bolton is telling us fits perfectly into the strategic scenario we've been analyzing since the foundation of the Colony."

"Ivan, you also know that we are not yet prepared to openly confront the Council. Militarily, we are vulnerable."

"Agreed, but if Severs is moving against us, we're left with only two choices – opposition or submission. And, I firmly believe you are not inclined towards the latter."

"Surrender will never be an option as long as I'm Chairperson. We came to Mars to give humanity an opportunity for a new evolutionary future, not to repeat the terrible mistakes of its tortured past. Providence may not be our constant ally, but integrity will be our enduring legacy. The destiny that awaits us shall be met with inspired resolve, and we will shoulder no pangs of regret."

Bolton thought to himself that if Jones had spoke that publicly in front of the Martian people, it would have gone down in history as one of the most memorable speeches made in the long fight against human oppression. Her powerful words had given him goose-bumps and strong feelings of admiration. Bolton understood now why she had elicited such great fear in Janus Krichek.

"Well then," Tcholich observed, "our course is set. All that remains to be worked out is a plan on how to execute it."

"We'll take that up shortly," Jones informed him. "In the meantime, what do we do with Mister Bolton?"

"If we detain him, Severs will get suspicious and start making official inquiries. That would alert the Council and ruin any chance we might have of countering their move."

"On the other hand," Jones rejoined, "Bolton may be lying. His story could be a ploy to lure us into taking preemptive action so that the Council would have justification for using military force to seize control of the Colony. Releasing Bolton now would allow him to notify the Council of this conversation, and that could prompt them into aggression much sooner than might have occurred otherwise. I say again, the Council is fully aware that this colony is currently unprepared for war. We need more time."

"Time is a luxury we may not have, Carolyn."

"What do you suggest we do with you, Mister Bolton?" the Chairperson posed.

"That depends, Madam, on what you intend to do. If it were up to me, I would quarantine the *Hesperia* immediately after she assumes orbit and wouldn't do anything to arouse suspicion in the interim. Undoubtedly, Janus Krichek will react violently; however, it will take at least two Earth months before the Council's fleet could be assembled, provisioned, and transported to Mars. You would have that much time to make preparations."

"Ivan?" Jones prompted the Minister of Science.

"I concur we should conceal our foreknowledge of Severs' coup, and that means releasing Bolton. But, let's discuss the *Hesperia* in private with our military and foreign relations advisors."

"Alright, I'll accede. Mister Bolton, you are free to go. I'm placing an enormous amount of faith in you, and that is making me uncomfortably anxious. The welfare of our entire population is reliant upon your sincerity and discretion. For their sakes, I hope those attributes of yours are able to carry the burden. If we manage to survive this impending crisis, there will be an outpouring of gratitude which itself bears a great responsibility. We shall see if you are worthy of that as well. Perhaps it is not coincidence that the Colony and your life have reached a crossroads at the same time. From now on, our fate will also be yours.

The Chairperson's homily brought tears to Bolton's eyes. She was right. His life would never be the same again. The humble orphan who had succeeded – in part – by acquiescing to a corrupt society, was now committed to an actively prominent role which philosophically and tangibly opposed it. The task was daunting. His future seemed as frightening this day as it had nearly twenty-six Earth years earlier when the teenage Marc Bolton was marooned on that lonely San Franciscan hilltop surrounded by turbulent floodwaters. Back then, good fortune came to his rescue. This time, he knew it would take more than that.

Instead of returning to work, Bolton withdrew to his room. He was mentally exhausted and needed some downtime to collect himself. After a typical workday, he normally listened to music or watched a popular Martian television show before having dinner. But today, he just sat motionless on his bed with all the lights turned off. Bolton was always prone to introspection. He believed it was a necessary instrument of self-improvement, and that people could not accurately evaluate the outside world without first being able to objectively critique themselves. However, this tendency towards self-reflection occasionally strayed into moroseness and depression. It was his greatest weakness.

Two mours later, the telecall device activated and Bolton reluctantly got up to answer it. "Hi Sirtes, how are you?"

"I'm a little tired. I had to replant the entire tomato shelf today and haul all the waste over to the recycling station. It wore me out! Your room looks really dark, Marc. What are you doing?"

"Just resting, it was kind of rough in the Ministry today."

"What happened?"

"I've been ordered to return to Earth."

"They're sending you back now? But you haven't finished the project yet. I thought Minister Tcholich was smarter than that."

"The order was issued by the *Terran Council*."

"Oh, I see. Are you taking the next transport then?"

"Yes, the Hesperia is due to arrive on the nineteenth."

"Three days... I didn't think it would end so soon, Marc."

"Nor did I, Sirtes."

"Look, I want to see you. I'm coming over right now, okay?"

"Sure," he said.

Bolton considered whether or not he should inform Sirtes of the looming danger to the Colony. His reluctance did not stem from a worry she might accidentally alert John Severs by spreading the news around, since he knew that she wouldn't, but because he didn't want her to be scared. Besides, there was nothing that could be done to avoid whatever was about to happen. She couldn't escape, she couldn't do anything to protect herself, and neither could he.

The buzzer sounded and Bolton opened the door. Sirtes stepped in and gave him a gentle kiss on the cheek.

"I have a confession to make," Bolton admitted. "Twice today, I had to utilize my telepathy."

Sirtes closely examined his face and replied. "I sense you employed it with great care and wisdom. Regardless, you have already learned everything I could teach you. From this day forward, you shall use your own judgment. I am very proud of you."

"And I am eternally grateful, Sirtes. You have completed me in a way I never would have thought possible. It was a personal awakening that few are fortunate enough to experience."

"Although, there is something else you are struggling with. Isn't there?"

"Yes... yes there is."

"You are hesitant to share it. That's alright, I won't ask you to."

"No, you deserve to know the whole truth. But, it would be more meaningful if I didn't have to explain it verbally."

"Come, let's sit down," she suggested.

The nuance of interpersonal telepathic communication had been learned well by Bolton. No longer did he have to probe Sirtes' mind in order to read her thoughts. They opened up freely to each other allowing the exchange to flow naturally. Periodically, the rate surged too fast for Bolton to absorb, or lasted so long that he became mentally fatigued. Sirtes, however, was very perceptive. When he tired, she would pause for a moment or interposed with speech instead. Following their review of the pending John Severs coup, the couple laid down beside one another in quiet contemplation.

"Marc," she spoke after the temporary lull, "there is one ray of sunshine in the midst of this dreadful news."

"What is that? Damned if I see any."

"We know the *Board of Regents* will not willingly relinquish the Colony under any circumstances, and the delegation aboard the *Hesperia* is not large enough to seize control without the element of surprise."

"So?"

"So, that means you will be staying safely on Mars for the foreseeable future. The Hesperia will not return to Earth, and therefore, neither will you."

"It will be a brief reprieve, Sirtes. The *Terran Council* will be back by the spring, and they will arrive in force. There will be little to stop them, and my name will be near the top of their target list. I do not find that an illuminating prospect."

"Until then my dear, you will be here with me. And, that makes me extremely happy.

Bolton looked caringly into her loving eyes, and tenderly stroked her long silky hair. Their kisses intensified more passionately while their mutual embrace grew tighter and tighter. Muscles strained against one another as beads of sweat formed in the rising heat of intimate play. Emotions intertwined telepathically merging into a singularity that matched the unity of their physical bodies. Deeper and deeper they plunged, into the innermost regions of their sensual beings. The interplanetary interlude went late into the night, and it shattered a terrestrial myth that sex on Mars was a lackluster affair.

High above the blood-red Martian countryside, a creature was observing with grand approval. It transmitted a communication across the boundaries of space and time, to a far off world skeptical of the human experiment. The message simply stated: "Phase two is complete."

Chapter 8
Conflict at One-Three-Three

On Phi nineteenth, the interplanetary transport ship *Hesperia* maneuvered into Martian orbit after an uneventful four week journey from Earth. Aboard her, the *Terran Council* delegation impatiently awaited orders to descend to the surface and reassert the terrestrial authority which they emphatically represented. It was headed by the enigmatic Yasmin Blecht, a longtime associate of John Severs who craved power and fortune much more than any personal commitment to duty. The delegation she assembled for this mission reflected the various facets of her character. The administrators were opportunistic yes-men who refused to consider the consequences of their actions because – in their view – a well-developed sense of morality was an inconvenient human flaw. The security personnel were ruthlessly sadistic individuals, and the assassins were coldly efficient killers who seemed oddly benevolent when not performing an assignment. When aligned for a single purpose, this collection of civilian soldiers produced a truly formidable team. Had the *Board of Regents* not been alerted to their operation, it would have been eliminated in one swift stroke.

As the occupants of the huge ship recovered from deceleration sickness, two *Rigel* class space cruisers and six laser-equipped shuttles suddenly appeared on the *Hesperia's* radars and quickly formed a perimeter around it. A collision alarm sounded in the transport's command module. Captain Kurt Smithers looked towards his junior officers manning the scanning stations for an explanation.

"What is it, men?" he barked.

Lieutenant James D. Jefferson, son of the infamous general who led Janus Krichek's military campaigns in the 2060's, studied the display screens and reported. "Sir, there are eight ships moving into attack position. They are surrounding us. Two of them are heavily armed..."

The communications officer interrupted the lieutenant. "Captain, we have received a request from their lead ship to establish an audio communication link."

"Route it to my command station, Sparks."

"Yes Sir," acknowledged Ensign "Sparks" Ribbenhower.

"I am Commander Trenton Manbury of the cruiser *Cromwell*. Your vessel, the *Hesperia*, is to be interned by the Martian Colony as part of an official investigation into its passengers and cargo. You are ordered to surrender immediately. A boarding party is standing by to assume temporary control."

"Commander, this is Captain Smithers. You might remember me from your days as a cadet at the Bathurst academy."

"Yes Captain, I remember. What is your reply?"

"Trenton, let's not be hasty now. You and I both know the Colony has no authority to commandeer the

Hesperia. It is state property of the *Terran Council*, and operated by the Interplanetary Space Agency which has jurisdiction above the one-hundred mile limit. If the *Board of Regents* has questions about our shipment, they can take it up through the proper channels."

"Captain, you will use decorum and address me as *Commander*. I am not here to engage in diplomatic debate. I have my orders and they are resolute. Once again, will you surrender your vessel?"

"My apologies Commander, I meant no disrespect. It is unclear whether I have the authorization to unilaterally comply with your demand. If you would permit me to contact my operational headquarters, I'm sure we can get this cleared up in an hour or two."

"You have two of your minutes to comply, Captain. If you have not surrendered by then, or make any attempt to escape, we will open fire on the *Hesperia*. Our lasers are now locked on to your command module and power generator. For the safety of your personnel, I urge you act promptly and wisely."

"Alright Commander, please stand by." Smithers switched off his communications microphone and visually scanned the bridge area. He saw mostly youthful faces peering up at him in fear, who were still suffering from the effects of deceleration. Even though he would be charged with dereliction of duty - at the very least - if he voluntarily relinquished control of his ship, this Captain was not about to sacrifice the lives of his crew just to save his reputation.

"Sparks, transmit a message to the command center notifying them that I am surrendering the *Hesperia* immediately to superior Martian forces, and attach all log entries since our last report."

"Yes Sir!"

An aggressive sergeant manning the weapons console jumped to his feet and challenged the Captain. "Will you hand over this ship like a frightened rabbit? I say we fight! The spirit of General Jefferson will guide us to glorious victory!"

"Guards!" yelled Smithers, "Arrest that man! There will be no more senseless talk. We are outmanned, outgunned, and unable to escape. There's only one course of action left. Chief Petty Officer Richfield, make preparations to be boarded."

"Yes Captain."

Smithers turned the communications microphone back on. "Commander Manbury, we are standing down. I'm turning you over to our Operations Chief who will coordinate docking maneuvers. I trust you understand what this act means to both of our careers."

"I most certainly do, Captain, and I hope you understand that I take no pleasure in it whatsoever."

Down on the surface, John Severs was awakened by the door buzzer. He got up out of bed and opened the door to his room. Standing outside were four armed deputies of the Regency Police.

"What are you men doing here?" he demanded.

"You are under arrest, Mister Severs," one of the men informed him.

"Preposterous! What's the charge?"

"You will be formally presented with the specifications of the indictment by the Board members. Please get dressed so we may proceed."

Severs was handcuffed and taken to the *Board of Regents* main assembly chamber where an emergency session was called by the Chairperson.

Upon his arrival, Carolyn Jones brought the meeting to order. "Be seated everyone... thank you. John Severs, as a member of the *Board of Regents*, you are hereby charged with willful violation of your oath of office. Count one: Acts committed to subvert the entrusted administration of the Martian Colony. Count two: Acts committed to undermine the trust granted to this body by the citizenry of Mars. Count three: Acts committed that threaten the collective health and welfare of the people. Upon resolution of these allegations, you shall be turned over to the Ministry of Justice to face general charges of conspiracy, espionage, and sabotage. Considering the serious nature of this arraignment, you are to be detained by the Regency Police until the Board completes a comprehensive review of the evidence and determines appropriate punishment if you are found guilty. Do you have anything to say for the record?"

"Yes, I have something to say." Severs jumped up from his seat and slammed his handcuffs on the table.

"First of all, you don't have any evidence against me. These are just trumped-up politically-motivated charges for which you will all dearly pay for very soon."

"If you are referring to your collaborators aboard the *Hesperia*," Jones responded, "I'm afraid they won't be able to help you. The transport ship, and the *Terran Council* delegation it carried, has been interned by the Colonial Fleet. Prior to your arrest, Commander Manbury notified the Board that Yasmin Blecht confessed to her role in the coup attempt and named you as the co-conspirator who would assume autocratic power over the Colony. At the present time, all delegation participants are being identified and efforts are in progress to expose all your operatives on the surface."

Severs was smugly defiant. "You are sadly mistaken if you think you've won. The Council will send an invasion fleet and there's nothing you can do to stop it. Remember this day Honorable Board Members! Remember the day when you let a tired old woman sign your death sentence! When the time comes, you'll all be crawling on your knees for me to save you. Mark my words! Mark my words!"

Jones nodded to the deputies. "Take that bitter, contemptuous man away."

No one in the chamber was fearful of John Severs. He was neither respected nor appreciated by the Board or its staff personnel, and most considered him a loudmouth braggart devoid of any redeeming characteristics. However, his prediction of a full-scale invasion from Earth did send shudders through the assembly. Everyone was of the opinion the *Terran Council* would probably react that way, and there was no doubt the puny military forces available to the *Board of Regents* would be egregiously overmatched. Unless a negotiated settlement could be reached, the Martian Colony – as it had existed – was in great peril.

The Chairperson stood up to address the assembly. "Every civilization reaches a defining moment through crisis. Ours is now upon us. The danger we face is both real and profound. It threatens not only the lives of our people, but their very right to exist as citizens of Mars. To prevail in the coming fight, our skill and determination will be put to its ultimate test. We must succeed, and we will succeed. The fertile ground we have sown on this planet cannot be allowed to wither. It is our duty to mankind, ladies and gentlemen. So, stand up and meet our antagonist with irresistible resolve! I know I can count on each and every one of you. Redemption, we will achieve!"

A boisterous round of applause reverberated throughout the chamber.

At the same time Carolyn Jones was giving her rousing speech to the *Board of Regents* assembly, there was a more contentious gathering taking place tens of millions of miles away on Earth. Janus Krichek had called a joint meeting of the *Terran Council's* top political and military experts after receiving news of the *Hesperia's* capture. The enraged Head Council was berating all those who had planned and supported the John Severs coup plot.

"Councilman Walters! You assured me this mission would achieve complete surprise. But, it is clear now that it didn't. The Board was waiting for the Hesperia. How can you explain that?"

"Your Honor," Bernard "Bernie" Walters reluctantly replied. "We took all necessary precautions to maintain secrecy. Very few people knew about this ahead of time, and we're certain that whoever it was that betrayed us was not on the Hesperia or even the Earth at the time."

"Why are you certain of that?"

"Sir, any communication originating from those locations that could have warned someone on Mars would've been detected by our surveillance systems."

"Are you suggesting the traitor is one of our agents on Mars?"

"That is the only possibility left, sir."

"I can't believe it!" Krichek insisted. "I know John Severs. His loyalty is unassailable, and I'm convinced he wouldn't have confided in anyone he didn't explicitly trust."

"What about that treasonous bastard Marc Bolton?" one of Walters' aides suggested.

"Bolton was deliberately kept out of the loop," Krichek's Chief of Staff William McKinsey replied. "No way he's the source."

"Well, somebody ratted us out," the Head Council asserted. "And, you people better find out who it was pretty goddamn quick! Have we heard back from Severs yet?"

"No sir," answered McKinsey. "He hasn't responded to any of our calls, and we haven't been able to reach anyone from his ground team."

Krichek was incensed. "What the hell is going on over there? If I don't start getting some answers soon, some of you at this table will have serious cause for regret. Major James Francis!"

"Yes your Honor."

"You call yourself a *strategist*?"

"That is my occupation, sir."

"Maybe you should find another line of work. Wasn't it you who said the *Board of Regents* would react passively to a hostile takeover attempt?"

"Sir, I respectfully..."

"Excuse me your Honor," McKinsey interrupted. "We've just received a communication from the Martian Colony."

"Let's see it then," Krichek instructed.

Everyone turned toward the large overhead monitor, and the jumpy images came into sharp focus. It was the stoic face of Carolyn Jones, Chairperson of the *Board of Regents*.

"To all the people of Earth and beyond: As of this terrestrial date, January twelfth two-thousand-seventy-eight, the Colony of Mars declares itself a free and independent state. All existing public and private affiliations, whether they are explicit or implied, are hereby dissolved. We claim as our sovereign domain the Martian ecliptic plane from one-point-three to one-point-seven astronomical units from the sun, and having a vertical extent of point-five A-U. Although we mean you no harm, and will not take any steps towards aggression, we are prepared to defend against intrusions into our spatial province. Until the time when the people of Earth have expelled the yolk of despotism which is corrupting their governments and institutions, we will limit all interactions between our respective worlds. Until that day, we Martians bid you farewell."

When the monitor went blank, the Head Council erupted like an angry volcano. One of his great eyebrows was cocked high as if it were a guillotine poised to execute its deadly function. His lips contorted into a thin stubble-strewn line across his mouth, and his massive jaw muscles constricted grinding his primitive teeth against each other. The great leader's breaths became forceful and deep, and his eyes fixated on the initial target of his rage.

"Guards, put Councilman Walters under arrest! You, my friend, are responsible for this outrage! It was you who talked me out of seizing the Colony with a relatively small strike force. Now we'll have to commit the bulk of our fleet, and that will give them time to prepare. You incompetent fool! Guards, arrest Major Francis while you're at it. I have no more use for strategists."

A bloodcurdling chill ran through the veins of Krichek's subordinates as the two men were taken away. They all feared the Head Council would target more scapegoats until his ire subsided, and that wasn't likely to happen anytime soon. In the interim, it was best for everyone to lay low and keep silent.

"Would anyone like to suggest how we should proceed?" Krichek asked sarcastically. The question was met by an eerie stillness and downturned faces. "Fine, then I will. We will not lose Mars to a bunch of idyllic dreamers. Doing so would not only be economically damaging, but would also demonstrate weakness which could embolden our enemies here at home. The moment has past for subtle stratagems. A more direct approach is needed. We will retake Mars. Admiral Orizuna, I'm placing you in tactical command of the invasion force. How long will it take to mobilize the fleet?"

Admiral Tinichi Orizuna, whose family history was replete with distinguished military men, arose to accept the prestigious assignment. "I am honored, Head Council. If I'm allowed the new battle station which is nearing completion, it will require three months. If not, I can be ready to sail in six weeks."

"How would you deploy the battle station?"

"Sir, my plan would be executed in four separate phases. Immediately upon arrival at Mars, I would secure the surrounding space with a cruiser squadron which would destroy or capture all colonial vessels confronting the fleet or trying to escape the planet. After that was accomplished, I would move the battle station into orbit to surgically disable their surface defenses without causing too much collateral damage to civilian structures. Then, the occupation force would be transported to the surface in stages to systematically seize control of key locations and isolate the rest of the Colony. Finally, the remaining strongholds would be mopped up individually or left to wither on the vine if they prove too costly for a conventional assault."

"That's an excellent plan Admiral, positively excellent! It's bold, direct, and methodical – exactly what I've been hoping for. Now, can you assure me that the battle station will perform as expected? And if so, what is your estimate of when the Colony would be totally subdued?"

"Your Honor, the battle station is heavily armored and therefore impervious to attack from below by surface defenses. Its vulnerability to orbital weapons and space ships will be wholly offset by our cruiser screen. Considering three months for mobilization, one month for rendezvous, two weeks for phase I, up to four weeks for phase II, one month for phase III, and no more than three months for phase IV, I can say with confidence that Mars will be under total control by mid-fall and under effective control before the end of summer."

"Splendid. What is your assessment of the Colony's ability to improve their military capabilities in the next four months?"

"Sir, they could possibly strengthen their ground-based laser weaponry and construct fortifications to impede our occupation force; however, they have no current production capacity to build the number of spacecraft required to mount a credible defense. They also have no missile systems, no nuclear weapons, no land army, no legitimate air force, and there are no foreign allies which could assist them. I must conclude that the military capability of the Martian Colony is extremely limited, and will remain so for several years."

"That was my estimation, as well. Admiral Orizuna, you shall have your battle station. Plan accordingly, and begin mobilizing the fleet. You will receive full cooperation from my staff. If you encounter any problems that could even remotely jeopardize this operation, you are ordered to inform me personally. Now if there's nothing else, this meeting is adjourned."

Carolyn Jones brought together the first ever meeting of the *Board of Regents* war council on Phi twenty-second. It consisted of all Board Members sans the imprisoned John Severs, some representatives from their individual staffs, the Ministers of Science and Justice accompanied by their personal attachés, the highest ranking military officer in the Colony – Commander Manbury and a few of his key subordinates, selected departmental personnel who had displayed an aptitude for strategy and tactics, and one former analyst of the *Terran Council* – Marc Bolton. From a strictly military point of view, this group was rather anemic and would have been soundly ridiculed by the likes of Alexander the Great, Napoleon Bonaparte, and Erwin Rommel. But, it was all the Board could muster.

The Chairperson began the proceedings. "The war council is now called to order. Our newborn *Independent State of Mars* must fight for its survival. The issue presented before us today is the process of how to achieve it. This problem will be the most challenging we have ever faced, but I am confident we will prevail. You are the best and brightest minds on Mars."

"Before we get started, I ask you to welcome our newest citizen Marc Bolton. You have all been briefed on his remarkable story that described the circumstances of his journey from Earth, and how he saved us from a malicious attack by our terrestrial antagonist. He has accepted the dual position of Advisor to the Board/Special Projects Coordinator. We are fortunate to have him."

The round of applause that followed was almost deafening, and it was accompanied by numerous cheers such as 'Bravo!' and 'Hear! Hear!' Bolton himself was noticeably embarrassed. He shook hands, mumbled several utterances of 'thank you,' but respectfully declined to give a speech.

When the ruckus subsided, Ivan Tcholich stood up to assume his role as meeting director. "Alright, let's get down to business. Commander Manbury, please list our combat assets."

"Our space-mobile inventory includes," Manbury began with his distinctive Queen's English accent, "three cruisers, ten shuttles, and the interplanetary transport *Hesperia* which at this time is virtually crewless. Lieutenant Colonel Ferris will detail our static defenses."

"We have eleven ground-based lasers to defend against orbital attack. Eight are obsolete infrared types, and three are newer and more effective ultraviolet weapons. They are positioned primarily to protect our municipal and industrial infrastructure, and that means the whole of the southern hemisphere is essentially defenseless."

"Additionally," Manbury appended, "the infrared weapons' combat range is quite limited and all the laser sites are vulnerable to counter-fire due to their exposed mountings. We also have thirty-five rocket planes restricted to atmospheric operations. They could be armed to defend against a land invasion, but that would require several months to fully implement."

Tcholich shook his head in dismay. "It isn't much, is it gentlemen? Mister Bolton, please explain what we are up against."

"The *Terran Council* has twenty-one space cruisers. Of which, ten are the new *Capella* class. These are vastly superior to our *Rigel* class ships, having greater speed, endurance, armament, and protection. They have five remaining interplanetary transports, and one orbital battle station of immense power currently under construction. There are scores of shuttles and smaller vessels, although the bulk of these could not accompany the main fleet to Mars because of their limited speed. I would hazard to guess that at least two-thirds of this inventory will be assembled into a task force."

The meeting turned silent except for a smattering of disconsolate groans.

"Can you speculate on their plan of attack?" Tcholich inquired.

"Yes Minister, but I cannot claim any professional military expertise. I'm sure Commander Manbury's opinion is more valuable than mine."

"We will get to the Commander in a moment. Please continue."

"Alright sir, their tactical plan presumably depends on whether they want to employ that new battle station or not. Construction was scheduled to be completed by the end of January, and it should take an additional month to perform a shakedown and conduct operational trials. Without the battle station, they would compensate by including a greater proportion of their cruiser strength in the task force. Regardless, they would probably use their *Swallow* fleet formation, with a fighter squadron of light cruisers forming the head and wings, the heavy bombardment group comprising the central body, and the transports at the rear as the tail of the formation. The fleet would complete deceleration in the vicinity of a million miles from Mars. Their initial objective would be to destroy our space vessels as these pose the greatest danger to their fleet. Next they would form a perimeter around the planet, and move the bombardment group into low orbit to systematically disable our surface defenses. After that, the transports would launch a division-sized infantry detachment for a direct ground assault. Then, it would only be a matter of time before the end came."

Ivan Tcholich rubbed his chin in contemplation. "It is a very simple plan, is it not Mister Bolton?"

"Yes sir, conventional military doctrine prescribes a conservative strategy when opposed by a vastly inferior foe."

"What is your opinion, Commander Manbury?"

"I completely agree with Bolton's appraisal. It is exactly what I would do, and it is exactly what I expect their fleet commander will do – who by the way is likely to be none other than Admiral Tinichi Orizuna."

"Orizuna, isn't he the one who put down the Siberian Revolt a few years back?"

"Yes he is, Minister Tcholich. I actually served on his staff as a young ensign right after graduating from the academy, and I can tell you this about the man. Orizuna is a deliberate and thorough tactician. He detests the rash impulse to attack without meticulous preparation, much like George B. McClellan in the American Civil War. If he is placed in command of their fleet, he will hold out as long as he can to procure more firepower. For this reason, I'd like Mister Bolton to give us additional information about that new battle station."

"Mister Bolton?"

"She's a monster, Commander. I worked on developing several components of her propulsion system. In essence, the battle station is an orbital weapons platform designed to attack ground targets with relative impunity. It bristles with an array of particle-beam guns and the latest mark-ten lasers. Her keel-bottom, or underside that faces a planet's surface, is heavily armored with composite materials such as depleted uranium-titanium alloy, boron carbide, other advanced ceramics, and hardened steel plate. To my knowledge, there is no directed-energy weapon in existence capable of defeating it. Conversely, its roof and sides are relatively unprotected, and the battle station itself is very difficult to maneuver. In open space, a nimble warship like a cruiser would find it easy prey."

One of Manbury's executive officers, Lieutenant Lauren Jenkins, proposed an idea. "Commander, we could station our cruisers at a safe distance until the battle station tried to maneuver into orbit. They could attack it in transition with a series of high speed runs and then accelerate out of the range of their fleet."

"That's an interesting suggestion Lieutenant, but tactically impractical. Bolton is right. Their *Capellas* are faster and have longer range weapons. Our cruisers would come under fire long before they could get close enough to the battle station. It would be a massacre."

"There's got to be something we can do," Tcholich exclaimed. "We need answers, people!"

"A head-on attack while their fleet is decelerating?" Jenkins posed.

"Lieutenant, think for a moment. They will not be decelerating close to Mars as a civilian transport would. Our ships would be detected before they could get that far out. However," Manbury continued, "I wonder if we can devise a way to ambush them from behind while they're in transit?"

"From behind?" repeated Jenkins. "That means our cruisers would have to cover a tremendous amount of space, and perform the equivalent of at least three standard velocity changes. Can they carry that much fuel, and how could they achieve the element of surprise?"

"The fuel problem is solvable one way or another, even if it means aerobraking through the atmosphere on the return to Mars. But your second concern is spot on, Lieutenant. Without the element of surprise, an in-transit interception of their fleet is simply out of the question – if we could just think of a way to do it."

"What seems to be on your mind Mister Bolton?" Carolyn Jones observed.

"Oh, I was contemplating whether we could use an asteroid to conceal our cruisers until they were in position to ambush the Council's fleet."

"What asteroid Mister Bolton?" Jenkins quizzed him. "We don't even know when they will launch or what trajectory they'll take. Besides, most asteroids are in the main belt outside the orbit of Mars. How could they be useful?"

"I think I know what he's driving at Lieutenant," Ivan Tcholich implied. "We wouldn't look for an asteroid to hide our ships behind. We would maneuver one in the direction of their fleet."

"That's correct Minister Tcholich," Bolton added. "We have spent an Earth year developing the technology to move asteroids as part of the *Archimedes* project. I propose we locate a medium size rock in close proximity to Mars, say one half mile in diameter, and move it into a parallel solar orbit as soon as possible. Commander Manbury, is it true that we will be able to detect the launch of the Council's fleet from our communications satellites?"

"Yes, there's very little chance that we wouldn't. We continuously monitor most spectral emissions from Earth. The simultaneous launch of an entire fleet's worth of ships would be hard to miss."

"Good, then here is how we would utilize the asteroid. Once the launch of the Council's fleet has been confirmed, we plot an interception course for the asteroid and send it on its way. Following close behind will be our cruiser force. As long as they maintain a tight formation in an antipodal position relative to the opposing fleet with the asteroid as the relational sphere, then they could not be directly observed. After transposition, our cruisers would execute an engine burn to alter course and catch the Council's fleet from behind. This would give them a legitimate chance to achieve surprise, and allow them to attack from a point confronted by the fewest number of opposing weapons."

"Is that practicable, Commander?" Tcholich prodded.

"His idea has several outstanding variables which would all have to work out favorably to produce the desired result," Manbury explained. "The asteroid's trajectory must be calculated and executed with great precision. The timing of each step in the operation must be perfect. Our cruiser force would have to be extremely diligent to stay in tight formation, keep the correct orientation, and not use up all their thruster fuel in the process. Furthermore, their time-over-target, or T-O-T, would be limited due to the velocity difference – necessitating a highly accurate attack since they wouldn't get a second chance. Then there is the most uncertain issue of all – the possible detection of our first and second engine burns and how they might be interpreted."

"Commander, even though our cruiser force couldn't give away their position by communicating directly with Mars, we could still send them regular or periodic intelligence reports of the enemy fleet's status," Jenkins proposed.

"That's true, Lieutenant. Although, not via standard military channels because line-of-sight transmissions would also give away their position. We would have to encode the messages and broadcast them over the Solar System Alert System, which means there is no guarantee that our cruisers would pick them up."

"Well Commander, what is your recommendation?" Tcholich pressed him. "Will Bolton's plan work or not?"

"Sir, I would estimate the odds for at least partial success to be no more than fifty percent. That said, it is a brilliantly innovative concept that gives us a real opportunity to defeat their fleet where the other ideas we discussed do not. My recommendation is that we adopt this strategy and make it work."

"What is your opinion, Lieutenant Colonel Ferris?"

"I'm for it, Minister Tcholich. The logistical problems of Mister Bolton's plan are not insurmountable. Also, I have some thoughts on how we can obscure the first engine burn from detection by masking it with a dust shroud."

"Excellent, and what do you have to say Lieutenant Jenkins?"

"Sir, while I consider this plan inherently problematic and obviously risky, it does appear to be our best option. I think we should try it."

"Is there anyone here who wants to cast a dissenting opinion or has any other questions? Alright then," Tcholich continued. "With the permission of the Chair, we shall move to further develop and implement Mister Bolton's plan which will be codenamed *Operation Midway*."

"The Chair agrees," Carolyn Jones announced.

Ivan Tcholich paused for a moment to collect his thoughts, and then proceeded. "Under the directorship of Bess Harcourt, Marc Bolton will coordinate all efforts to locate and maneuver a suitable asteroid. Trenton Manbury will command the cruiser force. Lieutenant Colonel Ferris will be in command of all planetary defenses, and is responsible for devising a backup plan to be carried out should the ambush of the *Terran Council's* fleet fails. Overall command resides with the leadership of this war council. We all have a lot of work to do, so I suggest we get started. Our next meeting will be scheduled for one week from today. You are all dismissed."

The ensuing Martian days were feverish in the former colony. Mobilization efforts were in full swing. Everyone and everything that could contribute to the coming military campaign was employed for combat duty. Regional command centers were setup to facilitate local defenses and make emergency preparations. The lowest subsurface levels of the cities, industrial centers, and transportation hubs were stockpiled with food, water, and other essentials for use as refuge shelters. Although the denizens of Mars were accustomed to living in a hostile planetary environment, the imminent prospect of full-scale war with Earth was unnerving even to the most stalwart among them.

On Phi twenty-sixth, Marc Bolton and his team of technicians were hurriedly completing the final details of a mission to send five automated *Archimedes* robots towards an insipid stony asteroid named Miramicus by the 4th of Chi. Roughly six-tenths of a mile in diameter, it orbited eccentrically around the sun currently about twenty-two million miles from Mars.

Trenton Manbury entered the study room. "Bolton, may I speak with you in private for a moment?"

"Sure Commander," Bolton replied as the two men walked out into the hall.

"I wanted to notify you in person that the Chairperson has approved my request to have you assigned to my command staff just before we launch the cruiser force. You will be given a temporary commission of lieutenant, junior grade. You may contest this assignment if you wish to."

"No Commander, I will not contest it. However, I'd like to know why you requested me. After all, I'm no warrior."

"Perhaps not, but I couldn't think of anyone else more valuable to this operation than the person who conceived it. The logistics of intercepting a fast moving interplanetary fleet with a rock the size of a small mountain, while trying to stay hidden behind it, will push my crews to the limit of their capabilities. We will need all the help we can get."

"Not to worry Commander, I am confident we can do this. It will also be an honor for me to serve with you. I just hope you're not expecting me to learn how to salute anytime soon!"

Manbury laughed heartily and shook Bolton's hand.

On Alpha 6th, year fifteen, Sergeant Miles O'Keefe was monitoring the graphical display of data down-linked from the orbital communications satellites dedicated for Earth observation. Protruding from the rim of the third planet, he saw a large unidentified energy disturbance. After completing a detailed analysis of the anomaly's electromagnetic spectral emissions, O'Keefe identified what had caused it. He immediately notified his superior that twenty space ships had left Earth orbit and appeared to be on an intersecting trajectory with Mars.

Aboard the *Cromwell*, Commander Manbury and acting-Lieutenant Bolton were discussing tactical deployments when the news reached them.

"Sir, we've just received a priority message from Surveillance Ops," exclaimed the communications technician.

"Send it over here Petty Officer," instructed Manbury.

After reading the text displayed on his monitor, Manbury turned towards his newest junior officer. "It's started, Marc. Twenty separate tracks have been confirmed. The four larger ones must be their transports, and possibly the battle station."

"Agreed Commander, which means they have an escort of sixteen cruisers. Does the message specify an e-t-a or their exact trajectory?"

"No, but that information is forthcoming I'm sure."

"I can do a quick calculation," Bolton declared as he switched the monitor over to a real-time map of the inner solar system. "We won't know their terminal velocity for a few hours, but let's assume they launched with the battle station. That beast is so massive that it will slow down the entire fleet. I doubt they'll reach one-hundred-seventy thousand miles per hour. Hmm, that should give us a minimum of twenty-three Earth days before they would decelerate."

"When is Miramicus due to arrive?" asked Manbury.

"Alpha nineteenth," answered Bolton.

"That's cutting it awfully close, Marc."

"I know, but we still have time if there are no more delays and we expedite the refueling interval."

"What if they sailed without the battle station at maximum speed?"

"In that event, I'm afraid we'll have to change our plans Commander. But, let's not worry about that until we get confirmation. Whatever happens, the *Hesperia* will be a sitting duck in orbit. If worse comes to worse, she might be the only avenue of escape for our people – well, for some of them anyway."

"I've already anticipated that. Her new crew is getting a crash course in operational navigation as we speak. I put Lieutenant Jenkins in command, and gave explicit orders to take any steps necessary to keep the ship out of harm's way even if it means leaving orbit."

Three hours later, Commander Manbury telecalled Bolton who was resting in his quarters. "We have confirmation, Marc. The fleet's speed is one-sixty-eight-point-nine. It looks like we were right about the battle station."

"There's a chance now, Commander. After rendezvousing with Miramicus, we'll have roughly a week to maneuver behind them, change course, and accelerate to attack the rear of their formation. It won't be easy, but we might just be able to pull this off."

"There's no more doubt in my mind, acting-Lieutenant Bolton. Those bastards won't know what hit them!"

Bolton gave his commander a traditional military salute which was returned with an enthusiastic grin. He knew better, however. Combat commanders are inclined to be eagerly optimistic in the presence of their troops when battle is near, because a leader who exudes a lack of confidence is likely to ruin their aggressive spirit. Commander Trenton Manbury wasn't about to risk losing that advantage as it was the only one he could truly count on.

Alpha 27th was a stormy winter day for the fledgling Martian nation. High winds had kicked up a menacing cloud of dust and ice in the northern hemisphere that interfered with communications between the planet and its intrepid warriors moving against the invading fleet from Earth. An impatient Ivan Tcholich was pacing back and forth in Lieutenant Colonel Ferris' defense command center.

"What is the damned problem, Major Nausbaum?"

"Some of our transmitters have been damaged by the storm, Minister Tcholich, and severe atmospheric ionization is inhibiting all communications over a thousand mile wide area. The entire system is being affected. Until the storm blows over, there isn't much more we can do."

"Have you tried rerouting the command link to one of the eastern industrial centers like Pasteur?"

"No sir, they are not authorized to military channels."

"Well, I'm giving them authorization now! We've got to get this latest data on the Earth fleet to Commander Manbury straight away. Don't just sit there, man, get on with it!"

"Yes sir!"

Meanwhile, millions of miles closer to the sun, Manbury's three cruisers were struggling to stay in tight formation behind Miramicus as it plunged headlong toward Admiral Orizuna's powerful fleet. The irregularly shaped asteroid produced unpredictable gravimetric effects that required the ships to continually use their thrusters to maintain the correct position. This was complicated by Miramicus' end-over-end rotation, even though the rate of spin had been greatly reduced by the *Archimedes* robots.

"Commander, have we received any additional reports on the exact whereabouts of the Council's fleet?" Bolton asked with some trepidation.

"No, damn it! We haven't heard from Mars in the last eighteen hours. We're crawling along at fifty thousand miles per hour, and have used up most of our thruster fuel hiding behind that big unsightly rock in front of us. Pretty soon, we won't be able to hold this position. And if our course is off by even a degree, we'll never be able to intercept their fleet."

"I know, Trenton. But, we need to be patient. Our calculations couldn't be that far off. Besides, we can't risk exposing ourselves by making a course correction at this late stage. Trust the good work we have already done. Believe me, we'll find them soon."

Six hours later, Admiral Tinichi Orizuna sat confidently on the bridge of the cruiser *Monmouth* with his executive officer, Vice-Admiral Vladimir Lorinov.

"I don't understand it, Admiral," said Lorinov. "Our long range scanners have detected only minimal activity around Mars. The Colony must've discovered by now that we're coming. Why haven't they deployed their ships? My gut instinct tells me something's afoot."

"Worry not, my friend," Orizuna reassured him. "The reason why we are not seeing much activity is due to the fact that the Colony has so few assets with which to mount a defense. Had they launched their pitiful cruiser force to attack us in transit, we would have observed it. Is that true or not?"

"Yes sir, we should have been able to detect such a launch. Although, I keep wondering what that diffuse energy reading was that our scanners picked up seven days ago beyond the orbit of Mars."

"Vladimir, analysis concluded it was asteroid debris excited by that solar flare we recorded a couple of days earlier. Are you getting cold feet?"

"No sir, I just don't want us to get..."

"Mid-range contact, bearing forty-two degrees starboard, negative three-point-eight degrees ecliptic latitude, range eight-one-six thousand!" the excited radar operator announced loudly.

"What?" Admiral Orizuna exclaimed. "I want visual identification, men. Snap to it! Get those scopes powered up!"

"It looks like an asteroid, Admiral," a young corporal proclaimed.

"Verified," his station officer added. "It's about one half mile wide."

"Give me its course," Lorinov demanded. "Is there any danger of hitting it?"

"No sir," answered the navigation officer. "The fleet will clear it in one-point-nine hours at a distance of six-two-five thousand."

Orizuna was livid. "Vice-Admiral, how could your people chart a course so close to an asteroid that big without knowing about it?"

"It's not on any of our charts, Admiral. It must have been perturbed from its stable orbit in the main belt by a collision. Maybe, that's what caused the diffused energy reading we saw last week."

"If it was knocked out of orbit, then there may be smaller pieces of the asteroid directly in our path. Initiate a ninety degree forward scan immediately," Orizuna ordered.

"Sir, I must advise you that a ninety degree scan will expose our position to any ships in the vicinity," Lorinov warned.

"Your concern is duly noted. Now, follow my orders Vice-Admiral."

On the bridge of the *Cromwell*, no one was aware of the Earth fleet's proximity. Hiding behind a rock is a double-edged tactic. Your opponent cannot see you, and you cannot see them. The uncertainty of the situation was trying Trenton Manbury's patience.

"Marc, our computer projections indicate we've just about reached the point of intersection. We can't afford to wait too long. Maybe we should risk sneaking one ship out into the open so we can get a good look."

"Commander, the opportunity we're counting on will be lost if we reveal ourselves too soon. Please give it a little more time. I don't know why, but it doesn't feel right to me yet. Anyway, we are not scheduled to execute our attack run for another three Earth hours."

"Alright, alright, we'll wait."

A few moments later, Ensign Robert Wilkins was called over by the operator manning the ship's passive scanners. The two men appeared puzzled by the strange signals being displayed on the monitor.

"What is it, Wilkins?"

"Sir, we are encountering energy waves from every direction. But the readings are confusing and we can't pinpoint its source. The waves cover the U-H-F and V-H-F bands between fifty and five hundred megahertz with varying wavelengths in the point-five to five meter range. I've never seen anything like it."

"We found them!" Manbury cried out. "The Council's fleet is actively probing the space in front of them with their radars."

"What are they looking for, Commander?" Bolton inquired. "Could it be us?"

"No, they wouldn't be broadcasting their position if they knew we were here; and, there's no way they're getting any radar returns from our ships with that asteroid between us. I'm certain now that Admiral Orizuna is commanding their fleet. His cautious nature has led him into a critical mistake. When his sensors picked up Miramicus, he perceived the possibility of collision with asteroid debris to be a greater threat to his fleet than an unlikely surprise attack by us. We have him now! For the next few hours, his attention will be focused to his front and not on his rear. Wilkins, overlay those passive radar plots on the big screen with our course projections."

"Yes sir. Carry on, Petty Officer."

When the merged images displayed on the large overhead monitor, it was obvious to everyone exactly where the enemy fleet was.

"You see that, Bolton? There's only six-hundred thousand miles of separation. If that isn't hitting the bulls-eye, I don't know what is. Well done, acting-Lieutenant, very well done!"

"Thank you, sir."

"When's the optimum time to begin our attack run?"

"Let me do a quick calculation," Bolton paused. "It looks like two-point-eight Earth hours, sir. That's assuming a one-point-seven-five hour engine burn to produce a terminal velocity margin of twenty thousand miles per hour relative to their fleet, and putting us in firing range inside of thirty-five Earth hours. I can give you the precise figures shortly."

"Outstanding Mister Bolton, see to it immediately."

"Yes Commander. You know, I'll be sad to leave Miramicus behind. It will feel like throwing away an old security blanket."

Manbury laughed jovially. "My goodness, man, it's just an ugly rock!"

On the early morning of Alpha 29th, at an empty spot in space 1.33 astronomical units from the sun, three colonial cruisers closed in on their unsuspecting quarry. Trenton Manbury was correct. Admiral Orizuna was oblivious to any threat to his rear. All the weeks of meticulous planning and hard work would now coalesce onto a single moment in history. The fate of an entire planetary society and a feared authoritarian regime would depend on the outcome of this imminent armed conflict. It has been said that only soldiers fight wars, but it is the children of war who ultimately bear the greatest burden of its legacy.

"Look at that!" Manbury declared. "Three big fat transports at the end of their formation."

"That's the *Maxwell Montes* to our left, the *Argyre* in the center, and the *Triton* on the right," observed Bolton.

"The sun is almost directly behind us, men. They are brightly illuminated while we are obscured by its glare. I doubt they'll be able to see us until we get into firing range. Lieutenant Preston, send visual signals to the *Canberra* and *James Bay* to target the transports on the left and right respectively, and we will attack the one in the middle."

"Yes sir, at once!"

"Ensign Ramirez, aim our forward lasers on the *Argyre's* power generator just aft of the fuselage."

"Acknowledged, target confirmed."

Bolton's eyes began to water, and he quickly wiped them dry. As he looked at the glistening *Argyre*, he fondly remembered Sergeant O'Mara, Doctor Raystreet, and that magnificent listening room he so enjoyed. They would all be gone soon, and the spilling of blood would soil Bolton's hands perhaps more than anyone's.

Aboard the *Monmouth*, Admiral Orizuna received an emergency message from Earth informing him that their long range sensors had detected three unknown vessels trailing his fleet. Immediately, he ordered visual observers in the transport ships to corroborate the report. Just as their sightings were being routed up the chain of command, two scarlet-tinged beams shot out from the *Canberra* and crashed into the junction between the *Maxwell Montes'* power generator and fusion engine. Two compartments in that section ruptured, causing a mixture of pressurized air, coolants, and radioactive fuel to gush from her hull like an angry torrent. The huge ship was mortally wounded, and she tumbled end over end into the blackness of space – never to be seen again.

Meanwhile, the inexperienced commander of the *James Bay* impetuously decided to strike at the base of the *Triton's* habitat ring supports. His first shots caused only minor damage allowing an alert gunner manning the transport's top rear laser turret to return fire. Almost simultaneously, the *James Bay's* second salvo and the first from the *Triton* found their marks. Two of the supports for habitat ring four were sheared away causing it to break loose, and the ring spun wildly into the rest of the ship. The resulting explosions were horrific, sending pieces flying in every direction as the great transport vessel ripped itself apart. The *James Bay* fared no better. Lieutenant Raintree and his command crew were killed instantly when the cruiser was struck squarely in her bridge. Thirty seven crew members in the engineering hull were trapped when the passageways to the escape pods depressurized. They all suffocated several hours later.

Commander Manbury was very proud of Ensign Ramirez's expert aim. His shots were evenly spaced, striking an eight foot wide section of the *Argyre's* power generator. Bursting deuterium storage tanks blew into the breached hull and completely destroyed the reactor's cooling system. Within seconds, a gigantic explosion disintegrated the entire aft portion of the transport. What remained was thrown forward, and Bolton could see streams of gas erupting from holes punctured in the habitat rings.

A panic induced shock gripped Admiral Orizuna aboard the *Monmouth*. The attack was so sudden and precise there wasn't time for his cruisers to double-back and engage the enemy. The only immediate action available was to fire at them with his leading ships as the colonial vessels sped past his now disorganized fleet. Several of Orizuna's cruisers had to maneuver out of formation to evade the destruction at the rear, which essentially took them out of what was left of the battle. Sensing his commander's emotional paralysis, Vice-Admiral Lorinov seized control of the situation.

"Lock tracking computers onto their flight path!" he ordered authoritatively.

"It's no good sir, we can't get a fix. There's too much radar interference," the weapons officer reported.

"Well, use visual targeting damn you! I want those ship destroyed!"

"Yes sir! Sighting coordinates are coming in now sir!"

At that moment, the two Martian cruisers were performing a maximum engine burn to streak past the fleet at the highest possible speed.

"There they are! Fire!" screamed Lorinov.

Violet-hued beams leapt from the *Monmouth* and four other ships that managed to react in time, but their vengeful fusillade was hastily executed and poorly aimed. One glancing hit was registered on

Canberra's armored undersides. The ship sustained no appreciable damage. Before any more effective shots could be fired, the colonial cruisers had accelerated out of range.

Admiral Orizuna sat motionless as damage reports and retaliatory pursuit requests poured in from the fleet. He did not react and appeared to be oblivious to them. Lorinov did not press him either. Both men understood the mission was over. Without the supply of fuel and provisions carried aboard the transports, his ships could not safely return to Earth if they went chasing after their tormenters. In addition, there was no longer any infantry force to invade the Martian surface. If the fleet continued on to Mars, they would be trapped in orbit with insufficient food and water to survive until they could be relieved from Earth. Whatever damage they could do to the Colony's defenses before their inevitable surrender, seemed pathetically insignificant.

"Vladimir, do we have enough fuel for a direct return to Earth?" Orizuna inquired meekly.

"No Admiral, we don't. The *Capellas* might be able to if they took a low speed circuitous route back, but not the other ships. The battle station *Champion* is particularly limited in the number of standard velocity changes it can execute."

"Do you have any suggestions, Vice-Admiral?"

"Well sir, considering the positions of the outer planets, we could plot a gravity assisted course around Jupiter for a free return to Earth. That option would expend the least amount of fuel."

"It would also take longer... months, in fact. We don't have enough provisions to last that long."

"We might sir, if we implemented a strict rationing plan and devised a way to recycle our water. Regardless, I regret to say there are just no other options, unless you want to consider splitting up the fleet."

"Vice-Admiral, I will not sacrifice half the fleet only to stay alive long enough to face capital punishment on Earth! Make preparations for Jupiter. We are going home together."

The celebration aboard the Cromwell was spirited and distinctly unmilitary. It was a grand release of the fear the crew harbored leading up to the battle. The odds were stacked heavily against them, but they somehow managed to prevail. Though the old warhorse Manbury needed no such purge of emotion, he nevertheless had the wisdom to let it run its course. Mars had been saved. Discipline could be shelved for a while.

Retiring to his quarters, Marc Bolton was also filled with emotion. But, his feelings were not of jubilation. The sorrow and guilt from the loss of 6300 souls weighed heavily upon him, and no amount of justification seemed to help. He concluded that he lacked the inner strength of great leaders who could cope with the responsibility of such tragedy. In reality, he was just torturing himself. The price of human life is never cheap.

So ended what on Earth became known as *The Conflict at One-Three-Three*. On Mars, it would be remembered as the *Battle of Miramicus*. The outcome cultivated the growth of a new civilization, and spelled doom for an old one. For countless eons this pattern has repeated itself in the disagreements between men because the primal urge often wins out over rational thought. But from now on, mankind would have an alternative evolutionary path to try and correct that flaw.

Chapter 9
Of Worlds and Time

It wasn't until the tattered remnants of Admiral Tinichi Orizuna's fleet arrived home in the winter of 2078-2079 that the scale of the defeat was realized by the public. Of the original twenty ships, only nine returned safety to Earth. The surviving crews were severely emaciated, although the admiral himself, Vice-Admiral Lorinov, and the rest of his staff were not among them.

The tricky maneuver around Jupiter proved far more perilous than was anticipated. In order to alter their course back towards the inner solar system, the fleet needed to reduce its speed. The only way to do this quickly without exhausting their fuel reserves was to use a technique called *aerobraking*. This entailed flying through the upper layers of Jupiter's atmosphere at the *periapsis*, or low point, of their elliptical orbit. The resulting drag on the ships would slow them down; however, it required great precision. The battle station *Champion*, the latest development in military technology, was too unwieldy to attain the proper trajectory. Its angle was too steep, and the massive vessel plunged into the swirling clouds of the giant planet taking 904 people to their deaths. The *Rigel* class cruiser *Ramilles* suffered an engine malfunction and failed to escape Jupiter's gravity. Two other ships overshot and were flung out into the outer solar system. The *Callisto*,

Kaiser, *Klamath*, and Orizuna's flagship *Monmouth*, got close enough to Earth for orbital acquisition - which in fact - they never ultimately achieved. All transmissions from those ships ceased before their scheduled course adjustment.

Unfortunately for Janus Krichek, the death of his fleet commander eliminated the possibility of using him as a scapegoat. Only officials still alive could be held accountable for the colossal disaster, especially the one who had authorized it. There were many who suffered recrimination, but the axe fell heaviest on the Head Council himself. On August 15, 2080, Krichek's two decade long reign as absolute ruler of Earth expired at the end of a hangman's rope. Ironically, the very military establishment which had vaulted him to power became the instrument of his demise. Throughout history, the armed forces who ostensibly serve their commander-in-chief have sometimes turned violently against them in the face of collective adversity or personal disagreement. Marcus Licinius Crassus was murdered in 53 B.C. after his Roman army was routed in an ill-conceived campaign against the Parthians. The July Plot in 1944, that nearly killed Adolf Hitler, was undertaken by high ranking members of the German General Staff. Under mysterious circumstances, American President John F. Kennedy was assassinated on November 22, 1963 after he openly defied the most powerful military-industrial complex of the 20th century.

The legacy of the one and only Head Council would not be fondly written in the pages of history.

The man was a megalomaniac of the highest order, on par with the most notorious in that genre such as Hitler and Joseph Stalin. The degree of misery he inflicted on most of the world's populations was unsurpassed by even those two hated dictators. Just in the 2060's alone, entire nations were systematically wiped out of existence. In Krichek's defense, some would say no other leader ever faced more daunting societal problems than those which plagued mankind during his rule. To this, there can be no doubt. However, his methods were atrocious and his motivations were pathologically self-serving. For Janus Krichek, one personal goal outweighed everything else – to be the first conqueror of the entire world.

The *Terran Council* did not last long after its leader's death. No one had the courage to try and assume the unenviable position of Head Council in that hostile political climate. The organization itself degenerated into impotency, and regional military regimes seized control in North America, East Asia, and Central Europe, where most of the world's wealth was concentrated. Elsewhere, feudal systems reminiscent of Medieval Europe sprang up around the globe – particularly in South America and Africa – to bring some sort of structure to impoverished localities. Considering the escalating environmental degradation which was placing increasing burdens on food, water, and energy supplies, this inefficient patchwork method of planetary governance was destined to fall apart.

The situation on the fourth planet from the sun contrasted sharply with that of Earth. Mars had finally ridden itself of the terrestrial yoke that had hung like dark cloud over everything its people were trying to accomplish. The former colony was now free to develop the civilization envisioned by its founders. Trenton Manbury and Marc Bolton were canonized as heroes, although the fanfare was much more modest and subdued compared to what would have occurred on Earth. The pair traveled from place to place receiving honors and giving speeches to grateful onlookers. The mayor of McLaughlin, an émigré from Brazil prone to occasional silliness, garishly bestowed the title of *Manbury of Miramicus* to the Martian fleet commander who was less than enthralled by the label. During a tour of Maggini, industrial workers shouted 'Vive le Libérateur!' everywhere the rather embarrassed Marc Bolton went. These harmless displays of affection were cathartic for the Martian people, and it was understood they had earned the right to a little frivolity.

There were also subtle cultural changes that took root on Mars in the aftermath of the great battle. It quickly became passé for the citizenry to use the words 'colonist' or 'colony' in reference to themselves or their newly independent state. They were now self-identified *Martians*, separate and distinct from their Earthly cousins who just happened to share a common lineage. This sociological disassociation manifests itself when one group wants to see themselves as different from another competing group in order to promote a feeling of self-esteem. In other words, a man can value himself more if he becomes the opposite of the person he detests. History is replete with examples, but perhaps none more poignant than the plight of the Black Man in post-colonial America. The subculture they developed provided the equality and acceptance which were denied to them by the larger White-dominate society. So too, the people of Mars were compelled to be different. Although, this alienation of one's own ancestry did run contrary to the commonly held belief that Martians were somehow ethically superior. Instead, it was stark evidence that the Apple of Mars hadn't yet fallen very far from its human tree.

That shortcoming aside, the *Independent State of Mars* achieved successes in the subsequent years that could only be dreamed about on Earth. Poverty did not exist. Malnutrition and disease were almost unheard of. Quality education and healthcare were universal, and everyone worked in some capacity to benefit society unless they were incapacitated. The elderly became teachers, and there was a new appreciation for the arts that had been almost absent in the early days of the Colony. Of all the lessons learned from Earth history, the most valuable was that uncontrolled economic growth driven by greed could not be sustained. It eventually leads to destructive conflict, and brings out the very worst of human nature. What the founders of Mars had created instead was not nirvana. In fact, the very concept of a corporeal paradise was absurd to the Martian psyche. But, they did manage to create a truly egalitarian society, and it was patently obvious they intended to keep it.

After the euphoria of victory settled down, Marc Bolton retreated from his public persona. He quietly continued his work for the *Board of Regents* and Ministry of Science, but otherwise kept a low profile. The dramatic personal changes he had experienced combined with the great responsibilities he had incurred, made Bolton emotionally distraught. He felt lingering guilt over causing so many deaths, and he worried incessantly about the future of Earth and those he left behind. Additionally, he still hadn't resolved what had propelled him to this fantastic Martian adventure, and that profoundly frustrated him.

Bolton's emotional self-flagellation could have easily spiraled out of control had it not been for the stabilizing influence of Sirtes. She was the anchor that kept him from drifting away from the banality of everyday life. Her style wasn't to push, scold, or coddle, but to always be there for him. Sirtes knew that Bolton was fully aware of his depression, and that he had the capacity for self-correction. He just needed a tether to keep from straying too far before his practical sensibilities asserted itself. Sirtes was no ordinary woman, and the good fortune of having her was indicative of just how lucky Bolton's life seemed to be.

This post-war period also saw Bolton renew his relationship with his lifelong friend Han Li, who was still on Mars when the hostilities began. He was now a Martian citizen working for the Ministry of Science as Director of Atmospheric Research & Planning. Han's main office and residence in Lowellton were both within walking distance of Bolton's, which allowed the two men to spend a lot of time together.

Early one morning, Han stopped by his friend's room unannounced. Bolton awoke from a restless sleep, slipped on a pullover shirt, and ran his fingers through his coarse hair to make himself more presentable before opening the door.

"Good morning, Marc."

"Hi Han, what time is it?" Bolton grumbled as he rubbed the sleep from his eyes.

Han looked around the room and saw clothing and miscellaneous household items scattered everywhere. "It's time to get up. I thought we could have breakfast before going to work. This place is a mess, Marc. Do you ever intend to clean it?"

Embarrassed, Bolton cleared off one of the recliners so Han could sit down and then fell back down on the bed.

"Alright Marc, this has gone far enough! What the hell is bothering you? The whole damned city is asking questions. Why are you withdrawing from them? Even Sirtes has expressed concern, and she is the last person who would talk behind your back."

Bolton massaged the back of his neck in exasperation. "I'm not cut out to be a public figure. I just want to be left alone."

"Don't bullshit me, Marc Bolton! That's not what I'm talking about and you know it. Look at yourself, you're a wreck. I think I'm entitled to a little honesty here. Now, what's really going on with you?"

Bolton fought off the urge to rebuke his friend with stubborn denial. "If you must know, I'm having trouble coping."

"With what?" his guest asked emphatically.

"With myself," he cried out, "and what I have done!" I didn't have to come to Mars. I could've stayed home with Christine where I belonged. But even if I hadn't, I still could have done what I was told and stayed out of this Martian business. Maybe that would have saved all those lives lost in the battle, and kept the Earth from deteriorating into anarchy. Those people who died, Han, they weren't our enemy. They were people just like you and I. Why did they have to pay for my arrogance?"

"You did not act out of arrogance, Marc."

"No, what would you call it then? "This telepathic power was put into my head, and I had the audacity to play God by rationalizing that it was the quote, right thing to do. Ha! No man should presume to know what's right for anyone other than himself. I never wanted it. I never wanted any of this!" Bolton started shaking and covered his face with his hands.

Han was surprised to see Bolton in such a deeply serious emotional state, which he would have never thought possible knowing his friend as he did. His confrontational approach had drawn it out, but now it was time for Han to tread more lightly.

"Well, I agree with you. You did assume a great deal of responsibility, maybe more than you had a right to. But I'm certainly glad you did, and there are a half a million people on this planet who feel the same way. I hope you're not inferring that they are all wrong."

Bolton did not respond.

"Had it been me in your shoes," Han continued, "I wouldn't have had the courage to put my life on the line even for the noble cause you faced. Janus Krichek's evil pursuit of power would have devastated this civilization. The *Board of Regents*, the departmental Ministers, and all their key supporters, would have been summarily executed. A puppet government would have been installed to brutally suppress the populace which would have resulted in even more killings. Demoralization would have reduced economic productivity, causing the Terran Council's regime to implement forced labor practices and harsh quotas. The quality of life would have degraded, the death rate would have climbed, and there would have been widespread suffering. Eventually, Mars would have become nothing more than an impoverished slave colony. And meanwhile, the people of Earth would've been no better off than they are now. If I had been in your shoes, Marc, we would now be discussing the ruination of two worlds instead of just one."

"Describing my actions as courageous is a real stretch, Han. I was as trapped by the circumstances as anyone, perhaps more. Also, I don't believe you would have acted any differently."

"Assuming that's true, would you have cast the same amount of blame onto me as you have on yourself?"

Bolton thought for a moment, but couldn't come up with an answer.

"We both know you wouldn't have. That begs the question of why you've been punishing yourself so."

"Do you have an answer for that too?"

"No, I don't. But, I know your guilt is completely misplaced. Do you remember what my mother told you when you felt the same way over the loss of your family?"

"Yes Han, she said that life sometimes affects us in ways we cannot control. People grow as individuals not by avoiding adversity, but by learning how to cope with it."

"Indeed. She also said that your personal tragedy gave you the strength to succeed. Marc, we all marveled at the sense of duty and purpose you developed as a young man. Mom was so proud of you. She always thought that by overcoming so much, you would one day achieve true greatness. And, it is evident now that her prophecy was correct."

"Be strong yet humble, she used to tell me. I've tried to live by those words."

"You have, my friend, and you may be called on once again to be strong."

"What do you mean?"

"The Chairperson is gravely ill. Her doctors don't know how much longer she can hang on."

"I'm sorry. I heard she was sick, but didn't know it was that bad."

"There's more, big guy. The Board is considering nominating a new Chairperson. Rumor has it that your name is at the top of their list."

"You must be joking!"

"I'm afraid not. There's been a lot of discussion about it inside the Ministry."

"They can't be serious! I'm not qualified for that job. Besides, Ivan Tcholich is next in line, and there isn't a person better suited to take over."

"Maybe, but Tcholich wants to remain where he is. He and the other Board Members have a very high opinion of you."

"I'd like to stay where I am too!"

"Relax, this is all just speculation. But if the call to duty does come, it's not in your nature to shriek away from it. Now, will you please get dressed so we can go to breakfast?"

That evening, Bolton and Sirtes went to dinner at a little family-run café on level one called *The Deimos*. The menu reflected a style of cuisine common in the eastern industrial complexes, heavy into poultry and tubers, which Bolton likened to French country cooking on Earth. It was a nice change of pace from the fresh green vegetable and tank-farmed fish entrees peculiar to Lowellton.

After discussing the ordinary events of the day, the subject of Bolton's early morning conversation with Han came up. Sirtes was pleased that her lover was not only willing to discuss his psychological conundrum - a critical first step towards healing, but was also now open to admitting the emotional reasons which had triggered it. Although she knew he would progress to this point eventually, it was a big relief to actually see it occurring.

"Well Marc, it sounds like Han knows you very well. Did you take what he said to heart?"

"Yes, I'm trying. The enormity of everything that's happened to me here on Mars was overwhelming. I was so concerned with everyone else, I kind of lost track of myself."

"Those who cannot help themselves are unable to help others. Isn't that how the saying goes?"

"That's true, Sirtes. I'd like to get your opinion on the other matter as well."

"You mean the possibility of being nominated as Chairperson?"

"Yes. I'm sure it is way too premature to be contemplating this, but I'd like to know how you feel about it regardless."

"Is it not more important how you feel?"

"Sure it is, but I don't know how I feel about it right now. My life is changing so fast I'm not even convinced I'm in control of it any longer. You understand me as well as anyone could, perhaps even better than myself. You are privy to my most innermost thoughts. Your opinion matters and I am in need of it."

"I believe you would make an excellent Chairperson," Sirtes said with a serious expression, "if you were at peace with yourself. Unfortunately, you are not. The war was a great burden on you, but it's over now and yet you continue to torment yourself. The reasons why are buried deep inside you. I have sensed them for some time, but wouldn't dare probe your mind to bring them to the surface."

"Perhaps now is the time."

"Are you sure, Marc? It may not be pleasant."

"I'm sure. I can't carry this weight forever. Without a resolution, it will destroy me."

"As you wish, but let's finish dinner first and go to your room."

The two had hardly picked at their food beforehand, and it didn't take long after that for them to give up and leave the café. That was a shame, the rosemary chicken and caramelized sweet potatoes were delightful.

In Bolton's room, Sirtes took him by the hand as they sat down facing each other. "You know how this works," she implied. "Take a few moments to clear your mind. Relax... that's good. I'm going to make some mental suggestions. As the thoughts coalesce in your mind, allow yourself to explore them freely. No inhibitions - let them take you into yourself. Yes, it is a tranquil place I see..."

Beyond Sirtes' crystal clear eyes, Bolton found himself back on Earth. He was lying on a beach lined with palm trees softly swaying in a warm breeze. His memory recalled it was the inland sea parkland south of Sutter City. Christine was beside him reading a book while snacking on fresh strawberries. Their relationship was new, and the love they shared was innocent and unbounded. There was never a more pleasant time in his life so fulfilled with youthful exuberance. Then, there was a mysterious figure that repeatedly came to him in his dreams. It was both familiar to his soul, yet unfamiliar to his consciousness. The strange being did things to him. There were reoccurring nosebleeds and spontaneous blackouts. It beckoned him irresistibly to follow a higher calling. Mars was his ultimate destiny, and he must leave his terrestrial life behind. As Christine's face faded from the images, intense pangs of guilt ripped through his suddenly quivering body.

Sirtes immediate broke off contact and tightly embraced her subject. "It's over. It's over now, Marc. You're here. You're here with me. Come out of it."

Bolton's shaking subsided as he opened his bloodshot and watering eyes. He was disoriented and extremely confused, but otherwise unharmed by the hypnotic-like telepathic experience.

"How do you feel?" asked Sirtes.

"Okay, I suppose," he replied.

"It looks like we've discovered what's been bothering you, and I must say it's a shocking revelation. Do you remember what transpired?"

"I think so. Were you able to get a visual representation of that creature, or whatever it was?"

"Yes, Marc. It wasn't human, that's for sure. I've had some prior telepathic interactions with others who claimed to be alien abductees, and the beings I saw in those sessions looked similar to yours."

"Has it been controlling me?"

"Even though I'm not certain, I would have to say no. My impression is that it gave you something which was an essential part of itself. I realize that doesn't make much sense, but I got a strong feeling that the two of you moved closer together somehow."

"Like I was changed in its image?"

"Possibly, but I just don't know. The memories you have of it are buried deep in your subconscious. Neither of us was able to perceive them very well. However, wouldn't you say that the creature's intentions seemed benevolent?"

"Yes Sirtes, I agree. Although I am feeling great anger towards it, aren't I?"

"You blame it for interfering in your life which took you away from Christine. There was no mistaking that emotional response, Marc, as it was the most powerful connection we shared."

"I'm worried about her."

"Then why don't you try to find her? I know you've been thinking about it."

"How can I return to Earth? I have no ship, and they would kill me immediately upon my arrival should I be able to get one. I'm pretty sure I'm at the top of their most wanted list."

"Considering everything you've accomplished in the last three years, I'm confident you could. If you don't try, it will haunt you for the rest of your life."

"And if I find her, then what? Do I stay on Earth, or bring her back to Mars? What will happen to us, Sirtes? I don't want to be apart from you."

"What will happen, will happen. We'll never be truly apart, my love. Our souls have intertwined beyond the limitations of physical space. You could never completely leave me as I could never completely leave you. But, we must each chart our own courses. If you must go back to Earth, then I can live with whatever results."

For the first time since the *Battle of Miramicus*, Marc Bolton had a renewed sense of purpose and direction. His guilt was now gone. There are dragons within each of us that can only be slain through confrontation. Hiding one's head in the sand will not make them disappear.

On Chi 22nd, 16, Marc Bolton visited Carolyn Jones who was convalescing after receiving another bone marrow transplant. She was always very thin, but the figure lying before him was distressingly emaciated. Her dense grey hair had fallen out from the radiation treatments, and the rich booming voice that had inspired so many was now laboriously weak. It was apparent that the end was near for the regal matriarch, and this greatly saddened Bolton; although, he tried his best not to show it. The Chairperson deserved respect, not pity.

When she opened her eyes to see her latest visitor, a beaming smile lit up that wrinkled face. Jones had become extremely fond of Bolton. He had risked his life to save her greatest love. Mars was everything to the Chairperson. She was in college when her parents died, and a devoted career in politics got in the way of marriage and children. Jones' dedication to a uniquely Martian civilization was paramount, so everyone who contributed to it earned her admiration. But, there was a special place in her heart for Bolton that had grew into an infatuation of sorts after the war. Unbeknownst to anyone, she had written a sealed decree to be opened upon her death that mandated the construction of a thirty foot tall stone monument on the surface of Lowellton in honor of him.

"My goodness, it's Marc Bolton!" she exclaimed with a crackled voice.

"Hello your Honor."

"Please, no more formalities. I'm an old woman who has little time left for official etiquette. My friends call me Carolyn."

"Thank you for that, Carolyn. One day I would like to talk with you at length, if I may, to get your reflections of your remarkable life and momentous achievements here on Mars."

"That would be nice, but it'd have to be soon. There isn't much time left."

Bolton looked sad, and couldn't find any words to reply.

"Don't worry yourself, Marc. All things come to an end in their own time. My life has been full and satisfying. There is nothing I can imagine that has been left undone. You should be happy for me."

"Forgive me Carolyn, but I do not feel happy right now."

"It will pass. Did you know the Board is convening this afternoon?"

"Yes, I heard. I wanted to speak with you about that. I would like for you to withdrawal my name from consideration as a nominee to succeed you as Chairperson."

"I've already cast my vote, but why do you wish to decline the nomination?"

"Being nominated for the Chairpersonship is the highest honor I can envision. However, the candidate must be worthy of such consideration. I must tell you now that I am not."

Jones swallowed hard in reaction to a surge of physical discomfort. "Please explain," she uttered feebly.

"Amongst other reasons, I plan to return to Earth. I must find out, first hand, what has become of the people. There are a few whom I was intimately close to. It is unsettling not knowing their fate."

"Is this easement of your conscious more important than your duties here?"

"No, it is not. However, I'm concerned that the performance of my duties will suffer without a resolution to this internal conflict within me."

"I see. How do you propose to garner passage without approval from the Board?"

"Err, I had assumed that..."

"You know," she interrupted, "there may be an opportunity here. Given the fractured political situation on Earth, we might be able to reestablish ties with some of our former allies. This would be mutually beneficial and could help stabilize their social structure. But, we'll need a competent envoy able to negotiate in that tumultuous environment. Do you have any ideas where we could find such a qualified person, Marc?"

Bolton was in so much awe of the Chairperson that he was nearly speechless. Here was a woman on her deathbed still capable of the most consummate political savvy and sophistication. He knew she was under no illusion that a diplomatic mission could possibly achieve any meaningful result; but, it would give her the pretense necessary to justify Bolton's transport to Earth. In essence, she was granting her final wish in gratitude for his service to Mars.

"Would I suffice?" he replied.

"Yes, I believe you would. Here are the stipulations. Contingent upon Board approval, a suitable vessel will be procured and manned by an all-volunteer crew. The ship itself will be commanded by a fleet officer, although you will be in charge of the overall operation. Your task is to establish contact with individuals and organizations specified by the Board, and anyone else you deem necessary, for the purpose of developing formal relations between the Independent State of Mars and the peoples of Earth. However, you are ordered to undertake no action that would needlessly jeopardize the safe return of your ship and its personnel to Mars including yourself. Furthermore, you are authorized to provide transport for terrestrial persons seeking immigration to this planet within the logistical constraints of your vessel."

Jones gasped briefly to catch her breath and then concluded. "Do you consent to these parameters?"

"I do," Bolton acknowledged.

"Very well then, you will be notified of the Board's decision. Also, I have a strictly personal request to make."

"Yes, Carolyn."

"In the event the Board confirms your nomination today, I want you to accept it."

"I promise I will."

"Thank you, Marc. That's very reassuring to me. I will make arrangements for Ivan Tcholich to temporarily assume the Chair if I pass while you're away. When you return, a general election for Chairperson will be held."

"If that day comes, it will be the saddest of my life."

"That day will come," Jones murmured softly as she stroked Bolton's hair.

He kissed her on the cheek and departed. That evening, the headline news story described the unanimous vote by the *Board of Regents* confirming Marc Bolton's nomination to succeed Carolyn Jones as

Chairperson. All across the Martian world, the voices of approval sang out in unison.

Chapter 10
Lost Souls of Planet Earth

"Telecall for you Sir," Han Li's administrative assistant informed him.

"Thank you, Terry. I'll take it over here."

"Good day to you Han," Marc Bolton gestured through the electronic imaging device.

"Hi Marc, I'm a little busy at the moment. Can I call you back?"

"Sure, but I really think you'll want to hear this soon."

"Alright, go ahead."

"How would you like to take a trip to Earth?"

"Marc, I don't have any time for tomfoolery right now."

"I am quite serious, Han. The *Board of Regents* is sending a small expedition to Earth in an attempt to reestablish diplomatic relations wherever possible. I need able volunteers to flesh out my staff, and thought you would be interested."

Han was temporarily stunned by the news. "Are you leading this expedition?"

"Of the overall mission, yes; but, Captain Manbury here will have operational command." The image of Trenton Manbury moved into the frame as he stood beside Bolton."

"Captain!" exclaimed Han. "It is a great privilege to meet you. Congratulations on your recent promotion, although many of us thought you should have made admiral."

"Well, thank you Mister Li. But, you understand that military ranks have become largely symbolic since the end of the war. And, it is certainly a pleasure to meet you too. Marc has told me much about you."

"Then, with all due respect Gentlemen, both of you should realize my skills aren't suited for this mission. I am no diplomat, have no tactical or strategic qualifications, and am not an official government representative. I'm just a scientist. And forgive me for being frank, but this undertaking sounds incredibly dangerous. Earth has military factions who would probably open fire at the first sight of a Martian ship. How could you possibly negotiate in that hostile climate?"

"Han," replied Bolton, "I'm afraid you don't understand. This isn't a high level operation. We will have to sneak in, make direct contact with selected people, and avoid being discovered by anti-Martian groups. But, you're right that it will be exceedingly hazardous. You must decide if the chance to see your family again is worth the risk."

"Oh Marc, that's hitting below the belt. If I did find my family, could they return with us to Mars?"

"If we succeed and are able to accommodate them, then I would say yes."

"How do you propose we get down to the surface undetected?"

"Mister Li," Manbury interjected, "I have a plan that just might work. General Brookfield, who was a close personal friend during my academy days, is currently in command of the Moon Base. Our intelligence reports indicate he has refused to align his forces with any political entity on Earth. He is protecting his aloof independence with a ground based laser powerful enough to deter any act of aggression, which by the way was partially developed by Mister Bolton. If I can convince him to help us, we'll have no trouble getting transport, identity papers, letters of transit, and perhaps even regional visas to move around more freely."

"You should also know Han," Bolton added, "that it's likely to be a one way trip if General Brookfield is not amenable."

"Granted, but I know Brookie," Manbury continued. "He is an unabashed, though eminently practical opportunist. When the *Terran Council* dissolved he lost his allegiances, and has been reluctant since then to commit to a new ally until he's sure who will emerge into the strongest position. He is known to despise his nominal superior in the *North American Alliance*, General George Peckarie, the former army thug of Janus Krichek. Half the space fleet is under Chinese authority – Brookfield's ideological nemesis, and the logistically vital space station *Liberty* is controlled by the radical *European Confederacy*. These three powers are vying for supremacy. They neither coordinate their activities nor share any information. Tensions are so high that even a minor abrogation of the Rotterdam agreement could trigger outright war. Brookfield is hungry for a fourth alternative, and I intend to give him one."

"Well Han, what do you say?" Bolton asked.

"I am not a brave, adventuresome man. I also believe the two of you are crazy to attempt this insane mission which risks so much for the chance to attain so little. It is understandable why an out-of-the-closet idealist like Marc would want to, but I thought you would have better sense Captain. What motivates you?"

"Duty, Mister Li. The people of Earth are slipping over the edge of a horrendous abyss. Even if we can only save a few by throwing them a lifeline, then the effort will have been worth it. The costs to our moral character will be infinitely greater if we don't try. Pragmatism may be smart, but it isn't always the right thing to do."

"Han, no one will condemn you for declining to volunteer for this operation," Bolton contended. "We will respect your decision. It's completely up to you."

"I can't believe I'm going to say this, but... when do we leave?"

On Psi 21st, the cruiser *Cromwell* was 32 hours away from the Moon Base. Six hours earlier, Captain Manbury had sent a communiqué to General Brookfield requesting 'safe harbor' under section K of the 2065 Honolulu accords. The provision stipulated that all spaceships, aircraft, and oceangoing vessels on diplomatic missions would be afforded temporary sanctuary by each of the international and interplanetary treaty signatories. Manbury knew that invoking this immunity clause would allow his ship to safely acquire lunar orbit, if in fact it was still being recognized. Since he did not know the current status of the treaty following the *Terran Council's* downfall, Manbury's action was a bit of a gamble.

One of the problems associated with communicating through space is the time delay. Even at the speed of light, standard two-way audio/visual communications are impractical at distances greater than a few hundred thousand miles. Outside that range, various asynchronous digital transmission methods are used each having different formatting, compression, and encryption techniques. For these to work properly, the sender and receiver must be 'on the same page' so to speak with respect to specific radio frequencies and protocols. Additionally, a sender would not know if their message was even received unless some form of confirmation was returned. The highly directional transmission Captain Manbury sent over a secure military channel reduced the chance of detection by unwanted agents, but was also the most uncertain means of contacting General Brookfield.

"Damn!" shouted Manbury as he banged his fist in frustration on top the control console. The *Cromwell's* bridge personnel didn't react however, as they were accustomed to his occasionally impatient outbursts. "We should have received a reply by now. I may have over-estimated the firmness of General

Brookfield's neutral stance. If he sold out to the highest bidder, we're in trouble. Lieutenant, plot a return course around the sun as soon as possible."

"Yes, Captain."

"Wait a moment, Trenton," Bolton countered. "Are you sure they're monitoring that communications channel? Can't we try another?"

"The two-two-two-seven-point-five-one-four megahertz decimeter wave has been the official Moon Base military channel for over twenty years. Even if Brookfield has aligned his command politically and switched his primary communications, he'd still be monitoring that channel. Unfortunately, we don't know the other secure channels Brookfield might be using; and, contacting him via the low frequency civilian analog bands would broadcast our arrival all over planet Earth."

"It's possible our transmission was obstructed and they never received it."

"Yes that's possible, Marc. But, there aren't many obstructions in open space. I'm sure they received it."

"Are you suggesting we quit?"

"No not yet. We have another twenty-seven Earth hours before deceleration. Lieutenant, how much longer can we hold this course before altering it for a free solar return trajectory back to Mars?"

"Seven Earth hours, sir."

"Alright Marc, if we don't get a reply by fifteen-hundred G-M-T we'll retransmit the message. That will give them four Earth hours to respond. Otherwise, we abort the mission at nineteen-hundred.

But, I will not attempt to put this ship into lunar orbit without getting some indication of Brookfield's intentions. It's just too risky. Agreed?"

"Thank you Trenton, I trust and accept your judgment. Assuming General Brookfield received our first message, I wonder why he hasn't answered."

"Brookie is a wily old cuss. Provided he's still operating independently, he just might want me to sweat for a while and force my hand. I'm sure he's correctly deduced that we need something from him, or else we wouldn't be knocking on his door. Although, I doubt he has any clues as to why we actually came. The General probably thinks I made enemies on Mars and am seeking political asylum under his protection. By granting it, he hopes to get the *Cromwell* in exchange. That would be big a prize for him."

"And, if Brookfield is not operating independently?"

"In that case my friend, the only communication we're going to get is the belligerence of a laser blast rammed down our throats."

"Captain, there's a message coming in now sir."

"Read it aloud, Andreotti."

"To Captain Trenton Manbury of the Martian space cruiser *Cromwell*. Your request for safe harbor is acknowledged and denied. The *North American Alliance* has decreed non-recognition of all preexisting treaty commitments to which it specifically has not signed. However, I may grant you temporary sanctuary under the condition of special privilege if you expound your diplomatic mission. We await your prompt reply, but do not attempt orbital acquisition without authorization as your vessel will be fired upon - General Harold T. Brookfield, Moon Base Commandant."

"Thank you, Ensign."

"What do you make of that blustery admonition?" inquired Bolton.

"Ah Brookie," Manbury chuckled. "The term 'special privilege' refers to an old naval provision allowing combat commanders to disregard operational orders if they encounter advantageous and exploitable circumstances in the normal pursuit of their stated objectives. This was necessary before the advent of radio when ships were at sea and incommunicado for long periods of time, but is now a rather antiquated concept. What the General is really saying, is that he's willing to negotiate in person if we can convince him it's to his benefit."

"I hope what's beneficial to him isn't too expensive for us, Trenton. Also, his deference to the Alliance's authority concerns me. Are you sure Brookfield is acting autonomously?"

"There's always a level doubt in intelligence work. But, we've had the Moon Base under remote surveillance since before the war. There is every indication that Brookfield's association with the Alliance is a superficial façade of convenience. He is in a very strong relative position and they know it. This message reinforces my belief that the General is acting to his own interests. And worry not, Marc

Bolton, my plan to entice him shouldn't be too costly."

"Ensign Andreotti!"

"Yes Captain."

"Transmit the following message to the Moon Base: To General Brookfield. Our diplomatic mission is confidential and must be discussed with you in person. If this condition is unacceptable, we shall return to Mars without further ado. Awaiting your decision – sincerely, Captain Manbury commanding."

"Yes sir, right away."

"You didn't offer him anything," observed Bolton.

"No, but I remember what my father taught me. The largest fish in the lake won't be lured in by a simple offering of bait. He got big because he was wary of all-too-easy meals. The king is a predator who must hunt for his food. By feigning casual indifference, we present ourselves as worthy prey. That's when the monster is most likely to strike."

"Ha, ha, ha," Bolton giggled. "Trenton, you do have a flair for the poetic metaphor!"

"Receiving another message now, Captain," Andreotti announced.

"Go ahead, Ensign."

"Captain Manbury, the confidentiality of your diplomatic mission is disturbingly inopportune in light of current events. However, in the interests of interplanetary relations, I grant you sanctuary for a period of seventy-two hours so that we may explore the substance of this matter in private. Continue on your present course. Space Operations will contact

you shortly to coordinate your orbital approach –
regards, General Brookfield."

"Trenton, I would've enjoyed going fishing with
your father," Bolton offered.

"I didn't. He was an obnoxious, drunken old
buzzard with a penchant for brazen exhibitions of
flatulence. And, he liked to put live worms in my
hair when I wasn't paying attention."

The *Cromwell's* bridge crew broke out in laughter.

Marc Bolton was resting in his quarters when the
Cromwell settled into lunar orbit late the following
day. Through his viewport, the surface of the Moon
appeared much closer than he had noticed when
orbiting Earth or even Mars. It also was whizzing
past him at an unusually high rate of speed. From a
distance, the Earth's single natural satellite looks
featureless aside from having varying shades of grey.
But up close, it has much more character. There are
innumerable mountain ridges sitting atop crater filled
highlands. The dark, placid lunar maria are
surrounded by bright blankets of impact ejecta, and
the sunlit horizons contrast sharply with the cold
blackness of space.

The personnel assigned to meet with General
Brookfield were also the ones who would travel to
Earth if the mission progressed that far. They
included Captain Manbury, Marc Bolton, Han Li,
Ambassador Arum Pagnatan, special envoy Bernardo
de la Rosa, and staff assistants Willard Mounthaven
and Ululani Palakiko. Lieutenant Commander Jacob

'J. J.' Rosenberg was placed in charge of the *Cromwell* with specific orders to protect the ship and crew at all costs.

The seven passengers descended to the lunar surface in the *Cromwell's* tiny command staff ferry. It was a tightly cramped, but smooth ride down that provided a good view of the sprawling Moon Base. Bolton noticed that the landing bays were more robust than those at the Sharonov shuttle terminal on Mars. Heavy steel-reinforced concrete sliding doors covered the bays at the surface. Below them, a second set made of molybdenum-alloy enclosed the pressurized airlocks. There were an array of cranes to move large cargo items, and a light rail system connected the site at its lowest levels. Armed guards watched stoically from almost every corner of this military fortress. Bolton surmised that the landing bays were designed to withstand multiple direct hits from laser fire.

Due to the Moon's weak gravity, less than half that on Mars, everyone was required to wear ankle weights as a safety precaution. These were supplied to Bolton's team during the orientation process. Han Li complained bitterly that the weights were too uncomfortable and not necessary. He decided to shut up when a guard pointed a weapon at him. Afterwards, they were taken to General Brookfield's administrative headquarters.

"Trenton!" Brookfield rejoiced as the seven Martians entered his spacious office. "It's good to see you after such a long time."

"Greetings General, allow me to introduce you to Ambassador Pagnatan, Mister de la Rosa, Mister Li, assistants Palakiko and Mounthaven, and this is the leader of our mission… Mister Marc Bolton."

"Welcome ladies and gentlemen. Bolton, Bolton, hmm… that name sounds familiar. Oh yes, I remember. There was a technologist with that name from the *Terran Council* who helped develop some of our most important projects for the Moon Base. Would you be him?"

"Yes, that was me sir," Bolton answered as he formed a first impression of the General. Brookfield was shorter than average with thinning grayish-blond hair, a fair complexion, and delicate facial features. He certainly didn't project a physically imposing presence, and his personality seemed equally unpretentious. However, Bolton did perceive an aura of cunning intelligence much like that of a shrewd businessman. Because everything depended on the General's cooperation, Bolton decided to telepathically monitor his thoughts as subtly as possible.

"How remarkable," Brookfield noted, "that a person dedicated to technical scientific service on Earth would one day head an obviously perilous diplomatic mission for Mars."

"Fate is often remarkable General, as well as unpredictable."

"So they say," Brookfield added sarcastically. "Sergeant, that will be all for now. Close the door behind you."

"Sir!" the guard snapped to attention before leaving.

"Please be seated. Well Trenton, how do you like it on Mars? You've made quite a name for yourself, although it is a rather infamous one on Earth."

"They appreciate my efforts, General."

"I recall your tendency to provoke your superiors was not at all appreciated during your fleet assignment. Didn't they banish you to Mars as punishment?"

"Hardly banished sir, I consider it one of the greatest decisions in military history."

"I suppose it was at that," Brookfield confessed with noticeable amusement. "Now, what can I do for you fine people? I'm sure you didn't travel all this way just to be neighborly."

"General," Bolton replied, "we need transport and official authorization for a short trip to Earth of about two weeks."

"You must be out of your mind, Mister Bolton. I can't authorize the transport of Martian nationals. Any one of the three major powers would have you arrested, at the very least, immediately upon your arrival."

"We would also need false identity documentation."

"Oh, my goodness!" barked the General. "Since you must comprehend the gravity of this request, I presume you are prepared to offer something in return?"

"Yes we are, General," Manbury interceded. "We're aware of your squabbles with the *North American Alliance*, and appreciate your advantage of remaining effectually independent until the political situation on Earth sorts itself out. However, you risk losing your logistical support the longer this situation drags on. Sooner or later, the Alliance will get frustrated and cut you off. We might be able to help. Ambassador, please explain our offer to the General."

"With pleasure, Captain," Pagnatan complied. "General Brookfield, the *Independent State of Mars* will supply you with the food, water, fuel, and technical support necessary to maintain your Moon Base operations for a period of ten years. In exchange, you will pledge to commit no act of military aggression – except for those measured responses necessary for legitimate defense – and accommodate all diplomatic efforts by the *Board of Regents* to reestablish positive relations with the peoples of Earth."

"Thank you, Ambassador, for that gracious offer. But unfortunately, the good captain's analysis of my situation is in error. Although there have been occasions of minor dispute, my relationship with the Alliance is on solid ground. They realize the Moon Base is the most critical asset in preventing all-out world war. It's absurd to think they would abandon us just because we are uncooperative from time to time."

"I see you haven't lost your affinity for expedient understatement, General," Manbury said in rebuttal.

"Do not provoke me, Captain! It is you who are in a precarious position. The Alliance would be quite pleased if I presented them with your ship and delegation as conciliatory offerings. I suggest keeping those offensive remarks to yourself."

"Please calm down, Gentlemen," pleaded Bolton. "General, like you, Captain Manbury is a redoubtable line officer. I'm sure you understand working in the field under stressful conditions requires a direct, confrontational approach that is not particularly suited to subtle negotiation. He simply wants us to skip any unnecessary posturing and lay our cards on the table."

"Alright Mister Bolton, but I'm holding the top hand here. You need me more than I need you. Without my assistance, you'll never make it to Earth safely. Conversely, my logistical issues can be resolved without any help from Mars. So, unless you want to sweeten the pot, this game appears to be over."

"No sir, it is not over. We know about the ultimatum you received from General Peckarie several days ago."

Brookfield was caught completely off guard by Bolton's remark, and looked as if someone had just stolen all the clothes off his body.

"What, ah... are you referring to, Bolton?"

"In a personal communication, General Peckarie informed you the Alliance will suspend all resupply shipments to the Moon Base if you do not relinquish command by the end of the month. We are also aware that you secretly contacted Danh Tho Huong and Ulrich Huber, of the Chinese and European foreign ministries respectively, in attempts to secure alternative logistical support. However, both of those governments declined because you refused to allow them administrative control over your operations."

"How could you possibly know that? Not even my senior staff officers were privy to those communications."

"We do not reveal our intelligence sources, General. Regardless, you are in an untenable position. You cannot survive more than a few months without resupply, and all your accessible Earthly providers want to relieve you of command. You should be thankful for our arrival at such an opportune time. We offer a viable replenishment option, and we'll let you keep your post. All you have to do in return is help with our diplomatic activities, and remain militarily neutral. Isn't that a good deal?"

Mister Bolton, I've never liked being pushed into a corner. It compels me to act irrationally. I'm inclined to put you Martians in confinement and confiscate your vessel. But, my better judgment tells me that won't solve any of my problems. I'll agree to your terms if the Moon Base is recognized as a sovereign interplanetary entity, and that my governing authority is acknowledged as resolute."

"Ambassador, can we consent to that?" Bolton asked.

"Yes, I believe so. We can have the documents drawn up as a contractual treaty between the *Independent State of Mars* and whatever name General Brookfield chooses for his new military regime."

"May I suggest," Manbury proposed, "that the General delay any publicly announced declaration of independence for the Moon Base until after we complete our current mission on Earth?"

"No problem, Captain," Brookfield acceded. "And, I'm sure I can come up with a plausible cover story when the Alliance starts asking why there is a *Rigel* class cruiser orbiting my base – which they are certain to do at any moment."

"Excellent," Bolton concluded. "Well, it appears we have an agreement. Unless someone has anything else to discuss right now, we should get on with our preparations. Is that okay with you, General?"

"Sergeant!" yelled Brookfield.

"Yes sir!"

"Have these people ushered to the officers' guest quarters, and assign them a personal aide."

"Yes General. Please follow me folks."

Bolton's team was escorted to a rectangular living space with a row of partitioned bunk beds and a single bathroom. At one end was an open area having a table with chairs and a telecall device mounted in the wall. These officer guest quarters were austere even by Martian standards, and left some members of the group wondering how Spartan the enlisted persons' lodgings were.

"If there's anything else you require, press this button on the telecall," instructed Private Cedrick Williams. "When I'm off duty, either Private Jamison or Private Singh will be your aide. You should all get a good night's sleep. Tomorrow, you start two weeks of e-gac. We'll wake you at zero-six-thirty."

"Thank you, Private," Bolton replied. "But, what is e-gac?"

"I'm sorry, that's short for E-G-A-C, or Earth Gravity Adjustment Conditioning. Your bodies are too frail for the Earth's deep gravity well. E-gac is an intensive course in centrifuge training, cardiovascular and muscular exercise, and a strict mineral-rich diet. It isn't pleasant, I can assure you. Will that be all, sir?"

"Uh… yes Private. That will be all. Good night."

"Good night to you, sir."

"E-gac," Bolton fretted as he sat down beside the table. "Egads!"

"I've been through it once before," Manbury explained. "The first week is really tough, but you'll get used to it after that."

"Captain, do you think we can trust Brookfield?" de la Rosa asked.

"No, but we don't have any other choice. The General is an extraordinarily pragmatic individual, and we gave him his best option. Unless he gets a better one before we return to Mars, he should remain cooperative. Marc, I presume you got that information about his private communications through telepathy. Did you also get any reading whether he'll stay committed to the agreement?"

"Brookfield's thoughts were consistent with his words. Although, there is no way to predict what he will do in the future."

"I can," Han Li said in jest. "He won't play poker with telepaths anymore!"

Chapter 11
Escape from a Burning House

E-gac was as unpleasant as Private Williams warned it would be. Bolton and Ambassador Pagnatan suffered the most ill effects, having multiple bouts of dizziness, nausea, joint pain, and insomnia. But, the symptoms gradually subsided so that everyone was in reasonable shape for the trip to Earth. It was decided that Captain Manbury would remain behind on the Moon to keep an eye on General Brookfield, and act as a central command center for the mission.

Transportation to Earth was provided by an aging SSETM (Single Stage Earth to Moon) rocket-assisted aerospace plane (registry number E-14), whose initial role as a trans-lunar transport had since been supplanted by the P.S.C.S. system; and, which was currently employed as a space taxi for high ranking military officers because of its ability to take off and land non-stop. The E-14 was crewed by pilot Major Sizwe Mabuza, copilot Captain Katie McDonald, Chief Engineer Randolph Quivers, and four security guards. Brookfield had authorized the flight as a training exercise, and had convinced the *North American Alliance* leadership that the *Cromwell* – in orbit around the Moon – was actually the recovered cruiser *Wellington* lost during Admiral Orizuna's ill-fated maneuver around Jupiter.

The three day voyage to Earth was uneventful other than a brief challenge by a patrolling Chinese cruiser whose commander wanted to know the purpose and destination of their flight. The E-14 landed at the spacious Sutter City airport without incident. Before departing the ship, plans were finalized detailing how the mission would proceed. Ambassador Pagnatan and assistant Palakiko would attempt an arduous expedition to Mexico City aiming to establish contact with the pro-Martian revolutionary organization *Mundial de la Libertad*. Special envoy de la Rosa and assistant Mounthaven would travel to New Vancouver in a parallel endeavor to reach a similar but smaller and widely scattered group in British Columbia. Han Li would go to Boulder, Colorado to recruit some of his former scientific colleagues for immigration to Mars, and also look for his family. Bolton would try to find any ex-*Terran Council* representatives remaining in Sutter City who might be willing to serve as peace-seeking political liaisons for Mars, and of course, locate Christine Bakerman. The E-14's crew would stay behind to look after the ship and prepare it for a return flight that everyone hoped would occur.

The first two teams left for the airport terminal followed shortly thereafter by Han and Bolton, the latter of whom labored to walk in the Earth's mighty gravity.

"Geez Han, it must be ninety-five degrees here. I don't ever remember it being this hot in December."

"Yeah I know, Marc. It's almost Christmas for goodness sake. Hey, see that pillar of smoke off in the distance? It looks like a pretty fierce fire."

"That's in the direction of the magnetic train terminus, as I recall. I wonder what's going on."

"Central American terrorists," interjected a young woman walking behind them. "They've been blowing up bombs all over the city for months now. That pile of rubble on the hill to the northwest is what's left of the old *Terran Council* headquarters complex. A hundred and forty people died in that blast, bastards!"

Bolton realized his former office was in one of those buildings. "What do the terrorists want?" he asked.

"Been out in space a while, huh?" she observed. "They want something no one will ever see on Earth again, at least not in our lifetimes… democracy and freedom."

"Isn't the Alliance trying to protect the people?" Han inquired.

"The Alliance?" she said indignantly. "Boy, you two must've been away for a long time. The Alliance doesn't care about the people, and they aren't capable of protecting them even if they wanted to. This society has deteriorated into a state of lawlessness like the old Wild, Wild West. Everyone is out for themselves."

"We've been working on the Moon for several years now," Han submitted.

"Military contractors, huh?" the woman surmised. "Well, you guys better be careful around here. It's not safe, and make sure you're inside before the curfew. This is my gate. Good luck to you!" she shouted while veering away.

"What time is the curfew?" Bolton yelled.

"Twenty-one hundred hours… sharp!"

Taking seats in the terminal lobby, the two ill-at-ease Martian men scanned the overhead departure schedule. "There's one, Han… a ten-fifteen flight to Boulder. Will you be alright by yourself? I mean, I could go with you."

"I knew this mission would be dangerous when I signed on. Besides, you have your own objectives, Marc. I'll be okay. You better get going."

"Sure Han, but don't forget to use the emergency beacon if you lose radio linkage with the ship. I'll see you back here next week."

"Best wishes, big guy."

An hour later, Bolton's taxi stopped in front of the residence Christine was living in when he was sent to Mars. The building was boarded up, and there were homeless people sitting on its walkways. The *Grasslands Café* across the street, one of her favorite restaurants, was now an empty lot. Disheartened, he told the driver to move on.

They next arrived at his old apartment near the top of one of Sutter City's panoramic hills. Bolton got out of the car, paid the driver, and thanked him for his service. He gazed down to the grassy parkland at the edge of the inland sea, noticing that it had been overtaken by rising ocean levels as the beach and adjacent picnic grounds were now gone. The once bustling hub of worldwide governance had become a dilapidated shell of a city. Vacant rundown buildings were everywhere, and the people seemed sluggishly drained of life. No longer did he hear the laughter of children reverberating through the neighborhood. A brownish haze was drifting over the city, and the air smelled of decay.

It was apparent that a few people still lived in the apartment complex, but most of the units had 'for rent' signs on them including his own. Bolton walked over to the main office and saw a thin elderly man sitting at the front desk.

"Is that you, Mister Thespianos?"

"Do my eyes deceive me or am I seeing ghosts? I never thought I'd catch sight of you again, Marc Bolton. What have you been doing all these years?"

"The *Terran Council* sent me away for a long time, and I've come back to search for my old friends. It's good to see you. How are you these days?"

"Not very well, I'm afraid. Life is getting really hard around here. My wife passed away some months ago, and my two sons were forced into the provisional army. They aren't allowed to communicate with anyone on the outside, so I have no idea what's become of them."

"I'm so sorry, sir. By the looks of the city, it seems most everyone is gone."

"Yes, they're gone. Some died from disease, starvation, or exposure. Those who could - packed up their belongings and moved to South America. Many more were taken by the Alliance as quote, 'wards of the state.'"

"Do you mean forced labor?"

"I do, but there were even worse fates than that. Those of us left behind were considered either too old or otherwise of little value. So, we're trying to carry on as best we can. It's a pretty hopeless situation. Sometimes I wish I would fall asleep and never wake up. That'd be a peaceful way to go."

"You were always a fighter, Mister Thespianos. It's not like you to just give up like that."

"Oh, I haven't given up yet. But, even the most optimistic of us realize now that the Earth is dying and our civilization is crumbling before it. We were entrusted with a great responsibility to which we have failed miserably."

Bolton nodded in agreement. "I want to contact my old friends and coworkers, if possible. Although, all the telecoms I've found were out of order. Can you help me, Mister Thespianos?"

"Sure, I have one in the back room. The system is technically still working even though it has clearly degraded. Several regions are currently inaccessible because their communication hubs were abandoned, and millions of terminal devices have fallen into disrepair. Official restrictions have also been put in place, and there have been numerous acts of sabotage. But, it's worth a try. Come this way."

Bolton spent the next hour trying to reach former colleagues and key individuals from the defunct *Terran Council* he thought might be amenable to association with Martian interests; however, all his attempts were in vain. These talented professionals, whom Bolton felt great respect for, were nowhere to be found. All the online data bases that should have contained their biographical information and personnel records were apparently purged, corrupted, or unavailable. To the general public, it was as if those people had never existed.

After some difficulty, Bolton managed to get through to an administrative staff member at the University of Georgia. He inquired about the whereabouts of Christine Bakerman, but was only told that she had resigned from her position in November 2077. Next, he searched for her parents who he knew had been living in Macon. Although he couldn't find a listing in that city, he did locate a residential entry for William and Marianne Bakerman in Boise, Idaho. It was a close enough match, so Bolton activated the telecall option. Within a few seconds, Christine's father's video image appeared on the screen.

"Bill Bakerman?"

"Yes... Oh, my god! Honey, come over here quick. It's Marc Bolton!" Marianne Bakerman ran from the kitchen to join her husband in the family room.

"Good lord!" she exclaimed. "My darling, we feared we'd never see you again. Where are you? You look awfully thin. Are you okay?"

"Yes, I'm fine. I am here in Sutter City on a diplomatic mission for the *Board of Regents*. It's so nice to see you again. How are you two doing?"

Marianne glanced towards Bill with an expression of deep concern, and then responded. "Well, we're doing as best we can, I suppose. My, my, the *Board of Regents*... how prestigious! Have you been on Mars all this time?"

"Yes, but so much has changed since I left. I need to discuss it with you and Christine in person, if I may. Do you know where I can contact her?"

"Christine is living with us, but she's at work right now. Can you telecall back later this..."

Bill Bakerman interrupted his wife. "Marc, this conversation could be dangerous for you and for us. We better end it now. Do you remember that nickname Christine used to call me?"

"How could I forget? It was..."

"Don't say it, son. Just look it up later, and you'll find a personal audio-only address. Call there tonight after nineteen hundred, but do so from a different device than the one you're on. Understood?"

"Yes sir."

"Good, until then... take care."

Bolton got caught up in the emotional moment of reuniting with Christine's parents, but suddenly grasped the nature of Bill's concern. It was foolish of him to reveal his Martian identity over the public airwaves. Someone was bound to be listening. In doing so, he may have compromised the safety of the mission and everyone associated with it - which now included Christine's family.

He walked back out to the front office. "Thank you for your help, Mister Thespianos. I appreciate it very much. I must leave now and return to the airport. Would you mind calling me a taxi?"

"It would be my pleasure if you let me give you a ride. I have an old rusty electric mini-car, but it still runs good. Come on."

"You are too kind, sir."

Bolton asked Mister Thespianos to drop him off at the *Mother Lode Eatery* two miles from the airport. Once a popular dining establishment of the local residents, the family-owned restaurant was now struggling to stay in business. However, it did have a few functioning public telecall devices in secluded booths. Bolton planned to get a meal, call the Bakerman's at nineteen hundred, and then walk back to the ship before curfew.

Due to the breakdown of centralized food production and distribution throughout the world, most people had resorted to growing their own. Gone were the days when wasteful western societies feasted lavishly on red meats, highly processed starches, and sugary drinks. The *Mother Lode Eatery* had essentially become a small farm that also served prepared meals. They raised poultry and goats, grew vegetables that did well in the long hot summer season, and had several varieties of fruit trees. Unfortunately for them, protecting the farm from the growing numbers of human and animal scavengers was proving to be an insurmountable task. They simply could not afford enough security to completely safeguard their business. To make matters worse, the well which provided their only source of water was drying up over time. The owners estimated their situation would become untenable within ten years. All over the Earth, similar stories of desperation were being played out in countless ways.

The meal Bolton decided upon was surprisingly enjoyable. It included handmade gnocchi (potato dumplings) tossed with a pomodoro sauce made from garden tomatoes and topped with fresh basil and goat cheese, a beautiful green salad in a light vinaigrette, and a glass of homemade Pinot Grigio. Bolton was so impressed by the quality of the food he made a special effort to compliment the chef and owners. He told them it was heartening that people would take such great care in preserving their culture in these arduous times.

Afterwards, Bolton went into a telecall booth and looked up the directory name 'Clover Honeysuckle' which Christine had given her father as a young child because of his habit of sipping on honeysuckle flowers when he worked in the family's clover fields. The nickname stuck, and Bill's relatives and close friends usually called him 'Clover' for short. It was not unexpected that Bolton found only one address listing under that name. He called it immediately. It was 19:07.

"Hello."

"Hi Bill, this is Marc."

"Are you alone?"

"I'm in a booth. No one can hear me."

"Good. Don't say anything that would positively identify any of us or our specific locations. We'll also have to keep this conversation short. I couldn't speak freely earlier today, but things are very bad here. Society is breaking down and the Alliance is using totalitarian measures to maintain control. I don't know how you managed to get down here undetected, but they will discover you eventually. Leave now while you can... please. Here's Christine."

"Marc, my love, I wish I could see you. Mama said you looked skinny. Aren't you taking care of yourself right? Talk to me."

"Chris, I'm so happy to hear your sweet voice again! I feared for so long that I never would. Don't worry about me, I'm doing fine. But, I want to know about you. Please tell me."

"It's been tough..." she stammered as tears began to flow. "They assigned me as a personal aide to the local base commander. He forced me to..."

"He forced you to do what, Chris?"

Christine began sobbing and could hardly speak. "They'll kill me if I talk."

Bolton felt a rage boiling inside him like he had never known before. "What's his name, Chris?"

"No, Marc!" Bill said sternly. "There's nothing you can do. Let it be."

"Yes, there is. I can take all of you away from this living hell."

"Is that even possible?"

"Definitely sir, I can jump on a flight and meet you in the morning."

"My sensible and loving wife, what do you think?"

"There's nothing left for us here, Bill," Marianne replied. "Marc's world will be strange to us, and we're probably too old to adjust to it fully; but, you know perfectly well what will happen if we don't leave. This might be the only way to protect our daughter."

"Yes honey, I understand. Alright Marc, we'll come. However, it would be better if you remained where you are. We'll try to get an early flight on Friday. That's Christine's day off, so she won't be missed until the weekend. Okay?"

"Excellent, that'll work. Our berth number is S-P-B-3-9. There won't be any way for you to contact me directly, so we'll have to setup a schedule where I can call you at this mobile address you have. We can start tomorrow night at the same time."

"Fine, hopefully I'll have the flight information by then. We should end this call now. Thank you, Marc."

"Darling, I knew you would come back for me!" Christine said proudly.

"I love you, Chris. We'll be together again very soon. I promise."

Bolton was so pensively troubled after the conversation his walk back to the E-14 was unhurried almost to the point of aimlessness. He managed to arrive four short minutes before the 21:00 curfew. Major Mabuza gave him a severe tongue lashing, accusing the mission's leader of needlessly imperiling the lives of the passengers and crew. Bolton didn't say a word in response. He just pulled down his folding sleeping platform from the interior hull of the ship, and tried to get some rest. Alas, slumber proved to be uncomfortably elusive. The inside temperature was only slightly less than the outside reading of 87 degrees Fahrenheit. It would get much hotter in the coming days.

Wednesday morning broke over Sutter City with a hazy, reddish-brown sky. It would be a busy day. Chief Engineer Quivers began coordinating refueling and maintenance operations with airport personnel. Captain McDonald monitored the airwaves to keep track of current events and assess the world's political situation. Major Mabuza ran diagnostic tests on the ship's computer systems, carried out regularly scheduled transmissions with the Moon Base, and generally supervised all other activities. Marc Bolton was responsible for setting up radio communications with the away teams.

At 9:10, Han Li was the first to report. He had successfully contacted two prominent climatologists at G.A.M.S. who were overjoyed with the offer of immigrating to Mars. Han had also managed to speak with his family, and was in the process of getting them transportation to Boulder. If all went well, he would return to Sutter City late on Thursday with at least five other passengers.

Special envoy de la Rosa checked in at 10:03. The afternoon of their arrival in New Vancouver, he and his assistant Willard Mounthaven had watched a newscast announcing the roundup and arrest of the *Occidental Democratic Liberation Front's* leadership and many of its key supporters. This was the group they were attempting to connect with. After confirming the story, and observing the omnipresence of the Alliance's security force in the city, they decided to terminate their operation and return to Sutter City on the next available flight.

Mabuza was reading a dispatch received from General Brookfield when Bolton's communications station sounded an emergency beacon alert at 11:20. The major hastily ran over to find out what happened.

"What is it, Marc?"

"The Ambassador's team issued a code eight-zero-one. That means they are in imminent danger and unable to use their radio."

"What are their coordinates?"

"Nineteen degrees, nineteen minutes, seven seconds north latitude, and ninety-eight degrees, fifty-two minutes, fifty-six seconds west longitude – let's see, that's Ixtapaluca southeast of Mexico City."

"Is there anything we can do to help them?"

"No. They have orders to destroy their equipment and identification documents if unable to evade capture by hostile agents. I have orders to abort the mission if the risk of exposure becomes too great."

"The Alliance will torture them if they're captured alive; and, that means the Alliance will find out about us."

"Yes I know, Major. Hopefully, we'll get more information from them soon."

"It better be very soon," Mabuza retorted as he handed General Brookfield's dispatch to Bolton. "Here's some more bad news for you."

Bolton read the communiqué to himself. Earlier that morning, a Chinese cruiser threatened to attack a cargo shuttle transporting deuterium to the Moon Base if the Alliance didn't agree to lift an embargo against its Japanese protectorate. General Peckarie not only refused to comply with the ultimatum, but promptly ordered Brookfield to destroy the cruiser. Not wanting to be the one who fired the first shot in another world war, Brookfield openly disobeyed the order. His message concluded with a warning that an enraged General Peckarie might punish his insubordination by seizing the E-14, and suggested they return to the Moon Base immediately.

"Well?" Mabuza asked.

Bolton paused for a moment. "We can't leave now, Major. There's one team in transit, another due back tomorrow, and a third group expected on Friday. Do you want to strand them here?"

"As commander of this ship, I am obliged to protect my crew Mister Bolton. If we are taken into custody, the fate of your people won't be any different. This is a question of practicality. We must save what we can while we are able to."

"Major, while I appreciate the concern for your crew, it is I who am in command of this expedition."

"With all due respect sir, I shall recognize no authority that requires me to needlessly sacrifice my crew!"

"Major Mabuza! You are way out of line!"

"Gentlemen, please!" Captain McDonald interjected. "Before either of you says something you'll probably regret, let me inform you what's happened since today's incident."

"Alright Katie, go ahead," Bolton said calmly.

"I've been listening in on the diplomatic channels I was able to decipher, and monitoring the international news chatter. It seems that the Chinese have already notified the Alliance that their cruiser skipper acted without authorization, and will be making a public statement to that effect within the next hour. Also, I have the distinct impression that the Chinese are not aware of General Peckarie's order to General Brookfield. Since the Chinese would likely react angrily if they learned the Alliance wanted to attack its cruiser, I'm sure General Peckarie intends to keep this secret; and, he won't be able to do so if he retaliates against General Brookfield. If I'm correct, the impending threat against us that General Brookfield initially feared may have been assuaged."

"Good work, Katie. Thank you," Bolton acknowledged. "Major, can you confirm the Captain's analysis by subtly asking General Brookfield to clarify his warning in light of these new revelations?"

"Yes sir. I'll get on it right away. I also wish to express sincere contrition for my earlier disrespectful behavior. It was unprofessional at best, and I would not blame you for reporting it to my military superiors."

"There's no need, Sizwe. You have a passionate commitment towards the safety of your crew. That is commendable. I assure you that I feel the same. However, I suspect we will face great peril before the completion of this mission. It will take all of us working together to see it through, and I'm confident that we will. Let's have no more talk of this. It's time to get back to work."

Major Mabuza stood at attention and saluted Bolton. "You can count on me, Mister Bolton, and my crew."

Captain McDonald's analysis turned out to be partially correct. The Chinese High Commission quickly released a public statement describing their cruiser commander's actions as 'irresponsible and unauthorized,' and that he had been relieved of all duties. Moreover, General Peckarie took no outward steps at retaliation towards his obstinate Moon Base commandant; but, inwardly the head of the *North American Alliance* was seething and General Brookfield knew it. He replied to Major Mabuza's query by reasserting his recommendation that the E-14 leave Sutter City 'at the earliest practicable opportunity.' When the emergency beacon alert code 899 was received from Ambassador Pagnatan at 15:51, meaning that the team was irreparably lost, everyone on the E-14 understood there was little time left to make their escape. Bolton would try to expedite Han Li's travel plans, but it was even more critical to do the same for the Bakerman's.

Marc Bolton began his 70 minute walk to the *Mother Lode Eatery* at 17:00 escorted by security guard Basil Bahar – a concession made to the rather insistent Major Mabuza. Although Bolton had been unsuccessful in reestablishing radio communications with Han Li before he departed, Captain McDonald was able to at 17:45. She exhorted him to get back to the ship immediately as they may be forced to leave at any moment. Han said he would try his best, but it was unlikely that his party could do so before midday on Thursday. A more upbeat development occurred at 18:37 when the de la Rosa team arrived back from British Columbia. Willard Mounthaven seemed particularly eager to make a quick getaway when he expressed the ominous prediction that 'this place is about to fall apart.'

Shortly after 19:00, Bolton went into a telecall booth at the restaurant and made an audio call to Bill Bakerman.

"Marc, is that you?"

"Yes Bill. Is everyone there?"

"Hi Marc," "Hello darling," Christine and Marianne said respectively.

"Hello, my loves. How are you doing?"

"We found out the airline services discontinued all direct flights from Boise to Sutter City last year," Bill answered. "So, we reserved a Friday afternoon flight to Salt Lake City, and will then transfer to a one a.m. Saturday morning flight to Sutter City. We should arrive there around two-fifteen a.m."

"Oh no, we'll probably have to leave before then. Weren't there any earlier flights?"

"No Marc. We got the earliest available flight. Airline service has been scaled back dramatically over the last few years, especially for non-hub terminals like Boise. That's the best we can do. I'm sorry. When are you leaving?"

"That's hard to say. We'll stay as long as possible, but we could be forced to take off at any time."

Bolton could hear Christine weeping in the background.

"Don't worry Chris," he reassured her. "I'll never leave you again, even if that means staying behind. But, let's try to think of how we can get you here sooner. There must be a way."

"I don't see how we can, Marc," Marianne postulated. "The magnetic train service out of Boise is shut down. We could drive our vehicle, but that would take two days and cause Christine to skip work tomorrow. They would instigate a search if she didn't show up, and low-level employees are not allowed to take impromptu time off. Even if she could, there's no way to be certain all the roads are passable. I doubt those rural routes are even maintained anymore."

"Not too good, is it?" Bolton said rhetorically. "I guess the only option left is to go ahead with your flight plan and hope for the best. Damn!"

"Wait a minute," shouted Christine. "Clover, what about Mister Startower?"

"That old coot," Bill replied sarcastically. "How could he help?"

"He does own a small airplane, and he is a pilot. Is he not?"

"He was a pilot, my dear, many years ago. Now he's just a drunk old recluse, and that plane of his is a relic. It has an outdated internal combustion engine with a propeller, for goodness sakes. It probably doesn't even fly!"

"Bill," his wife scolded him. "Isn't it worth a try?"

"Well sure, I can talk to him. But, why should he help us?"

"Just tell him the truth and see what happens. I've always known Mister Startower to be a warm, generous man. You might be surprised."

"Okay, okay. I'll go over to his house right now. I don't believe he has a telecall. Marc, can you call me tomorrow at noon? We should know what our plans will be by then."

"Absolutely," responded Bolton.

Thursday was full of anxiety for everyone hoping to leave the Earth aboard the E-14. Han Li managed to cut a few hours from his travel schedule, but his group of six still could not arrive at Sutter City before 17:00 local time. The Bakerman's were thrilled that their neighbor, the boisterously eclectic 72 year-old Charles 'Charlie' Startower, had agreed to fly them to that destination in exchange for receiving the property rights to the Bakerman's small adjacent farm. Because they had to wait for Christine to get home from work, the three hour flight from Boise wouldn't reach Sutter City until approximately 20:30 – much later than what Major Mabuza thought was safe.

Meanwhile, an agitated General Peckarie had been complaining vehemently about General Brookfield to his staff personnel at the *North American Alliance* regional headquarters in Springfield, Missouri. He was livid at his Moon Base commander's continual disobedience, and was hell-bent on punishing him; but had thus far been dissuaded from doing so by his policy advisors who considered it strategically unsound. That is, until Peckarie accidently learned that Brookfield was conducting a 'routine training operation' in Sutter City. He immediately ordered his staff to investigate it. The order was issued at 15:22 PST.

Colonel Andrews delivered an initial report of the E-14's official spaceflight plan to General Peckarie fifty minutes later. It was logged as an SSETM training mission with shore leave, having a seven-member crew and six passengers. Peckarie mulled over the names on the list while Andrews stood at attention.

"What can you tell me about this crew, Colonel?"

"Mabuza, McDonald, and Quivers are all experienced officers with fine records. Two of the enlisted men have long assignments in Moon Base security. The other two are fresh out of boot camp, so we don't know much about them."

"Experienced officers and a security team? That doesn't sound like a training mission to me."

"Yes sir. However, it's not uncommon for veteran flight personnel to sharpen their skills with practice missions, especially for SSETM crews. Also, it is just standard operating procedure to have an accompanying security team."

Peckarie was not amused by what he perceived as a condescending remark from the Colonel. He glared at Andrews rather intently.

"What about the passengers?"

"They're all private contractors for the *Lunar Consortium*, sir. Two made a brief trip to New Vancouver. One travelled to Boulder, and is currently aboard a returning flight. Another never left Sutter City, as far as we know, and the remaining two flew to Mexico City on Tuesday."

"Mexico City? Didn't we apprehend two terrorists there yesterday?"

"They're hardly terrorists, sir. We found two middle-aged women hiding out in a suspected *Mundial de la Libertad* safe-house without any identity papers. They were interrogated, but we haven't been able to corroborate their story."

"How many of the E-14's passengers are female?" Peckarie demanded.

"Uh... I believe... there are two, sir. Yes, they both went to Mexico City together. Their ages are fifty-three and forty-eight. Maybe..."

"Colonel!" screamed Peckarie. "I want to know who they are and what they were doing! I don't care if you have to torture and kill those bitches, but you better get them to talk pronto! Do you understand me?"

"Yes sir, right away sir!" Andrews uttered nervously as he tried to bolt out of the General's office.

"Colonel, you have not been dismissed yet! I also want you to have an assault team organized at the Sutter City airport, but make sure it is done out of the public view. I don't want to spook the E-14's commander before we can seize his ship. That's all, now get to it!"

Andrews snapped back to attention, and hastily left the room with the cadence of a speed-march. He paused momentarily to wipe his sweaty brow after rounding a hallway corner. It wasn't an easy task. His hands were trembling.

Han arrived at 17:14 with his father, mother, younger sister, and climatologists Marta Pickford and Rudolph Fierro. The E-14 had an exposed berth, being parked out in the open some 150 yards from its passenger gate. This arrangement was necessary because the high temperature exhaust of aerospace planes would damage buildings and could seriously injure people. Bolton was the first to see the group walking across the tarmac, and he ran out to meet them.

Jun Li was an imperturbable man in his late 60's who usually didn't have much to say. Part of the reason for his quiet disposition was that he never fully mastered the English language and was still uncomfortable using it in conversation. The other reason was his Buddhist belief that any truly precious idea can and should be expressed in just a few carefully chosen words. Jun's wife Mei-Li was his polar opposite. She was warmly gregarious, open to non-traditional philosophies, and was several years his junior. Their daughter Cynthia was just 19 years old, astonishingly naïve even for a late teen, and preoccupied with frolicsome activities. At least superficially, she seemed completely unconcerned with the very real dangers confronting her and the rest of the world.

When Bolton reached them, he was met by hugs, kisses, handshakes, and cheerful greetings. Cynthia embraced him around the waist and wouldn't let go. As they walked towards the ship, she pestered him with all manner of silly questions.

"Tell me about the Martian men," she giggled. "Are they cute, and all?"

"I haven't given that much thought, Cynthia. Really, I don't know. What do you think, Han?"

"Sorry there big guy, but you're on your own!" Han bellowed out in laughter.

"If they're anything like you Marc," she teased while squeezing him closer, "then they must be very handsome and charming."

"You sure have grown up a lot these past few years," observed Bolton.

"Oh boy, if that isn't an understatement!" Mei-Li exclaimed.

Over 1900 miles to the southeast, Ambassador Pagnatan and Ululani Palakiko were being mercilessly tortured by a handful of sociopathic *North American Alliance* intelligence agents. They bravely resisted their captors by giving false and misleading information, but the excruciating ordeal pushed the two Martian women to their breaking point. Soon thereafter, they tried to save themselves by telling the agents exactly what General Peckarie wanted to hear – that General Brookfield had sent them to form a working coalition with the Alliance's revolutionary enemies. The story was far from the truth, but it unfortunately implicated the E-14. Even more tragically, it failed to save their lives. Arum Pagnatan suffered a massive heart attack and died at 19:28 PST. Ms. Palakiko finally succumbed to internal bleeding, from numerous blunt force traumas, forty-five minutes later. Their bodies were unceremoniously dumped into a drainage ditch. General Peckarie was given a full report at 20:24. At 20:33 he ordered the Sutter City airport assault team to take the E-14 and its personnel into custody by whatever means necessary.

Charlie Startower taxied his four-seat single engine airplane to the Sutter City spaceport berths on the opposite end of the runway at 20:27 PST immediately after landing. His maneuver was a blatant violation of airport regulations, as the control tower had specifically instructed him to move directly over to the non-commercial aircraft parking section. Their angry radio commands went unheeded however, as Charlie had other plans. The cantankerous old pilot had no intention of paying the airport's exorbitant usage fees and mandatory refueling costs. After dropping off the Bakerman's near berth SPB39, he visually checked the runway approaches for any ground or air traffic and then proceeded to takeoff. As his antique plane accelerated past the control tower, Charlie gave them an arrogantly rude hand gesture. He had no use for airport authority whatsoever.

Major Mabuza was impatiently pacing back and forth outside the E-14 when Charlie's irreverent passenger delivery maneuver caught his attention. He rushed over to the ship's hatchway and yelled through the opening.

"Bolton, come down here quick! I think your people are here!"

Bolton and Han ran down the ramp and saw the Bakerman's walking towards their ship. Christine's long silky hair was flowing in the modest breeze.

"That's them! Major, prepare for departure. Han, come with me."

"McDonald, Quivers, fire it up... we're leaving!" ordered Mabuza. "Security team, arms at ready! Corporal Bahar, assist Mister Bolton. Daniels, Jasper, Torrio, form a perimeter around the ship. All the rest of you people, strap into your seats."

Bolton and Christine jumped into each other's arms. They kissed passionately in a tight embrace while Han greeted her parents.

"I worried I'd never see you again," she whispered.

"Me too Chris, but we are together again. I've missed you so."

"Excuse me Mister Bolton," Basil Bahar interrupted. "We need to get to the ship right now."

"Of course, Corporal," Bolton acknowledged as Bahar shepherded the group towards the E-14 glistening in the airport lights 75 yards away.

"You look great Han," Christine remarked as she kissed him on the cheek. "Do you like living on Mars?"

"Thanks Christine. You're as beautiful as I can remember. Actually, I love it on Mars. It is a peaceful place, although its charms aren't as flamboyant as Earth's."

"Mars is so distant in my mind," she daydreamed. "I just can't seem to hold onto the image... like a boat at the edge of the horizon that is sailing away."

Christine's inner thoughts unexpectedly coalesced in Bolton's mind. They were aloof, ethereal, and detached from the physical world. The visualizations were surreal and totally discordant with her personality. Bolton couldn't understand it at all, and he became instantly alarmed.

Suddenly, a megaphone amplified voice was heard coming from the passenger gate to Bolton's left.

"YOU PEOPLE WALKING ON THE TARMAC... STOP WHERE YOU ARE AND DROP TO THE GROUND NOW! YOU ARE UNDER ARREST. WE WILL OPEN FIRE IF YOU DO NOT COMPLY IMMEDIATELY!"

"Damn Ironshirts!" yelled Bahar. "Everybody run!"

The group ran as fast as they could to cover the last 40 yards to the E-14.

"I WARNED YOU! ALRIGHT MEN, FIRE!"

Basil Bahar was the first one hit. A 7.62 millimeter bullet struck his right hand and blew off his little finger, but the corporal kept on running. Almost simultaneously, a round passed completely through Marc Bolton's left thigh without touching the femur. However, the force of the impact knocked him straight to the ground. Christine stopped to turn back towards Bolton, and was shot below the sternum severing her aorta. She crumpled over in a heap a few feet away from her lover. The life of Christine Bakerman passed on almost instantaneously.

Seeing what happened, Bolton screamed, "No, no, no, no, no... oh no!"

Just then, Major Mabuza ordered the three other security guards to open fire on the attackers.

Although they didn't hit anyone, it forced the Alliance's assault team to take cover behind the buildings. That allowed their group to reach the E-14 without further casualties. Christine's lifeless body was carried by her grieving parents. Han and Basil dragged Bolton who was struggling to reach Christine.

Everyone was taken aboard the ship while the security guards kept the assault team pinned down. The airport sirens began to howl as Major Mabuza hollered at Basil Bahar who was at the bottom of the ramp preparing to fire his weapon.

"We're ready to take off, Corporal. When I give the word, get your people up the ramp and kick it away from the ship. But, be quick about it!"

"We'll never make it, Major! Someone's got to stay behind and keep them from shooting up the ship before it can get away. I will do it!"

"Are you crazy? I'm not leaving you behind!"

"Damn you, sir! There's no time left! Do what I say! I'm running out of ammunition!"

"Listen up you other men!" Mabuza barked. "Continue firing using a collapsing retreat stance! Do it fast, and do it now! Captain McDonald, get us out of here!"

The E-14 moved briskly up the taxiway and was soon out of range of the gunfire. When Corporal Bahar exhausted all his ammunition, he was slaughtered by massed automatic rifle fire - his mutilated right hand still gripping the trigger.

Major Mabuza instructed the security guards to wrap Bolton's ugly leg wound with a compression bandage, seal Christine's bloody body in a corpse bag, and strap both into sleeping platforms. He then rushed up to the cockpit where Captain McDonald was maneuvering the ship around airport maintenance vehicles trying to block the E-14's access to the runway.

"Oh shit!" Mabuza cried out as he secured himself to the pilot's seat.

"Major, look at that cargo plane landing," McDonald said while pointing upwards. "They're going to close off the runway after it clears."

"We'd better take off right behind it then."

"Sir, we could collide with it!"

"Would you rather stay here, Captain?"

"No sir."

"Then punch it, Katie!"

The E-14's engines screamed as the ship accelerated rapidly down the runway. In the distance, the large red and black striped cargo plane was still coasting to a stop and had not yet begun to turn.

"Airspeed is one-eight-five. Seven seconds to liftoff. We're not going to make it, sir!"

"Turn, damned you, turn!"

With the E-14 bearing down on him like a missile, the cargo captain released the left rudder/toe brake causing his airplane to veer sharply to the right and into an unpaved grassy area. His abrupt action was sufficient to avoid the collision, but put too much strain on the aircraft's landing gear which collapsed. Grass, dirt, sparks, and pieces of the undercarriage, flew all over the field as the E-14 roared off the runway behind it. The leader of the Alliance's assault team watched the E-14 climb steadily away until its rocket motors fired taking the ship out of sight and into space. He then radioed his superiors to report the outcome of the mission.

General Peckarie was not pleased when informed of the E-14's escape from Sutter City. Lacking the space assets which could intercept the ship during its passage to the Moon, he enlisted help from an unlikely source – his foremost antagonists in China. In exchange for the capture or destruction of the E-14, Peckarie offered some valuable territorial concessions in the western pacific. The Chinese agreed not only because they wanted those possessions, but because they hated the *Mundial de la Libertad* as much as the Alliance did. That underground revolutionary organization was supporting anti-Chinese rebels in Southeast Asia and Tibet whose numbers and effectiveness were on the rise. Peckarie had managed to convince himself, and the Chinese, that General Brookfield was now in league with terrorist groups threatening their authority. The world of power politics is quite bizarre, and often makes strange bedfellows.

Twelve hours after the deal was finalized, two renamed Chinese cruisers – the *Shaoqiang* and the *Xun* – converged on the E-14 from two different directions.

In a space battle between these ships, the E-14 was totally outclassed. It had no weaponry, no armor protection, and was far too slow to outrun the fleet cruisers. Even worse, the ship had no rearward sensory capability which meant that its crew was unaware they were being pursued; and since they were still over 60 hours away from the Moon, it appeared that General Peckarie's vengeance would be exacted upon the E-14's 'mutinous' personnel after all.

"Major, I'm picking up a civilian broadcast over the universal public information channel," Quivers informed him.

"Let's hear it, Chief."

"Acknowledged," the Chief Engineer flipped the speaker switch.

"... proclaim this declaration of independence, and hereby annul all political associations with terrestrial entities. From this date forward, the Moon Base shall be known as the *First Lunar Republic*. By virtue of this act, all foreign claims to persons and property currently within the lunar gravitational field must be..."

"That's General Brookfield!" Captain McDonald exulted.

"Be quiet Katie! We need to hear this," Mabuza scolded her.

"Furthermore, this pronouncement also serves to notify the interplanetary community that aggressive actions towards the citizenry of the F-L-R. will not go unpunished. We can and will defend ourselves. In the interests of peace, we…"

"Major, we have a single radar contact… bearing three-three-zero degrees, range one-seven-zero thousand and closing," stated Quivers.

"Three-three-zero degrees?" questioned Mabuza. "That's coming from the direction of the Moon."

"Yes sir. It has a radar signature of a mid-sized space vessel. I'm analyzing the configuration now… confirmed… it's a *Rigel* class cruiser."

"That has to be the *Cromwell*," McDonald proposed.

"Agreed," Mabuza replied. "But, why is it headed towards us?"

"I'm getting ship-to-ship communications now, sir. Shall I put it on speaker?"

"Go ahead, Chief."

"To the commander of the two warships intercepting the spacecraft E-14 - halt your pursuit immediately! This is Captain Manbury. Please acknowledge."

"Captain Manbury, I am Commodore Xiong Ts'ao. The E-14 has been declared a terrorist ship by the International Tribunal of The Hague. I have authorization to seize it if possible, or destroy it if necessary. Do you wish to assist us?"

"Commodore, the E-14 is sanctioned under the domain of the *First Lunar Republic* which recognizes neither The Hague Tribunal nor your personal authority. As a contractual representative of the F-L-

R., it is my duty to ensure that no one interferes with its mission operations."

Marc Bolton drifted into the cockpit. "What's all the commotion, Major?"

"Mister Bolton! You shouldn't be moving around, you'll start bleeding again!"

"On the contrary Captain Manbury, it is General Brookfield's rebellious declaration of independence that has not been officially recognized. Let's be reasonable. If you try to stop us, you'll only succeed in getting yourself killed. My cruisers have far more firepower than your single ship does. Give it up."

"Commodore, I must correct your assessment of the tactical situation. As we speak, the Moon Base's long range laser – which I believe you know as *Zeus* – is targeting your two vessels. This is your last chance to turnabout and return to Earth. I urge you to act smartly and with restraint."

"Apparently Mister Bolton," Mabuza described, "there are two cruisers – probably Chinese – that are chasing us. Your Captain Manbury has taken the *Cromwell* out of lunar orbit to challenge them, but is still too far away to employ his weapons. It also appears that General Brookfield is backing him up."

"How close are the warships?"

"Unknown, but I don't want to maneuver the ship just to find out. We may have to make a real fast engine burn. Katie, warm up the RAMS."

The commodore's voice once again came over the speaker. "Captain Manbury, I believe you are bluffing. Even General Brookfield isn't stupid enough to risk starting a war by intervening in an official government anti-terrorist operation. Regardless, I have my orders. This communication is ended."

"He's going to shoot!" Mabuza growled. "Katie, ten second burn… on my mark… three, two, one, execute!"

The E-14's rocket assist motors ignited less than a second before it was bracketed by laser fire from the two pursuing cruisers. All except one of the beams missed the ship. The beam that hit sliced into the E-14's vertical tail fin demolishing the atmospheric rudder, but caused no damage that impaired the current operation of the ship. Bolton, who had been floating freely within the cockpit, was slammed against the bulkhead dislocating his left shoulder. As the weapons crews aboard the *Shaoqiang* and *Xun* readjusted their aim to account for the E-14's velocity change, the powerful *Zeus* laser emitted two short but accurate pulses from the surface of the Moon. Both of the Chinese cruisers were instantly eviscerated killing their entire compliment of crews. Eighteen hours later, the E-14 rendezvoused with the *Cromwell* transferring its passengers over to the larger Martian vessel where Bolton's injuries could be properly treated and Christine's body could be held in decomposition-al stasis. Subsequently, the *Cromwell* served as a close escort for the E-14's return flight back to the Moon.

This seemingly isolated incident would trigger dreadful global consequences. Much like the volatile political situation that doomed Europe in 1914, the world was once again an explosive tinderbox waiting for a spark to set it off. The Chinese were furious at the loss of their precious cruisers, and suspected the ships were lured into a trap. They suffered another insult when General Peckarie reneged on the territorial concessions using the E-14's escape as an excuse. The ideologically zealous *European Confederacy*, always wary of Sino-American cooperation, saw this rift as an exploitable opportunity. Over the next few days, their efforts proved eminently successful – and led to the demise of planet Earth.

Chapter 12
Alien Origins

The *European Confederacy*, a loose association of like-minded nationalistic groups whose roots trace back over 150 years, was the jealous younger sibling of the tripartite ruling family of world powers. They had neither the conventional military might of the *North American Alliance*, nor the space assets and human resources of the *Asian Federal Union* (China). Additionally, the E.C.'s sphere of influence was smaller than their political rivals being geographically hemmed in from the east, west, and north, and bordering the chaotic African continent to the south. Despite their inferior position, the E.C. leadership was far more sophisticated in the skillful use of diplomacy than was either the reactionary Alliance or aggressive Chinese. They preferred a diffident negotiating style to conceal their motives, and were frequently able to pit their adversaries against one another. However, the E.C.'s greatest coup was the creation of the *International Tribunal of The Hague* (actually located near The Vaalserberg because of the *Great Flood's* inundation of the South Holland province). Ostensibly, the Tribunal was an impartial judicial body consented to resolve international disputes. In reality, it had been secretly composed of members belonging to the clandestine White Supremacist organization *Der Arischen Speer* which pervaded all levels of the E.C. government. The organization's founder Joachim Hueber, who just happened to be the Tribunal's Chief Justice, was a descendant of a 20th century ODESSA operative accused of smuggling Nazi SS officers out of post-World War II Europe.

When the rancor over the E-14 incident reached a fever pitch, Hueber used a front-group posing as a South American news agency to release a falsified document outlining a *North American Alliance* plan to weaken the Chinese space fleet piecemeal through subterfuge and false-flag operations. The A.F.U. responded by insisting the Tribunal immediately conduct a thorough investigation to uncover the source of the leak and the document's author – both presumably within the N.A.A. General Peckarie publicly called the Chinese demand a 'witch-hunt without merit,' and steadfastly refused to cooperate. The E.C. also rejected an official inquiry into the matter citing the 'dubious authenticity' of the document, which was a grotesquely duplicitous statement on their part. The Tribunal then formally denied the A.F.U.'s request on the grounds that the mandatory two-thirds member state threshold had not been achieved.

The Chinese High Commission went berserk. They unilaterally withdrew the *Asian Federal Union* from the Tribunal, declared the revelations in Hueber's fictitious document an 'act of war,' and promptly issued an ultimatum to the *North American Alliance*. General Peckarie accused the Chinese of using the world as a hostage in order to score political points, and referred to their ultimatum as 'premeditated hyperbole.' Two days later, he found out it was not.

Mankind's third and final world war started when the A.F.U. systematically attacked the Alliance's satellite defense system. The military operation was masterfully executed, and left the skies over North America open to aerial assault. The N.A.A.'s meager space fleet tried to mount a counterattack, but it was wiped out in short order. Complete domination of Earth orbit was subsequently attained when Chinese forces seized the *European Confederacy's* space station *Liberty* after its outnumbered combat vessels surrendered without a fight. This first phase of the war transpired in a lightning-fast six hours. Even the most cautious of General Peckarie's military planners were caught by surprise, while Joachim Hueber and his compatriots in the E.C. were utterly traumatized by the audacity and success of the preemptive strike.

However, the Chinese were about to learn the same lesson as did the Japanese after their December 7, 1941 attack on Pearl Harbor. The *North American Alliance* possessed an extensive array of conventional arms including mobile land, sea, and air forces, and a variety of missile systems. These weapons were based on generally outdated technology, but were still useful in at least some combat scenarios. Although the N.A.A. could no longer confront the *Asian Federal Union* in space – ground-based directed energy weapons having been largely retired decades earlier due to problems associated with atmospheric propagation (absorption, diffraction, scattering, thermal blooming, and turbulence) and the advent of 'hardened' space vessels such as cruisers – it did retain the capability of striking Earthly targets. The scariest weapon in their arsenal was the MANTIDS (Midrange Anti-Nation Thermonuclear Incendiary Delivery System) – a force of 48 highly maneuverable supersonic jet aircraft each carrying a guided missile having a single 25 megaton warhead. The planes were designed to take a circuitous ground-hugging route to their missile launch points making them (in theory) less vulnerable to orbital counter-fire. After launching, the missiles would independently zigzag towards their targets and then detonate at a predetermined altitude. Even though the Chinese knew the existence of MANTIDS, they drastically overestimated their own ability to shoot them down.

The second phase of World War III began the next day after Chinese surrender demands were ignored by Supreme N.A.A. Headquarters. The High Commission responded to that silence by pounding several 'soft target' radar sites into rubble, and warning the Alliance that more devastation was on the way if they didn't comply. General Peckarie could take no more. Against the will of his advisors, he ordered a quarter of the MANTIDS force to attack important military installations in Northeast Asia, which were appallingly located near heavily populated urban centers. The A.F.U.'s orbital lasers had difficulty tracking, and focusing enough energy on the agile, low-flying MANTIDS. Only three were shot down. The rest easily evaded secondary air defenses and obliterated a swath of territory from north-central China to the Korean peninsula. Some thirty million people were killed instantly by the voluminous mushroom clouds, and many more millions would suffer and die in the weeks ahead.

The staggered Chinese lashed out with everything they had. A firestorm of lasers and missiles rained down on North America like a cataclysmic meteorite shower. General Peckarie fought back, and his remaining MANTIDS laid waste to the rest of the East Asian continent. When the two antagonists finally exhausted themselves a few days later, planet Earth had been unrecognizably transformed. The equivalent of nearly 3000 megatons of TNT had been unleashed onto the biosphere. Over 500 million were massacred outright. The number of persons injured, displaced, or exposed to harmful radiation, more than doubled that figure. So much dust and debris was thrown up into the atmosphere that the only place left where one could hope to find blue skies was Antarctica. Global temperatures plummeted, and plant life around the world began to wither and die. It was the onset of a nuclear winter which would persist for decades to come.

Deep underground in protected shelters, the political leaders who started the war, their support staffs, selected military personnel, captains of industry, and the world's wealthy aristocracy, all cowered like frightened children hiding from an angry parent. There was no remorse, no introspection, no accusations, and no empathy for the billions struggling to survive on the surface. There was however, a tremendous sense of relief that they were among the 'lucky' few. If there was a single thing which could be rightly blamed for the worst calamity in human history, it would be the abject callousness of men obsessed with the allure of power. To these emotionally primitive individuals, life – and the environment which supports it – exists only for the purpose of profitable exploitation. And, it was this lack of evolutionary stewardship which inevitably proved to be mankind's undoing on the planet that first put forth his seed.

Everyone on the Moon was horrified by what they saw. The Earth was now a brownish-gray color with dirty-orange radioactive clouds roiling over the northern temperate zones. General Brookfield's fledgling *First Lunar Republic* would from here on be solely dependent upon Mars for its sustenance, should it wish to continue. On the Moon Base's primary observation station, an impromptu meeting gathered which included Brookfield, Trenton Manbury, and the surviving passengers of the E-14 mission.

"General, there is no reason for your people to stay here anymore," Manbury proposed. "We can send for the *Hesperia* and start the evacuation in a few weeks. Believe me sir... you will be welcome on Mars."

"Thank you, Trenton. That is a most gracious offer. But we signed a deal with your late ambassador, and I intend to stick to it. We will stay. Besides, Mars will need a base of operations once it's safe to return to the Earth."

"Our return to Earth may be a long time coming. I wonder what we'll find."

"Our legacy, Captain," Brookfield replied. "We will find our legacy."

Across the room, Han Li was viewing the ravaged Earth through an 11 inch Schmidt–Cassegrain reflecting telescope. Marc Bolton was sitting beside him in a motorized wheelchair.

"What can you see, Han?"

"I can't see much other than dark ugly clouds, big guy. There's an occasional glimpse of the surface, but not enough to make out any detail. Although, it looks like the oceans have lost all their color, and I noticed a flat white surface above the Arctic Circle which could be the reformation of an ice cap."

"How ironic," Bolton pondered. "Man causes global climate change through his own carelessness, and then reverses it only by destroying himself."

"Indeed. You know, Marc, I was always the eternal optimist. As a child, I remember reading a famous quote by President Kennedy. How did that go? Oh yes... 'Our problems are man-made therefore they may be solved by man. And man can be as big as he wants. No problem of human destiny is beyond human beings.' As an adult, I dedicated my life to science trying to develop technologies that could help people. And, I was captivated by J. E. Hutchins' theory that Humanity's aggressive primal nature was diminishing due to natural evolutionary changes. Now look at us. It is a humbling experience to have all your preconceptions shattered in a single stroke. Where do we go from here?"

"Han, do not let this tragedy taint your dreams so. It is that optimism deep inside you which will compel us to reach those grand horizons you see. Earth no longer holds our future. Like an adolescent bird, we have left the nest and must establish our own unique identity. The living universe will come to know us in time, and its judgment shall not be influenced by the mortal sins of the past… but by the righteous deeds of the present."

"You speak eloquently with great wisdom and perspective, my friend. Not at all like the self-loathing individual who I saw several weeks ago, or like a man who had suffered an excruciatingly painful loss. Has this experience changed you?"

"I don't know. Perhaps I just woke up. A moment before Christine died, our minds touched. She had tried to envision her life on Mars, but couldn't. It was then that she realized the end was near. Her thoughts were tranquil, accepting, and seemed to merge into a higher level of consciousness. The essence of her being had departed before that fatal bullet pierced her body. I've had time enough for reflection now. Christine would have chided me for being so presumptuous to believe that I alone was responsible for the dreadful events which have caused me so much regret. She always knew my behavior was driven by principle, and she loved me for it. I shall never forget that."

Han smiled ever so gently and rested his hand on Bolton's uninjured shoulder. "Nor shall I," he spoke softly. "When do we go home, big guy?"

"Tomorrow my dear friend, we leave for Mars tomorrow."

The *Cromwell* was in transit when the news of Carolyn Jones' passing was broadcast on Beta 14th, Martian year 17. Her last public statement was released the previous day. It was a moving appeal for humankind to finally learn the awful lessons of its hostile past, which included a stern condemnation of hedonism and violent emotion. She also endorsed Marc Bolton as the next Chairperson of the *Board of Regents*, calling him 'the embodiment of Martian ethics and culture.' Memorial services were scheduled for Gamma 16th, and the national election for Chairperson would be held two weeks later on Delta 1st.

The election itself was anticlimactic compared to the grand tribute held in recognition of Mars' beloved first Chairperson, with Bolton winning in a landslide against two less-than-determined opponents. There were several passionately delivered eulogies, but none more touching than was spoken by acting-Chair Ivan Tcholich who called Carolyn Jones the 'truest love of my life' and the 'courageous matriarch of Martian civilization.' A magnificently constructed solid stone mausoleum stood above her interment chamber in the heart of Lowellton, and it was fitting that Bolton gave his commencement address at that location. He concluded his unpretentious speech by intimating the people should be well served if his chairpersonship even came close to that of his noble predecessor.

So it was that Mars moved into the post-war era confidently with Marc Bolton at the helm. His first act called on the *Board of Regents* to approve the building of a monument honoring the four persons lost during the E-14 mission. It was approved without objection, and constructed on a hilltop outside the city suggesting the physical distance between Mars and the Earth. Christine Bakerman was laid to rest at the site, which Bolton visited religiously with her parents on the same day every month for the remainder of their lives. Sirtes often accompanied him on these treks, and claimed many years later in her memoirs that Bolton had regular telepathic conversations with Christine. This chronicle of her life with the Chairperson, titled *The Man who fell to Olympus*, was received by the public as symbolic folklore. Sirtes insisted the accounts were true, using her own telepathy as proof that Bolton's conversations were in fact real.

The tenure of Chairperson Bolton was marked by the steady and sustainable progress of Martian society through the implementation of sound government policy and several remarkable technological projects that justifiably amazed the young nation. The first of these was an expansion of the air/spacecraft construction industry. That was quickly followed by a joint Lunar-Martian program to research the development of antimatter energy production. In year 21, a planetary exploration plan was approved paving the way towards future colonization of the outer solar system.

However, the project having the most dramatic impact was expediting an existing plan to terra-form Mars. Initially conceived during the earliest days of the Martian Colony, it was revived by Han Li in year 19 when he succeeded the venerable Ivan Tcholich as Minister of Science who had retired because of health problems. Han's climatological research team, which included the Earth refugees Marta Pickford and Rudolph Fierro, established the scientific foundational merits of terra-forming technology. After an exhaustive review, the construction of five *matrix converters* was authorized. These giant fusion powered machines would vaporize selected portions of the rocky Martian lithosphere to release gases, primarily carbon dioxide and water, into the atmosphere. The gradual increase in atmospheric pressure and temperature would eventually allow liquid water and vegetation to exist on the surface. To the Martian people, who were constrained to living underground and in protected structures, the prospect of one day being able to roam freely on the planet was especially alluring.

After all the adversity that was overcome during the colonization of Mars, its inhabitants were finally reaping the rewards of their indomitable spirit.

Martians grew into a rather contented and distinctly honorable society of people. They understood the innate fragility of their world and never expected too much from it. On a visit to the Red Planet, Harold T. Brookfield – who had previously dropped his military title – once publicly expressed his surprise at the industrious and cooperative nature of the Martian citizenry. He admitted privately that he found this difficult to comprehend considering the absence of a profit motive in its economic system. A prominent member of the *Board of Regents* with him at the time, replied that the Martian sense of duty spawned from its cultural identity which sees mutual interest as necessary, and personal greed as antithetical, to the purposes of survival. Brookfield wasn't amused by the comment, but realized it wasn't intended as an insult.

Although Bolton never quite achieved the same level of prominence as Colony founders Carolyn Jones and Ivan Tcholich, and certainly not the hero status of Trenton Manbury, the Martian people nevertheless reserved a very special place in their hearts for him. To them, he was their quiet reserved father – a rock of sensibility and ethics standing strong against a turbulent and violent sea. The renowned cultural journalist Edwina Simmons wrote perhaps the most illuminating portrayal of the man just before his resignation from office on Upsilon 1st, 24: 'Though his aloof and sometimes brooding disposition didn't always satisfy the public's appetite for him, there was no one who embodied the quintessential Martian psyche as demonstratively as Chairperson Bolton. He is Mars as surely as its expansive and dusty volcanic plains. His reassuring shadow will cast far into the future of our world, unless we forget the sacrifices he made in saving it. If it can be said that Jones personified the hopes and dreams of Mars, Tcholich its vision and intellect, and Manbury its unconquerable spirit; then it can be said that Marc Bolton was the incarnation of Martian wisdom and integrity.'

True to his nature, Bolton never had much to say about the accolades bestowed upon him. In fact, he retreated from these public displays of affection whenever he could without offending anyone. His private time was spent mostly with his close friends and companions, first and foremost being Sirtes, Han, and Han's family. In an interview conducted a week after he left office, Bolton was asked what was the most important thing he learned from his eventful career. He answered thusly: 'At a certain point in my life, I finally came to grips with the idea that the older I got the more I realized how much I did not truly understand. Youth is susceptible to the arrogant expression of naïveté. Self-doubt afflicts the elderly when their familiarity with an ever-changing world begins to erode. Those middle years, when we interact with the universe to our greatest extent, we have neither the purity of youth nor the insight of maturity. That is the most important lesson I have learned from my experience.'

However, the story of Marc Bolton doesn't end here. His life could not be complete without reconciling a personal mystery that had tormented him since his days in Sutter City and beyond. What he discovered atop a frosted Martian summit was so profound he never mentioned it to anyone. Sirtes found out accidently though a telepathic exchange, but decided it was too sensitive to discuss with him openly. It was this incident which prompted Bolton to resign the Chairpersonship later that year. No one ever knew the real reason, except Sirtes.

On the morning of Omicron 5th, 24, Marc Bolton instructed his staff to make arrangements for him to be flown to the top of Pavonis Mons around midday. Han Li was leading a Ministry of Science team there studying the atmospheric changes produced by the terra-forming project. The Chairperson's staff advised Bolton that a man of 60 Earth years should not undertake such a physically demanding excursion unless he received the proper training. They pointed out it required a medical clearance, and at least a week of instruction in how to use the bulky environment suits necessary for the harsh conditions on the surface. Bolton stubbornly refused to listen to reason. He informed his staff that he was adequately familiar with the suits because he was one of its designers, and insisted they comply with his orders immediately.

It was a midsummer day on Mars. The forecast high temperature for Lowellton was a cool 43 degrees

Fahrenheit, although that would be downright balmy compared to the pinnacle of the Pavonis shield volcano where negative triple digits prevailed. But even that bitter cold wasn't the greatest danger to human beings. Without a pressurized environment suit, a person wouldn't survive long enough to freeze. Sudden exposure to the atmosphere would rip the air from the lungs and cause a very rapid suffocating death.

The VTOL (vertical takeoff and landing) rocket plane that transported Bolton set down on a small landing pad adjacent to the Peacock Research Station 14 miles from the southeast edge of the volcano's summit caldera. Escorted by two Ministry of Science field technicians, Bolton arduously descended down the dust covered service ramp to the station's single domed structure. Inside the airlock, he was too exhausted to remove his own environment suit and needed assistance from the younger technicians. Bolton's staff was correct, this was no place for unprepared visitors – let alone middle-aged desk jockeys.

Han opened the interior airlock door, and greeted Bolton with some biting sarcasm. "Your Honor… welcome to Tharsis!" he said while bending at the waist.

"Cut out the crap, will you Han?"

"May I be so bold as to inquire why the distinguished Chairperson flew all this way just to pop in on us? Surely, he has more important – and personally safer – matters to attend to."

Bolton ran his fingers through his matted graying hair, but didn't respond.

"Okay Marc, I'm sorry. But, you must understand this is an austere research facility for scientists, not a place setup to accommodate non-working visitors."

"I understand that, Han. Aren't you going to show me around?"

Han shook his head in an expression of disbelief. "Alright, come this way."

The year old research station had six rooms. The main level housed a kitchenette, a dining/meeting room, a bedroom with six bunks, a machinery room where the toilet and shower was located, and an office containing computer and communications equipment. A transparent observation deck full of scientific equipment occupied the smaller upper level. Bolton was eager to see the latter.

"This is a disappointment, Han. I thought we'd get great panoramic views from up here. I don't see anything except the local terrain."

"Pavonis, like the other shield volcanoes at Tharsis, are over two hundred miles in diameter and have gentle slopes generally less than five degrees. The geography is very different than the steep narrow peaks of Earth which provide the kind of breathtaking vistas you might have expected. However, I have some recent satellite photos here that are quite interesting."

"What is that greenish color at the bottom of Valles Marineris?" Bolton asked.

"That's a pool of melt-water. The white area surrounding it is the *Melas* glacier. There are larger ones farther east. By mid-fall, they will all freeze over. The green color is produced by a strain of algae unknown on Earth. We have no idea where it came from. I suspect that our terra-forming efforts revived a native species that may have lain dormant for millions of years, but we have no evidence to support that hypothesis so far."

"Fascinating, are there bacterial or other forms of life in the water?"

"No, and we don't anticipate the discovery of any non-photosynthetic autotrophs there either. Although, the scientific consensus believes that natural chemosynthetic organisms probably exist deep underground at least somewhere on the planet, as the odds in favor of such life is greater than that against it."

"The last status report you submitted to the Board specified a problem with the matrix converters. Would you elaborate on that, please?"

"Sure, they are emitting too much sulfur dioxide and other effluents. We are working to refine the process so that the percentage of desired products, namely carbon dioxide and water vapor, can be increased."

"I see. Can you also tell me more about the A-M-S initiative the Board is currently reviewing? I haven't had a chance to read any of the details yet."

"A-M-S, or more precisely the *Atmospheric Monitoring System*, is a proposed global network of spectrometers and other measuring instruments that will analyze the interchange of chemical elements between the atmosphere, lithosphere, and interplanetary medium. As I have stated publicly, this system is imperative for the long-term success of our terra-forming project; and, I strongly urge the *Board of Regents* to approve it without delay."

"Thank you, Han. Once the cost/benefit parameters have been established, the Board will act quickly I assure you."

"Uh Marc... forgive me for pressing, but what the hell are you doing here today? I just don't understand. This terra-forming project has been studied and debated for years. Everything we do, or plan to do, is thoroughly scrutinized by the public. My department does not withhold any information from the Board. Whatever you might learn by coming here could be attained by other means. I hope you appreciate my appeal for some sort of an explanation."

Bolton looked perplexed. "Han, please believe me. I didn't come here to check up on you or this project. It has nothing to do with that."

"Then, why did you come?"

"I thought about that a lot on the flight, and I can't say I know the reason."

"Are you feeling alright, big guy?"

"Yes, yes, I'm quite alright."

Technician Ariel Mapce broke in over the intercom. "Minister Li, please come to the com desk.

We're receiving a distress call from an unidentified aircraft."

Han and Bolton ran down to the main level. Mapce was having trouble modulating the weak signal through an unusual amount of static interference.

"Sorry sir, I've lost the transmission. It was barely audible."

"What was the message?" asked Han.

"I heard a voice say his rocket plane had lost power and was going down. He identified his position and requested immediate assistance. Here are the coordinates. I verified the figures, sir. The location is approximately two hundred miles due west. If he broadcast his flight registry code, I wasn't able to hear it."

"West, why would anyone be out there? Did you check the A-C-L?"

"Yes sir, the Airspace Control Log lists no authorized flights in that sector."

"This is damn peculiar. However, we are the closest official first response team and are legally required to conduct an emergency rescue operation. Ariel, notify all station personnel to prepare for immediate E-R-O. We're short a few bodies, so everyone will have to come along including yourself."

"Minister Li, someone needs to stay behind and maintain communications."

"The Chairperson can do that. Get to it now, Ariel."

"I could be more helpful if I went with you Han," Bolton suggested. "After all, I don't know how to run this station."

"There's nothing to do except man this com desk, Marc. Besides, you have not been certified for E-R-O as the rest of us have. As team leader, this is my decision to make. We'll contact you when necessary. Please relay messages to us that we haven't acknowledged, as our reception might be inhibited. We'll be back soon."

"Okay, good luck."

Bolton heard the sounds of rocket engines firing a few mins later. Looking out a small round viewing port, he saw the flat-black rocket plane lifting off the pad as it rapidly gained altitude. Soon, the research station was eerily silent except for the low-pitched hum of the air circulation system. He was completely alone now, over 40,000 feet high and nearly 3,000 miles from the city of Lowellton.

Sitting down at the com desk, Bolton reacquainted himself with the controls as it had been several years since he last operated any communications equipment. He quickly recognized the frequency scanner/signal strength displays, channel and analogue/digital mode selectors, recording and transmission switches, noise and encryption filters, and the status indicators of direct communication links. A standard procedures manual, and an anomalous signals reference guide, were accessible from the computer monitor's sidebar displays. It wasn't long before he became comfortable with the operation of this equipment.

As Bolton was skimming through the manual, he felt the presence of another person inside the station. Alarmed, he got up and walked out of the office. At the top of the stairs leading to the observation deck, he saw a frail humanoid figure looking down at him. A surge of adrenalin rushed through Bolton's body, but he did not move and did not utter a sound. Instinctively, he tried to read the creature's mind. Although he was unable to perceive any conscious thought, he could determine its emotional state. There was no anger, fear, or hostility emanating from this being. On the contrary, it imparted a strong sensation of dispassionate empathy which had a powerful calming effect on Bolton.

Then it spoke to him telepathically. Bolton recognized the words as sounds, but the creature had made no such verbalization.

"Hello, my son," the words conveyed.

Bolton replied in kind. "Hello," he said with his mind.

The Chairperson watched in awe as the humanoid figure slowly navigated itself down the staircase. Its head was disproportionally large with solid black eyes, and its wiry body was sheathed in a colorless form-fitting garment. The intruder had only a vestigial mouth, nose, and ears, was about 5 feet tall, and would weigh no more than 75 pounds on Earth. Its skin appeared leathery and hairless. To Bolton, the creature was strangely alien and familiar at the same time.

"Phase three of your evolution is here. I must reveal myself to you before leaving this timension."

Bolton was confused by the last word and assumed it meant *time-dimension*. "Where are you going?"

"Home," the creature replied.

"Do you have a name?"

"Ceros."

"I have many questions, Ceros. Who are you? Where do you come from? Why did you greet me as your son?"

"I understand. It was necessary to keep you from becoming aware of your true origins until the transition was complete. That task is now done..."

Ceros approached Bolton and lightly touched his forehead. There was a momentary spasm of pain, and then dormant memories streamed back into Bolton's consciousness. The alien being named Ceros had always been a part of his life. He knew him as the protective companion who watched over the dream-filled nights of his childhood. He knew him as the scholarly tutor who silently guided Bolton through adolescence. He knew him as the one who plucked his drowning body from the raging floodwaters that killed his family. He knew him as the surgeon who performed the operations that activated his telepathic mind, and which caused his baffling blackouts and nosebleeds. And, he knew him as the father who helped Bolton cope with the challenging travails of his adulthood.

Bolton opened his eyes. Surprisingly, he sensed a degree of apprehension in his unexpected visitor as if Ceros was unsure how Bolton would react.

"So, you are my father and I am not completely human?"

"That is a two-dimensional interpretation and only partially correct. Outwardly, you are human in every sense. Underneath that flesh and bone you are essentially Orinian, and it is that part of you which came from me."

"Have you been controlling my life?"

"No, but as your Orinian traits became progressively more prominent, they altered the decision making patterns you were accustomed to. It was only from your human perspective that it appeared choices were being made outside your control."

"Are you saying the events that brought me to Mars were purely random?"

"No, I was responsible for affecting those circumstances. However, your subsequent actions were determined completely by yourself. Your performance during this vital transition has been exemplary, and I couldn't be more pleased."

"What transition are you referring to?"

"This fourth transition of Homo sapiens was fundamentally intellectual. Primal instincts had to be surpassed by rational thought for the species to survive. The first transition was genetic, the second was social, and the third was technological. Unfortunately, we were unable to achieve the fourth transition on Earth. That is why we selected Mars."

"You manufactured human beings? Why, for what purpose?"

"There were many reasons, most of which you will have to discover on your own. But, our primary motivation was self-survival. I cannot explain further."

The Orinian turned and started walking back up the stairs.

"Are you leaving, Ceros?" Bolton asked.

"Yes, your friends are returning."

Bolton felt an intense sadness similar to the other losses in his life, because he knew he would never see Ceros again. But, there was also a great feeling of joy. A lifelong chasm between father and son had finally been bridged. Emotions can be very powerful, from which even an impassive Orinian wasn't totally immune.

Ceros stopped at the top of the staircase and observed the sun illuminating the brilliantly rustic Martian landscape.

"This planet holds much promise. Always remember, my son, what you see as the universe is just one face of a much larger reality. When you look at it, see it for what it truly is and not for what you wish it to be. Therein lays danger."

Marc Bolton watched Ceros disappear into some type of spatial vortex. Outside, he could hear the descent of rocket engines. He sent one last message to his Orinian father:

"What about the people of Earth? What about the people of Earth?"